W   ...: BOOK 4

Thea Atkinson

CHAPTER 1

It was obvious to Alaysha that she was no god. She had only to look around as she knelt on the forest floor where Yenic had died to know the truth. The redwoods were younger here just at the fringes of the highlands, the humus beneath her bare legs full of tender shoots fallen from nubile branches, hoping to sprout and become saplings themselves and further to tall, broad redwoods capable of cradling men in wooden lodges. An errant breeze whispered against her cheek, one that didn't move through the branches but seemed to come from nowhere. That small kiss of air was the final insight and Alaysha found herself reaching for the young girl that stood in front of her.

Tiny fists were clenched in effort at the child's sides as Theron, stoic, hardened old shaman that he was, fell to his knees and jammed his forehead into the humus of the forest floor in reverent surrender. A tumble of blonde curls framed Liliah's eyes and those shifted colour even as Alaysha watched from blue to green and brown and grey like a slick of earth oil on a puddle of water. *A witch knows another by her eyes*, Alaysha thought. But these were no ordinary eyes to reveal an ordinary witch.

That would have been enough of a clue for Alaysha to know she was a mortal woman after all and not the goddess come again as Theron would have had her believe; truly, it would have been. But the way Liliah's father clutched the knife he held at his side, his eyes a wild panic that the child he'd kept secret so long had finally been exposed, was even more telling.

Until then, Alaysha had foolishly allowed herself to think she might be Theron's goddess. Her own lack of humility sickened her now, and the hope that she could be something more than a mere weapon of destruction died in her chest even as Theron defected that foolish belief in the face of those remarkable eyes, supplicating himself before a child not even to her second season.

But it was more than that, more than the two of them offering their bald faith wholeheartedly to a child. Indeed. It would take more than simple surrender for Alaysha to believe that this waif could hold such power. No. She'd seen far too much in her brief time to be so easily fooled. For Alaysha to believe, it would take a demonstration of power far superior to anything she'd ever seen.

And come it had, its demonstration in the way Yenic's chest, immobile and frozen in death just moments before, began to rise and fall with the quiet rhythm of breathing. It was the way Alaysha's heart seemed to begin beating again after falling spasm in grief.

She stretched toward the child, loath to let go her grasp of Yenic's chest as she felt the newborn tremor of his heartbeat growing stronger, but wanting to touch this Liliah as well. Make sure she was real. She had to be real. Dear deities, let this all be real.

"You raised him," Alaysha said to her.

The girl offered a tentative smile, one that danced on her face as though she couldn't believe it either. "Me fixed it." Her tangle of curls caught a light breeze and stuck to her cheeks, catching in the silver of her eyelashes. Rather than pull the strands away, she licked them into her mouth and chewed on them. Now and again, a flash of tiny white teeth moved against the lips.

Alaysha felt herself nodding stupidly at the child in agreement. "Yes, yes you fixed it." A choke of laughter bubbled up to her mouth and she had to stuff her fist into it to keep from laughing straight out loud. Moments before so desolate and empty, and now so filled with unspeakable joy. It was too much. Way too much.

A thought occurred to her, that she who could give Yenic his breath, could take it away just as easily. She'd seen it herself, hadn't she? Felt it back in the Enyalian village when she had to fight with her own power in order to keep her own breath, in order to protect herself and the others, and ended up almost killing Liliah in the process. Alaysha's teeth bit down onto her fingers as she recalled it. Would the girl remember too and want her vengeance?

She scrabbled backwards and reached for Yenic, feeling for the solidness of him, the coldness of his inert form warming beneath her hands. Yes. It was fixed. But was that pulse in his throat consistent? Did it pause once or twice as his breath caught in his lungs? Would it stay fixed, or would the little goddess remember her injuries taken in the Enyalian village and take back what she'd done? Alaysha decided she wouldn't wait to find out.

She searched the faces of those around her for the man who had followed her through the burnt lands, who had sworn to protect her and stay with her, who had let her mark him as hers forever even though he had to share the honor with an Enyalian warrior.

"Gael," she said, seeking him, steady and stalwart Gael. Trustworthy. She found his massive frame already striding forward, pushing his sword back into its sheath on his back, reaching out for her. His face was a careful mask of stoicism, but his green eyes betrayed his own confusion and wonder. They'd seen so much together. Suffered together. He would understand.

"Help me." She tried to lift Yenic herself, but she was still so weak. The battle against Enud, against Aislin's brutal killing of a horde of highlanders had left her more exhausted than she could have imagined. The grief of Yenic's death drained her that much more. And his new life? That stress brought its own fatigue: a wonderful, leg shaking fatigue that robbed her of her ability to stand.

"I need to get him –" she sent a furtive glance toward the girl, afraid that if the child noticed, she'd begin to doubt the decision to revive him. "I need to get him somewhere safe," she said. Despite the child's face seeming so proud, so wanting to please, the father's expression hadn't yet eased away from its outright protective panic. There was something more behind the guarded look on his swarthy face that Alaysha didn't quite understand. And if this day had shown Alaysha anything, it was how quickly things could change.

Gael was already kneeling beside her; Alaysha had to drag her eyes away from the girl's stunning gaze to his. The stubble of his chin seesawed back and forth as he considered her. She thought he must have seen the anxiety in her; her face must look frightful for his jaw to be moving so frenetically. He wanted to say something, she was sure of it.

"Will you carry him for me?" She asked him before he could sway her with whatever reason was running through his mind.

His eyes bore into hers as he searched her face and she thought he'd refuse. "Please, Gael." She knew he would do anything to protect her, but did protecting Yenic count as part of that? She prayed it would.

"You don't know what he will be," the warrior whispered.

She put her palm on his bicep, feeling his muscles move beneath the supple leather. A strange current ran up her fingertips and traveled to a deep burrow somewhere within her chest. The mark, must be. She 'd used her magic and the ash of her sister's bones to join them, and she felt the connection like a bee knew its queen. She knew what he was thinking, that the magic from the girl was foreign. That they shouldn't trust it.

"He will be alive," she said to him. "Isn't that enough?"

His boots scuffled in the dirt in response, and when she expected him to heft Yenic off the ground, she felt his arms go around her instead and she was pulled, struggling, to her feet. She squirmed against him, searched his eyes, begging him silently to let her go, confused and angry that he would go against her.

His eyes pinned hers as he called out to Cai. Nothing more was said, but in an instant the russet Enyalian had pushed her way past, brushing Alaysha's shoulder as Gael held her close against his side. She was huge, as all Enyalia were, an almost burly quality to their sinews, but she was tall enough to carry it with grace.

Alaysha felt a tremor run through Gael, buzzing somewhere behind her ears. The mark again. For an instant, her body remembered its heated union with his the night she'd tattaued him and she had to brush it impatiently away. This was about Yenic, and she had no time for the arousal of a bond that had been spun by nothing more than magic. She couldn't let it befuddle her into forgetting that Yenic needed her.

"What are you doing?" Alaysha struggled even more against Gael's massive chest, afraid suddenly of what Cai might do to her bondsman. Cai was the more pragmatic of the two, and her dislike for men would allow her to harm Yenic without so much as a second thought if she believed his life put Alaysha in danger.

"Don't you hurt him." Alaysha put all of her energy into the order, hoping the connection she'd made with the woman, the same connection she'd forged with Gael on the same eve, would move through the Enyalian's arm like she could already feel it coursing through her and Gael. That, with the force of her desire, Alaysha could keep the Enyalian from striking him. Cai ignored her and knelt next to Yenic. Alaysha turned angry eyes back to Gael and didn't care that his face was working with emotion. She could hear the panic in her own voice.

"The girl fixed it," she said to him. "Don't you hurt him."

She was vaguely aware of Cai behind her, perhaps trying to force Yenic into a sitting position, perhaps pressing her broad palm across his mouth and nose so she could smother the breath back out of him. She imagined the worst, knowing how the Enyalia hated men, how Gael disliked Yenic. They would use this opportunity for their own gain. She could imagine how Yenic would struggle against the callused palm, his legs kicking, his lungs straining painfully.

Over Gael's shoulder, she could see Edulph grinding his too-straight teeth as he stared at her from behind Liliah. Theron, still prostrate before the child, was useless in his ecstasy. His blue veined feet stuck out from beneath him, filthy with humus and ingrained soil, the bottom of his sandals were worn so great holes gaped on the heels. Neither of them would offer any help.

Alaysha stepped down on Gael's booted foot as hard as she could with her own bare one, thinking her weight might offer the huge man some pain, give her a chance to wrest herself away. Gael didn't so much as wince.

"She will tie him, Alaysha," Gael said, his voice a hushing whisper, calming her, the soothing sound of a father to a newborn. "That's all." His eyes held hers with a steely compassion. "That's all."

Alaysha relaxed, realizing Yenic was safe for the moment. But how long would that last? She couldn't delay.

"Get him onto Barruch," she said against Gael's neck.

Together, they could flee this place. Find a land they could call their own. Now she was not the goddess Liliah, and she and everyone here knew it, she could be free of all those things that kept her bound to this motley war she'd been waging so fruitlessly and unwillingly.

She squeezed Gael's forearm. "You and Cai can be free after that. You can do as you will." She looked up at him and was surprised to find his face had grown hard and cold.

"I can never be free of you, Witch." He gave her a subtle but firm pull towards him so that she bent slightly backwards, her hips against his. "I thought you finally understood that."

His eyes searched hers and she realized she'd hurt him without meaning to. Something in the small of her back was urging her to reach out to him, let her fingers play against his chin and touch him where his warrior's brand was, to try and stifle the burning she felt on her own chin. Her tattau felt as though it was on fire.

"I just meant…"

His expression softened. "Magic such as the girl has shown can't be trusted. What if it's gone black? We can't know, Alaysha. Until your Yenic comes to, we must be careful." His grip loosened at the practicality of his words and she felt the sharp arch in her back release. "That's all," he said wearily, but it looked like he wanted to say so much more.

Magic such as the girl had shown. Indeed. Alaysha had seen nothing like it. While in her years as a weapon for her father, the Emir of Sarum, she'd seen men turned to leathered husks of flesh by her own power, seen women and children and yes her own sister singed to ash by some flame lit from within because of Aislin's magic. While witnessing the earth tremble, and the heavens open with rain, she'd not once witnessed such power as this girl wielded. Perhaps Gael was right to be cautious. She turned to where Cai was wrestling with the hemp rope on her belt. Yenic lay against her, his torso slumped forward just enough that she could pull his arms behind his back.

He'd been dead. Had been dead for whoever knew how long. To break the connection with his mother that allowed Aislin to channel destructive fire through Alaysha, killing dozens of innocent people, he'd taken his own life. She bit back the recalled image of his limp form draped across Bodicca's arms as she'd laid him on the forest floor just after the battle, when they all believed they were safe finally, of the blood seeping between his ribs right at the spot where his first mark darkened his skin. A froth of coughed-up blood bubbled on his lips.

She'd gone mad at the sight of it, and they'd let her grieve right there on the edge of the village, her knees buckled into the moss and the tears streaming over her cheeks. Behind her in a stand of centuries-old redwood trees, with heights soaring into the sky to harbor lodgings built of wood and timber and hemp rope staircases that slithered up the trunks of trees like the snakes, she knew there were several piles of ash. Too many to count: the manifested result of Aislin's fury. What Alaysha's power would have left as leathered husks of mummified people, Aislin had left nothing but ash. Power made possible by a connection she found through Yenic, and through him to the bond he had with Alaysha.

It had been strong, that bond. She'd forged it herself in her first week of life through the ministrations of her blood witch who knew the infant's memory would not let her forget unless she had a reason to live. A connection made with him through the fluid of her tears. But the connection made by those tears so long ago had lost their power now. In the face of death, magic trembled.

Looking at him now, and the shallow rise and fall of his chest as he lay there, she realized how devoid of life he'd been. And when the girl stepped forward telling her she could fix it, Alaysha didn't waste a heartbeat guessing whether or not it was so. She'd scrabbled aside, her knees catching on the pouch that hung still from her waist. She'd reached for it, and held it as though it was Yenic's lung, willing it to expand as the waif of a girl closed those brilliant eyes in concentration.

The wind came then. But not from the edges of the forest as a breeze was wont to travel, it came from within the small frame that stood before them. She opened her mouth as though to exhale and a twist of breath moved from her lips to gain speed as it caught air. No sooner did Alaysha realize the air came from within the tiny chest, than it absorbed into the space about them and swelled until it looked like heat waves from the burnt lands. Then it swelled even more until Alaysha felt the kiss of hot humid breath against her cheek. It shuddered across her skin, raising the smallest of hairs even as it made her skin whisper back to it like a lover joining its mate.

Her fingers clutching the leather pouch grew icy cold as though the breath from her lungs was pulled straight out from the tips before the breeze became a mighty wind that moved the trees and the grass and Alaysha's hair and even made Theron's cassock flap like a linen sheet on a hemp line as he stood with his feet planted deep into the humus.

When it gathered above them, all air seemed to grow stagnant and her lungs fought to expand. She saw each of them clasp at their throats, but even before Alaysha could bring her own power to bear in defence, the air returned and swept over Yenic's form so fast, so hard, it moved him a hand's breadth forward.

The girl had opened her eyes and Alaysha could swear the colors swirling within settled into a shadowed black for a heartbeat only before they moved back into the rhythm of colors curling around on each other. The child looked up at Edulph as though expecting praise.

"It's fixed," she'd told him proudly, but rather than looked pleased, Edulph only looked more afraid.

Alaysha had tested it immediately. She tucked her hair behind her ear and leaned over Yenic's mouth. She couldn't hear breath, but she could feel warmth. It was then that she knew the girl had indeed fixed him. She didn't question, only reached out hoping to touch the girl's leg, praying that what was done wasn't some trick of her grief.

So yes, it was indeed Magic such as they'd never seen. Wonderous magic. Even Edulph shivered in the face of it.

She sighed now, knowing Gael was right. "Let it be done," she told him. "We shouldn't take chances."

When he released her, she turned to see Cai squatting beside Yenic, a blade in her left hand poised and ready, her right hand gripping Yenic by the throat as he hunched against the boulder she'd leaned him against. Alaysha wasn't sure which threat was greater: the glint of the knife ready to disembowel the youth or the power of the broad hand ready to choke the air back out.

"Stand back, Cai," Alaysha told her. "I'm sure if he's not what we expect you'll have ample time to kill him again."

"Men are never what we expect, little maga," Cai said, a note of unexpected humor in her tone as her red brows lifted gracefully. "We must take the time to kill them whenever we're offered the chance."

Gael harrumphed but said nothing; Edulph shifted angrily where he stood, unable, it seemed to let the warrior's prejudice linger in the air.

"I would say the same thing of any Enyalian," he said, but there was no response from Cai to acknowledge she even heard him and if she did, Alaysha was sure that she stored the appropriate response happily away in her mind, counting another couple of teeth to add to the bracelet that had somehow grown thicker on her bicep. Alaysha dearly hoped the circlet wouldn't grow again to stretch across her thigh. She was tired of death.

"She meant no harm," Alaysha told Edulph, thinking to ease the tension so they could all concentrate on Yenic, but he only grunted in response.

"Theron," she addressed the shaman who had flung himself down in front of the girl when the winds had come. "Theron, get up. We might need you."

He mumbled something into the dirt and roots that sounded something like a refusal.

Alaysha turned her attention to the girl. "Ask him to get up," she said and as graceful as you please, the child rested her hand on the shaman's head. This only served to make him melt all the way onto the ground with his arms stretched out sideways. The girl giggled and clapped her hands together.

"Theron, she's a child. She doesn't understand."

He didn't turn his head sideways, so much as move his mouth so that it twisted enough to find the air. "A shaman such as us, aren't worthy to speak to the goddess. No. No we aren't."

"This shaman was worthy enough to save her life when it was in danger," Alaysha said, rebuking him. "Now get up."

Again, he refused, but this time Bodicca reached down and grasped him by the bicep, yanking him to his feet. He did everything he could to avoid looking at the girl's face, twisting his head and craning his neck until Bodicca gripped him by the chin.

"Your goddess might still be in danger, shaman. You'll do her no good this way."

A moment went by before he nodded silently. At that, Alaysha could feel the tension in the grove fall just enough that she could feel the hardness in her own muscles. Now all that was left was for Yenic to wake. To stare at her with those honey eyes of his and declare himself unchanged, undead, and unbound from his mother's magic. She tried to feel for the connection they shared, believing the coils they had about her heart would tremor again against hers, tightening her chest and reminding her how she'd once ached for him. She tried to remember what it was like to feel his living hand in hers, the sound of his voice and how it soothed her. She wanted to let her memory trail through images of their bodies joining, of his breath in her hair, her own smothered sighs of delight escaping to mingle with his.

All that came, unbidden, was the memory of his betrayals, the mistrust. She squeezed her eyes closed, willing those things back into the depths of her mind.

She sensed Cai's movement first. The Enyalian tensed, leaning forward, her fingers curling toward Yenic's throat once more as Yenic moaned quietly and then gasped, dragging air in as though he was clawing his way through several handspans of dirt and stone. His eyes flew open, darted about, taking in each face and feature. They passed over Cai almost lazily, flitted to Gael, then landed on Alaysha. She had to fight the urge to rush to him.

"How many seeds have you collected, Witch?" he demanded and for one heartbeat, confusion swallowed her relief. Her hand sped to her throat at the way he enunciated one particular word.

Before she could speak, Bodicca rushed forward and fell to her knees in front of Yenic. "My Emir," the old warrior whispered. "Yuri," she said, her voice hushed with reference, her fingers deftly laying her sword across Yenic's lap in deference.

Alaysha grappled for the pouch at her waist, squeezing it, feeling for the small seeds within that Theron had given her back in Sarum, the seeds that were the only remains of her father. "Take these," he'd told her as they'd rushed to escape the city. "They're of Etlantium." She heard herself gasp as she swallowed down the trapped air she'd drug in. She struggled to breathe again.

"Unfleshed no longer," Theron mumbled in wonder and she stared at him speechless, struggling to find comprehension and discovering only a sense of betrayal when it came.

Because only in then did clarity send a screech rushing through the confusion like a mouse being pinned by a hawk, its fear a primal, piercing thing.

Not Yenic in front of her, whole and breathing, not her beloved amber-eyed bondsman had this small goddess brought back, but her ruthless and commanding father.

CHAPTER 2

Alaysha's first action, without thinking, was to pull the sword from its sheath on her back and lunge for the man who had caused her so much pain and grief. Her sister, her mother, her nohma. The callous way he'd left her to suffer under Corrin's brutal hand. The way he used her as a tool to do his bidding.

The way he died without telling her he cared about her, without giving her a chance to force him to redeem himself, who left her alone to discover things about him both heroic and insufferable. In those moments, the bloodlust of vengeance took her mind and held captive her sword arm. She lunged for him, sword raising, hips set to swivel with all the force she could muster.

She felt hands on her before she had chance to swing and couldn't count how many fingers buried themselves into her skin to keep her from moving. Her heart hammered in her chest so much, tingling into her fingers so fiercely, they felt swollen with the need to strike something. She couldn't move against the hands that restrained her. She pulled in a deep breath, feeling more acutely the sword in her grip and then she let go the handle. Her jaw hurt and her throat burned and it was only when she heard the dull thunk of the blade hitting moss did she realize she had been screaming, that her face was wet with her own tears.

Yenic/Yuri sat placidly against the tree, his mouth a sardonic twist that dissolved for one breathtaking moment into something else. Something that made his eyes soften and fill with confusion. She was aware of her chest heaving, desperately trying to pull in enough oxygen to keep her from passing out, to keep her legs from trembling. If she heard her heart beat in her ears for one more moment, she would go deaf.

"Alaysha?" He ventured, and the tone was so much like Yenic's that even those holding her, both Gael and Bodicca, she realized, let go in surprise. A sob caught in her throat for how close she had come to taking the new life he'd been granted.

By the time she got to him, his eyes had rolled back and he'd slumped forward.

"What's happening?" She demanded from her knees, her hands already finding the back of Yenic's neck and the small of his back, pulling him to her. She had him now, she wouldn't let go. To think she had almost –

"Theron," she cast about looking for the shaman and found him still staring at the girl, his face a contemplative mix of elation and confusion. "Theron," she said again and he drug his gaze away to look at her. She didn't wait to give him a chance to lose himself in the child's power again. "Come, see what you can do for him."

It was Bodicca who got Theron moving. She was next to him so quickly and had him by the bicep, pulling him, almost impatiently flinging him toward Yenic's feet that Alaysha didn't see her move.

"See to him," the old warrior said. "The Emir needs you." There was tension in Bodicca's body, Alaysha could see it rippling through the muscles of the woman's cheek and jaw. It traveled down the cords of her neck and made the fingers curl and uncurl absently as though her hand, in concert with her subconscious, needed to strike something. Alaysha knew exactly how she felt.

They all waited quietly as the shaman ran his hands over Yenic's form. He prodded here and there, peeled back the youth's eyelids. Tapped his chest. It seemed even the birds waited with bated breath, their song evaporated forgotten in the trees. Alaysha watched a squirrel dart out from a burrow in the humus that blanketed the roots of a juvenile Redwood. It stuffed tiny paws against its cheeks, cramming its forage deeper into the pouch before digging those same paws into the skin of the tree and fleeing to the safety of its heights.

She was aware of scrawny arms creeping about her waist and she looked down to see Aedus on her knees beside her, leaning in, trying to comfort her or be comforted, Alaysha wasn't sure. She let the girl lay her head against her shoulder, let her own hand find the tangle of mud and hair that Aedus would never comb clean.

"He'll be okay," she told the girl.

"But who will he be?"

It was a good question and Alaysha wished she could answer.

Theron answered before Alaysha could form a response. "The man will be as the goddess wills, Oh, yes. Yes indeed."

It was a foolish response, one that put an edge in Alaysha's voice before she could stop it. "Do you think the goddess willed this, shaman?" Alaysha couldn't help the note of frustration she heard in her own voice. "Do you think that child really decided to bring back my father?"

"Me fixed it," the girl piped up from somewhere behind and Alaysha cringed at the naïve sound of the voice. She gave the girl careful study in those seconds, watched as the young face went slack but for a minute tic in her cheek that made the mouth lift at one edge in a perpetual half smile.

The fountain of frustration would not be strangled off and Alaysha dearly wanted to let it vent. She gave in wholeheartedly.

"Yenic is dead and in his place this child brings back the man who sought to kill her. To have me kill her. What do you make of that, shaman? What do you make of your goddess now?" Her palms hurt where her fingernails dug in. She had to consciously let her hands go limp and found Aedus's shoulder again, to keep from clenching her hands in fury.

He said nothing, infuriating Alaysha even more. She let go of Aedus and found her feet, peppering the ground with her footsteps as she reached for his wrist and twisted him to face her. "You worship a child with no understanding. Full of power and empty of wisdom. What kind of shaman does that make you?"

The old face with its black eyes never flinched. "Such a thing makes a shaman such as us only wonder what kind of witch condemns her maker." His eyes went as hard as flint as he pulled himself from her grasp to continue his examination.

"But it was Yenic," Aedus said, her attention still on the youth as he lay on the forest floor. "It was him at the end, wasn't it?"

"Yes," Alaysha said, telling herself she believed it.

"Then she did fix it," Aedus said. "It was just a mistake, the first thing."

Fixed it, perhaps. Alaysha watched as the goddess sat in the moss and picked at the ghost pipes that grew at the base of the nearest tree and started to cram a handful into her mouth. She lunged for the girl, slapping at her hands and digging out whatever flesh of the plant she could see with harried fingers, trying to extract the last of the powerful sedative from her mouth.

She stretched the girl's mouth open to peer in, making sure she had got the last of it. They'd collected ghost pipes on their journey to the Highland village, thinking that when Theron found a village with proper cook fires and proper utensils, he could better brew a sleep that could calm a giant even if his skull had to be cracked into. But Theron had not brewed the ghost pipe in the woods; it was too dangerous, too potent a root to use without proper measurement. They'd had to use Aedus's beetles to put the girl to sleep while they split her skull to relieve the built up pressure.

The girl could have eaten too much, swallowed some even, and who knew what would happen to her then.

That was when Alaysha realized it finally.

Only when she couldn't find anything more within the cheeks or squashed into the teeth, did she look up at Theron. "The girl is simple, Theron. You worship a simpleton."

Theron refused to answer and Alaysha grabbed for the mulch she'd extracted from Liliah's mouth and thrown on the ground. She shook the handful of wet and masticated plant at him.

"Do you see?" Alaysha turned to Edulph for confirmation because she knew she'd get no reaction from Theron. "I'm right, aren't I?"

Edulph had the grace to look at his feet. It was answer enough for Alaysha; fury rose into her throat.

"You knew," she accused Edulph. She wasn't sure what angered her the most at the moment: the fact that the girl, the one Theron called his goddess, was simple, that the simple girl had brought back the megalomaniac who was responsible for killing Alaysha's sister and hundreds of others, or that the girl's own father would be cruel enough to manipulate her in such a way.

Hauntings from her past fought each other for prominence: she heard again the dripping of sweating stone, felt manacles on her tender wrists, heard the almost sultry chuckle of Corrin's laughter in her ear.

"You knew she was simple and so you used her to your own gain, thinking her power could somehow make you more so, " she said and couldn't help thinking of her father as she said it, all the fury of her years suffering neglect and torment poisoning her tone.

"And what gain have I," Edulph demanded of her, the black line of hair across the top of his lip quivered. "Captured and tortured by the fire witch Aislin for this knowledge. Do you know what it's like to burn from the inside? Have you ever felt an invisible fire lick over your skin until it bubbles in pain, you have no idea where the next place will be, whether it will be your eyes that she sets to boiling next or your manhood. Skin, lungs, they are nothing to the thought that you might never see again, might never… " His gaze went hard as he looked at her. "Oh yes, I have gained." He bent to put his hands on his daughter's shoulders and squeezed protectively.

"I have suffered your slanders, your ropes tied around my wrists, your gags in my mouth. I have spent moons upon moons away from my daughter, hoping to keep you all from finding her because what will you do with her now that you know who she is. Would you protect her the way a father protects her?"

He turned the girl so that she faced into his belly, her arms going around him in a hug. For a moment, Alaysha felt doubt creeping in, but she pushed it aside with the memory of the cruelty Edulph had showed his own sister.

"No," he continued on, oblivious to what any of them might be thinking. "You will only use her way you have been used, the way you accuse me of using her because you know no other way of living."

"You're lying."

A bite of harsh laughter came from the man. "Yes, see?" He shrugged almost helplessly. "You'll never believe me."

She wouldn't be swayed by the passion in his tone. She remembered. A witch has a long memory, and each of his atrocities could be called to her in depth at whim. She selected one to throw at him. "You cut off your own sister's finger."

He chewed his lip guiltily; the moustache wiggled grossly. She took note of the way his fingers tightened around the goddess's shoulders. He wanted to deny it, but he knew he couldn't.

"And then you cut off your own men 's heads when they would lose a battle for you and put her finger in one of their mouths. You sent that grisly package to me through a man you forced to fight till he was nearly dead."

"But he's not dead." Edulph's voice was almost manic as he pointed at the spot where Yenic still lay unconscious. "He only just died and by his own hand -- until my daughter brought him back."

Alaysha choked at the words. "Brought him back? No. Not nearly Yenic did she bring back. Not nearly. His body, yes..." she thought she'd lose her voice and had to swallow down the fury and hopelessness that wanted to raise her bile. She felt her core shake and her legs tremble with it. She tried to focus on the fury rather than the hopelessness and stomped closer to him, thinking to pull each ounce of water from him in her rage, stare into his eyes as she did it, but Cai caught her elbow and snagged her close. Alaysha could have taken her throat out with her teeth.

"It's not your concern, Cai," she shouted at the Enyalian.

"Anything that puts you in danger is my concern, little maga." The large woman's voice was calm, even strangely soothing, and Alaysha had to force herself to remember all the ex-Komandiri of the Enyalia had given up to become her protecter: exile from her homeland, the circlet of teeth so broad they stretched around a massive thigh, the familiarity of command and knowing your place. She turned her attention instead to Edulph.

"He's the one in danger." She glared at the man as she spoke to Cai.

"And you think his little witch will just let you do him harm?"

Alaysha chewed her cheek. Her gaze went from Edulph to Cai and then to Gael. She couldn't look at Aedus. She was afraid of what the girl's face would reveal. It was true: if she harmed Edulph, how long would it be before the goddess turned her power on them?

She addressed Edulph almost calmly, but the way her fingers tore at her palms kept the edge out of her voice even if it did nothing to calm her anger. "I don't trust you and I won't let you use the girl."

"She's my daughter. I would never use her."

Alaysha knew better than to answer that; wasn't she Yuri's daughter after all, and where had that got her. Instead she pointed at Edulph's sister, the girl who had been the first to show Alaysha any friendship. Aedus stood twirling her quill blower in anxious hands.

"You threatened to kill her. Do you remember that? Her and my half sister and my entire homeland. Threatened to kill them all unless I would allow you to use me as a tool for your own gain."

"Not my gain--"

"You used my sense of compassion against me just as you're using this girl's compassion. We can't let you do that."

She could see him deflate, nodding at her as though he was weary of his own memories. It wasn't enough for Alaysha. Not nearly enough.

"You are more brutal even than Yuri. Even than Corrin. You're the same ilk. Men like you use others for your own gain no matter who you harm. You told me that. Do you remember? Your men were starving in the woods, ready to eat those disgusting dreamer's worms. You told me a man wins a battle by his brain, not his brawn. You told me nothing, no emotion, no sense of compassion, should get in the way. Just like Yuri did. You can protest love for the girl all you like. I'll never believe you." Her voice was trembling when she finished, a good match for her chin.

"Yes. I did all those things," he said. "All of them. I admit." His expression hardened again, and his fists clutched vehemently at the girl's shoulders. The girl beneath his hands squirmed but eventually her arms wrapped around his legs and he took a deep, shuddering breath.

"You have no idea who I was, what I endured at your people's hands. Yes. I am a ruthless bastard. As was your father, as was his scout, as was his scout's lover." His own voice sounded choked and Alaysha was forced to meet his eyes, wondering if it was the choke of emotion at last in his tone, but his throat convulsed as he swallowed forcefully and the determination came back into his voice.

"You pretend you're the only poor victim, when you know nothing of the pain suffered by others." he hooked a thumb at Aedus. "Did you ever ask her what life was like for her as a slave to your people? Did you never wonder why she would rather forage with dogs than live in a house with other slaves?" He flashed a contemptuous grin. "You don't know my truths. You only know my brutality, and I pledge to always be so...for the sake of her. Always."

All of the passion seemed to leave him when he finished, and in truth, Alaysha could barely keep the fatigue from her own legs. She sighed and searched for Gael's eyes amidst the slack jaws that Edulph had left when his words ran out. When she found the warrior's familiar grey green eyes, they were steely with determination and silent message: whatever you need from me, his gaze said, and she knew he meant it.

"Not today," she told him wearily and he gave a brusque nod in understanding. She pointed to Yenic instead, thinking there would be better times to wage this long-standing battle of wills with Edulph. The most important thing now was getting Yenic to safety. She'd deal with Edulph later, yes, but she would deal with him finally.

"Get Yenic to my tent," she said. "Theron can see to him there."

Without so much as a grunt of effort, Gael hoisted Yenic off the ground and up over his shoulder. Alaysha signalled to the others to head back to the highland village, but to Cai she had one last order.

"Take the girl," she said as she passed the Enyalian.

"And the man?" Cai bent her head toward Edulph much the same as Gael had, no doubt wondering the same thing.

Alaysha knew what the both of them wanted; no more than she did, truth be told. She let her eyes rest on Edulph for a moment, thinking. "Not today," Alaysha answered, giving Edulph a magnanimous smile that could have meant anything, but to Alaysha meant he would have his life for the moment.

He made a furtive movement forward, perhaps thinking to sway her with physical threat. It was foolish, of course, and he had to know it; Cai was in front of him before he was able to close the distance between his own two legs. He stepped to the right, leaning around the huge Enyalian, trying to catch Alaysha's eye past the woman's torso.

"You can't take her," he said.

Alaysha watched Cai begin a silly hand game with Liliah, but she knew the warrior's attention was not on the girl's fingers and not on whether or not she met the goddess's hands with her own.

"I can," she told him.

He reached to grapple the girl's hand away from the match, but Cai deftly swatted it away, making it seem no more threatening an action, than a move in the game. The girl giggled, a high, bubbling thing. Alaysha couldn't help smiling at the tinkle of sound.

Cai hoisted the girl high above her head and spun enough to make a grown man dizzy. Liliah's laughter soared to the treetops as her hair caught the air, sailing out around her like a billowing linen in the wind. When Cai stopped swinging, she plunked the goddess down onto her shoulders, breathless and giddy.

Alaysha couldn't help sending Edulph a triumphant look, and was more than a little surprised when he did not look impressed. Something in the way he stood, with the fat lower lip twitching, trying to keep itself from curving into a smile made her uneasy.

"I have the Emir's son," he said.

Alaysha thought she felt her throat close up at the words. The Emir's son. Her half-brother. The infant boy had gone missing from Sarum and his own cradle despite Yuri's vigilance with his favored heir. They'd been searching for Saxon for so long. She thought of the lovely Saxa, the boy's mother, the way the woman's graceful posture reminded her of a willow tree. Her gentle hands, her compassionate nature. She thought of how distraught the poor woman was when she discovered her son had been abducted. She realized she was glowering at Edulph.

He seemed pleased with her reaction, as she expected he might. "How much do you want the little bastard back?" He asked, then he quirked a hefty brow at her. "Your brother, isn't that so?"

"Gael will kill you himself," she managed to croak out.

He ignored the threat. "Give me my daughter and I'll lead you to the boy."

Alaysha was aware of Cai suddenly beside her, brushing against her. In her shock, she'd forgotten the Enyalian was even there. She felt the girl's bare knee against her temple as the warrior pressed close. Cai offered a silent, if not confused look. Alaysha knew that even if the warrior knew nothing of Saxon, she'd have understood the tension in the air and would be prepared to meet it. She took comfort in that, that she could have Edulph cut down where he stood, the arrogant look on his face dissolving into a mask of fear. She stayed the warrior with a lifted hand and turned steely eyes to Edulph.

"We will trade," she agreed finally, but she couldn't look at him long. The bush of hair, the stubble on his neck, the overgrown moustache leaking down into puddles of course and unkempt beard: all made her stomach burn. She made herself pay attention to the girl as she picked at Cai's hair, threading the red tresses through her fingers and giggling when it tangled and tugged back. Even so, while looking at Edulph made her angry, trying to look into Liliah's eyes made her queasy. Simple or not, this little girl was very powerful.

She would agree to the trade for Gael and Saxa's sake, but she would kill Edulph herself before she gave him back his daughter.

CHAPTER 3

The highland village was busy putting itself together when Alaysha strode back. She caught the scent of cook fires smoking to life and when she passed the first of the staircases that climbed into an ancient redwood by means of thick hemp ropes and slats of beaten wood, she told herself that those people glaring at them, were really staring at Edulph and not her. It galled her to think he'd found sanctuary here when she'd been tolerated at best. Did they not know what he was? Did they not realize all of this tragedy beset upon them was ultimately at his hand?

She surveyed what was left of the village, and what wasn't damp and wet from her released torrent of rain to save them from the Enyalia, was crushed and tamped down from the mad rush of escape from Aislin. Several piles of ash were being swept into hand thrown pots and covered with chunks of cork. Alaysha couldn't say how many of those piles had already been stored, or what had been done with them. So many people, she thought. So many bodies turned to ash just for being in close proximity to her. She thought of the fire witch who understood her power so completely she could burn a man to ash from the inside out. The way she targeted innocent people through the mark on Yenic's rib that tied Yenic to her through the bond Alaysha and he had shared from the time she was a babe.

She looked askance at Liliah as she rode Cai's shoulders back into the village. So much power in one little girl. No, not a girl. The goddess Theron had spoken of just outside Sarum when they'd been fleeing from Aislin's wrath. The goddess reborn. The goddess Liliah. She stole a look at Edulph: if he could be believed, he was her father and had done his best to protect her. It was an almost alien thought for Alaysha, one she would have given anything for that one time. To think: a man protecting his daughter. It was as it should be, except nothing in her life was as it should be. Why should this one more thing be so?

She supposed she should be thankful that Edulph didn't give her up to Aislin when he suffered in that pit, knowing that if the fire witch were to manage to find the girl, she would surely have killed her. She would only have to look at Liliah's eyes to know the child was the witch she sought, the goddess who had escaped her brother's clutches when he'd stolen greater Etlantium for himself.

She should be grateful the stupid man kept his daughter a secret from them all. Even if the child had never turned out to be a goddess after all but merely a powerful, terribly powerful witch, the possibility for danger at her hand was too great. How much damage would a conscienceless woman like Aislin do if she got her hands on such a powerful child, she could only imagine. A shiver of memory ran through her as she thought of all the things her own father had requested of her as his tool, his weapon. She thought of all those things as she looked at the girl and told herself to be relieved that the child was here with her and not with Aislin.

Still, even though they'd saved Edulph from Aislin's fiery torture in that pit deep within the mountain of Sarum, he'd known where Saxon was and kept it to himself. She couldn't feel anything but bitterness toward Aedus's brother. And she knew he deserved it. He had done nothing since he'd left his sister like a feral, unwanted dog back in Yuri's city of Sarum. He'd left a young girl to her own defences and devices while he escaped slavery and drudgery, and then returned to viciously cut off her finger in his drive to have his people released from Yuri's slavery. In theory, it might have been noble, that act, but it ended up as one more cruel deed in a raft of cruel deeds that weighed on Alaysha as heavily as the tortures her father's trainer had inflicted.

Her mind wanted to skulk down the dark corridors of her early memories to the place within the mountain that her father's trainer Corrin liked to call the bathhouse, but she was practiced at burying memories she didn't want to recall. She found her voice rather than think any further on the various tortures Corrin had used to smother her emotions. Instead, she called up that implacable ability he granted her through them to bite down hard on the taste of compassion.

"Bring the child to Aedus," she told the Enyalian. "I'll see to Yenic and the shaman."

"And then?" Cai eyed Edulph and Alaysha knew what was running behind the warrior's green-eyed gaze: Edulph's death. She wanted nothing better than to give the woman the order she was hoping for. Instead, she gave the next best thing.

"Watch him," she told her. "And I give you leave to do anything but kill him if he so much as displeases you."

A spectre of a smile appeared on the woman's face, showing all but her back teeth; the ones on her biceps rattled noisily as the warrior gave them a pointed shake. "It doesn't take much for a man to displease me." She jiggled the little goddess on her shoulders and made the child laugh, a dichotomous sound to meet with the threat in the Enyalian's voice. If Edulph understood it, he gave a surly pout but said nothing.

Bodicca and Gael had obviously made their way back to her lodging by the time Alaysha found her encampment. Yuri's old guard turned a spit over a cook fire where a skinned rabbit roasted, wild onions stuck into the crevasse between its ribs made the pungent smell of meat all the more welcoming. Someone, no doubt Gael, had drawn fresh water; it rested just outside the leather flap of the lodging and it was with a palpable relief that Alaysha cupped handfuls of water over her face and let it dribble down the back of her neck. She swallowed down a few mouthfuls of air and pushed her way inside, bracing herself.

"Has he awoke?" She addressed Theron first even though Gael sat sullenly next to the door. She didn't bother to ask if Bodicca had been inside. She could guess that the woman had immediately gone off to hunt, imagining that the Emir would be hungry after such a long death. Alaysha almost envied the woman for the simplicity of her loyalty.

The shaman squatted next to the rush mat where Yenic lay. Alaysha tried to ignore the pots of ash and blood that had been pushed almost forgotten to the side. She'd marked both Cai and Gael with that ash, the last remains of the twin sister she had no idea she'd had until Aislin had murdered her. That night had been the first she'd felt safe and at peace, knowing two stalwart warriors would be her companions until the day one of them died and released the magic that bound them together. The same type of magic, the same breaking of bond that Yenic had suffered, that released him finally in death.

That emotion, too, she swallowed down as she faced the shaman. "How is he?"

The shaman tilted Yenic's chin upward, probing behind the base of his skull with deft fingers before he answered. "This boy has stopped shivering, finally, but it took all of our skill, oh yes, and much more, to make the breath as regular as the heartbeat."

She wished the shaman could do the same for her own heartbeat. It fluttered beneath her skin like a moth discovering its beloved light was a lick of flame. "He lives?"

"Our goddess has indeed done her miracle, yes. Yes, yes."

"What happened?"

The scuffing sound of Gael's boots as he drove himself to stand came as her answer. "No miracle, that's for sure," he said.

Theron gave him quiet study for a short time before he spoke again. "A shaman such as us is no zealot, no. No. Your father should have taught you the way of things." The old head wagged back and forth in frustrated contempt. "He was ever a foolish man. Yes yes yes."

Gael ground out a sigh, and Alaysha could tell he was doing his best to keep his temper. Gael's father had been the clay witch's brother, but outcast and miserable, he'd found sanctuary in Sarum where he'd eventually been executed by Yuri for his brutality.

"We've been through this before," Gael growled. "He taught me nothing. You know this. I was given to Corrin and I took my mark and I never knew of my father's people until you told me. Yet you knew all along. You knew Saxa and I came from your witch's line and yet you kept that little secret to yourself too just like a child keeps a bauble until it suits him to share it. So it's you who is a foolish man. Yes. Oh yes yes."

Alaysha could see he was working hard to keep his emotions in check. None of this was something a warrior trained for. They saw a foe; they killed it. They heard an order; they obeyed it.

"Gael," she murmured, thinking she could meet his eyes and offer him the comfort of understanding she was just as frustrated as he was, just as exhausted, as tired, as afraid. She tried with all the compassion she could muster, but his face didn't release its tension even when she touched his wrist. She knew what she would have to tell him about Saxon would make that hardened face chisel even further to stone. She didn't relish the thought.

"Best we leave Theron to his work." She held the flap open, thinking to let him go first so she could come from behind him, so he wouldn't see the anxiety in her shoulders. Just when she thought he would duck down ahead of her and turn, he met her gaze, his own grey green eyes narrowed in suspicion.

"Something's wrong," he said and his fingers went to where she knew his mark was, just beneath his armpit, coated with honey to keep it from mortifying and covered with a linen bandage to keep it from abrading against his leather. His brow furrowed. "You're keeping something from me."

Is that what it was to be bound to an Arm of Protection? To have your emotions and your worries and concerns transmitted like ant antenna touching?

"I am," she said. She sent a fleeting look toward the shaman. "Best we keep our voices down and let the shaman tend to Yenic."

Gael gave her a sour, dubious look. "Yenic, Yuri, which one do you think the shaman will bring forth when those sleeping eyes open?"

Alaysha would've answered, told him she didn't think the shaman had that sort of power when Theron himself muttered beneath his breath, obviously intending to be heard but pretending to talk to himself as though that was all he was doing. "It's the goddess work, not ours. No no no." The litany of words turned to a sort of prayer that pushed Gael and Alaysha outside. She made him sit and he did so, right there on the hard ground without bothering to seek out stone or log. His long legs splayed out in front of him, his hand reaching for her.

She could almost feel lightning move between their fingertips as she reached for his hand. He pulled her down to sit between his legs, her back against his chest. He folded his palms over her belly.

"Whatever you have to tell me will hurt you less if I'm touching you." He sounded wary and she knew he deserved to hear about his nephew, but at the moment, all she wanted was to feel his arms around her. It felt safe there.

"What makes you think it will hurt?" Craven, she called herself, all the delays she could think of wouldn't stop him from being angry. He deserved that, too.

She could feel him shrug behind her. "My spine feels like water is running down it like a waterfall." He pulled her closer, and she could feel her back melting into him. She eased her eyes closed, pretending for a moment that she was someone else who could enjoy the feel of a good hard man behind her, who could enjoy the simple delicious feel of muscled arms around her waist. But that wasn't her reality. Hers was more complex.

"It won't hurt," she admitted, sensing him tense behind her. "It will make you angry."

"That would explain why my lower back feels as though it's a cache of sharp unyielding rock."

She could hear the feigned jocularity in his voice and tried to chuckle for his sake, he so rarely made jokes. She found she couldn't. "It's Saxon."

He took a long moment to speak and when he did, his voice was a hushed pained thing that revealed a desperate hope that the worst he'd been expecting, that he'd known was a possibility, would prove to be nothing but fancy. And now the moment had come when he discovered his worst fears were real after all. "He's dead."

She twisted in his arms to see he had clenched his eyes shut against the news. How strange it was to see them closed so tightly and yet his face look so terrifyingly calm. "No," she rushed to ease his pain, cursing herself for not starting with allaying Gael's fears, fears they'd all suffered since the boy had been taken. "He's alive. Very much alive. At least I think so. But you should know that Edulph has him." She pulled his hands tighter, thinking that she could protect him somehow from his own anger.

This time she felt every muscle in his body go tight. She expected him to strike out immediately to find the man foolish enough to admit abducting the boy. She wasn't sure whether she should be relieved or confused at his next words.

"Good thing we didn't kill him," he said but his words sounded clipped together, as though he was trying hard to dig them from somewhere within his consciousness and string them into a coherent sentence. "Is he friend or foe?"

"Edulph?" She shifted so she sat outside of his legs and let her own gather beneath her. She searched his face. "What do you think?"

This time when he answered, the pause wasn't quite so lengthy. "Foe." His eyes fluttered open and bore into Alaysha's. She wasn't sure if the squirming at the small of her back came from anxiety or something else, something she couldn't quite name…

"Then let's not waste our time fighting with Theron," she heard herself say.

She knew the shaman had kept far too many secrets from them, but he'd also been very useful in getting through the burnt lands. He'd repeatedly done his best to keep their hopes up when everything seemed hopeless. Plus, he'd done his best to help heal Bodicca and allow her to recover from the hideous wounds inflicted on her by her own people for the mere act of bringing Yenic into her world of women-only.

She was grateful for Gael's steely composure then. She'd been afraid he would storm for Aedus's brother and shake the information out of him. It was what Alaysha wanted to do, she had to admit to herself. But for the girl she might have done so. No, it would be more prudent to let Edulph think he had the upper hand. At least for now.

He had his broad hand on her thigh and was squeezing and letting go, almost as if he couldn't stop clenching and unclenching his hands and thought that perhaps touching her would help him eases tension. She had to bite back a whimper of pain and scrambled so that she was just out of his touch. He looked at her confused and she thought he would apologize for unintentionally hurting her, but instead he crossed his massive arms and stared broodily into the trees.

Alaysha scanned the tree line with him, letting her mind wander as she did so. As far as she could see, the Highland village rose and disappeared into the brush of branches. Wooden stairs climbed up tree trunks, joined themselves with hemp rope to neighboring trees, hiding secrets within, rising to places beyond where even a crow would dare fly. An entire village hoisted into the air with pathways and roads mapped out by branches and hemp rope. She'd not gone far beyond the village itself, and in truth, she hadn't even thought to climb each mountainous stairway up into the heights of those Redwood dwellings within the village that the people who had been named for. It was possible the boy was within reach. It was also possible that in Edulph's paranoia, he'd stolen farther than the Highland village, out into the uncertainty of the forest beyond.

When she looked again at Gael, Alaysha could see the muscles in his jaw working as she pushed herself to her feet, reaching down for him. She walked into his arms and felt his heart thudding within his chest, matching time with hers. She looked up into his eyes and thought for half a heartbeat that he would kiss her. She panicked, then, not sure what she would do if his mouth claimed hers.

"We will find him," she heard herself stammer. "He's of my blood too. We will find him if we have to peel the information from Edulph's tongue along with the skin from his body."

The moment passed, but his gaze still held her lips and the hand that had been on her waist had moved to the small of her back, pressing incessantly inward. "Spoken like an Emir," he said, his voice filled with something she couldn't name, something that sent her teeth into the insides of her cheek. She knew he meant it as a compliment, but it was a disquieting thought, and she tried on a tremulous smile for him. Thankfully, the sound of Theron's voice saved her from having to hold onto the effort when she knew it was failing at it.

"She's awake," he said, blinking at the sunlight.

"She?" she asked him, extracting herself from Gael's arms and taking reluctant steps toward Theron.

Theron shielded his eyes, the blue veins on his feet standing out as though he'd traced them with woad. Indeed, she noticed that's exactly what it was when she drew close enough that she stood next to him, the anxiety tightening the muscles in her throat. Her face must have been a complete mask of dread because he reached out to her almost compassionately.

"Yusmine," he said and as he did, she understood that the compassion was genuine.

"The man you knew as Yuri is the one who wakes," he said. "And such a man is, in truth, a woman."

CHAPTER 4

Yenic was sitting up when Alaysha burst into the lodging, Gael and Theron behind her. His face was the same as she'd ever seen it. His hair was still the color of straw. Those eyes of his, still like warm honey, rested on her and she thought for a moment he would call to her, reach out to her, and she knew she was ready to rush forward. Even the line of his mouth was the same, but the way he worked his features, the way he leaned forward as they entered the lodging, placing his hands, now untied, on his lap. Almost supplicating, those things were different. They weren't Yenic. Nor were they Yuri. And that made her legs turned to rods of iron.

She wiggled her toes, so much to divert attention in her body as to give her something to look at when she spoke. Something other than those hard golden eyes. "Theron tells me you are better."

Yenic rose to a trembling stand, spreading his arms out for balance almost as though he had forgotten how to use his legs. He stood there, swaying a bit, eyes focusing. She thought it might've been the heat that stole his strength; Theron had lit the brazier in the center of the room and sage smoked throughout the enclosure, cloying in her throat.

"Can we get you anything?" She tried again. It was painful, seeing him standing there, uncertain but very much alive, and knowing that the easiness they had finally found with each other was gone. She had to work not to twist her fingers together nervously.

"I'm fine," the person in Yenic's body answered, looking down at the occupied frame as though it was completely foreign. "Except I'm not sure...I don't know..."

"How you got here," Alaysha finished, guessing from the way the person who had been Yenic began to run hands over his body, touching here and there, inspecting the smoothness and the hardness of it at the same time, that having a body at all was quite an unexpected event. Gael either missed the significance of Yenic's actions, or he didn't care.

"Who are you?" He demanded. There was steel in his spine as he stood there, confronting Yenic. Alaysha almost felt sorry for the poor person. Then she remembered whoever was inside of Yenic's body, whether Yuri, Yenic himself, or some new woman, that person had some explaining to do. She braced herself, still hoping Theron was wrong, that the evidence of her eyes was wrong. She wanted to rush to him, ease him back down onto the thatch mat and tell him how relieved she was that he was alive. How grateful she was that he given his life to break the bond with his mother that also tied the fire witch to Alaysha. She wanted to tell him she loved him, and even that made her feel strange, as though she'd been caught doing something she shouldn't.

She opted to pull over the wooden bench that rested next to the wall. She carefully avoided the ink pot and bone needle that she'd used just the night before to mark both Gael and Cai as her Arms Of Protection. Something never before done in Theron's memory, or so he'd said, explaining that usually a witch had one protective Arm, not two. He'd warned them that the consequences of the strength of such a bond were uncertain. It was just one more thing to keep her awake, her mind running down wooded pathways that never resolved, that never took her home.

Together with Theron's aid, she helped ease Yenic down onto the bench and sat next to him, struggling to keep her arm from curling around his waist. She had to sit on her hands to keep them from twitching.

"Tell us," she said. "Theron seems to believe you are neither Yuri nor Yenic." She couldn't assess from the sound of the person's voice whether it was feminine or masculine. It sounded somewhere like a mix between her father and Yenic, and yet neither.

It was hard sitting up straight on the bench, but the person who had been Yenic didn't slouch. The frame stayed ramrod straight even as Alaysha struggled not to hunch over.

"I'm Yusmine." The person controlling Yenic's frame turned effortlessly toward Alaysha and regarded her for a long moment. "The person you knew as a man, as Yuri, was me. *Is* me. I spoke with a feminine voice when I was here before."

"What do you mean when you were here before?"

"The last time. The only other time." She looked confused for a second and her voice sounded thoughtful. "I suppose this is the third man, isn't it."

Alaysha stole a look at Theron. The shaman was rapt. Nodding without speaking, yet still his mouth worked in some sort of agreement. It was as though he understood exactly what Yusmine was saying. Alaysha noticed that he had indeed found some woad and had traced the lines and symbols onto his hands and feet. Not just the old blue veins of age, after all, but some sort of magic he felt he had regained. Disconcerted, she turned her attention to Yusmine.

"I still don't understand," Alaysha told her.

"I have been in your savage flesh twice," the woman said. "Once as Oracle to the Sisket. Once as Emir of Sarum. Those bodies are no more, but the spirit is the same." Her hands moved furtively to her chest, testing again, feeling around. The fingers rested on the place where her breasts would be but where Yenic's chest was smooth. "I had thought to be fleshed by now, but it seems I am a man again." She regarded Alaysha with a look of near resignation.

The eyes were not warm honey, after all, Alaysha realized. They were darker, almost as though the honey had been burned over a brazier. There was a crystalline facet to them. What warmth came from color, the shine made cold. Even so, they were not ungentle eyes.

"Theron used that same term," Alaysha mused aloud. "Fleshed."

"It's a simple term, really." The woman shifted on her seat. "She reached out briefly, almost awkwardly, and her fingers met Alaysha's skin on her shoulder. There was a pinch, just enough to pull the skin away but not enough to hurt. "It's this savage flesh, that we take on. Like your jerkin, or your shoes." The woman picked at the leather at the edge of her shoulder, then pointed to Gael's boots. "The goddess gave us to this flesh so we could walk your earth as one of you."

Patient determination: that was what was needed. Alaysha needed to find a way to explain to this woman at the body she was in didn't belong to her, would never belong to her.

"This body was not made by the goddess," Alaysha explained, assuming that therein lay the loophole. She tried to be gentle, but she needed to be firm. "This body was born of a woman; it's not yours."

"Of that I have no knowledge," Yusmine said, waving away the thought as though it was inconsequential. "I only know I'm here." She tried to smile, but the lips only tilted at the corner lazily the way Yenic would have smiled. Alaysha's breath caught in her throat. She had to look away and found Gael's eyes, those green as moss and grey as a stormy sky eyes, urging her on, giving her courage. She thought she could feel a charge moving between them, like the rush of a river finding its way to the wide waters.

"And what of the seeds?" Alaysha wanted terribly to know. "You asked me – Yuri asked me – how many--"

Yenic's body went rigid. "You have collected them, haven't you? Each one?"

Alaysha found herself stammering. "Every time I – every time someone dies, when I find their seeds, I pick them up. Yuri used them as a count to see how many enemies died at my hand." Died at her hands for him, she reminded herself.

"I remember," Yusmine said. "But not when *everyone* dies, surely."

Alaysha remembered the Enyalian warriors who'd invaded the Highland village in retribution and seeming vengeance, those women she had killed and who had no seeds to collect when she'd drawn their water, how she'd laughed at the strangeness of it. "No. But some."

"It's ingrained in you, you were compelled to collect them much the same as the man you know as Yuri – myself – was compelled to gather the temptresses." A pained look came across Yusmine's face, then. Almost as though she was thinking of the things Yuri had done when he couldn't have the witches he wanted and instead decided to assassinate them, and felt regret. She shook it off quickly and faced Alaysha again.

"Those seeds are the spirits of Greater Etlantium. Of each of Liliah's children forced to be born over and over again in this savage world without being properly fleshed. We're trapped here, as she trapped herself to escape her brother." Yusmine tried to move herself down from the bench so she could sit on the broader, more stable ground. Theron rushed to take her arm, to ease her beside it. He passed her a hammered goblet filled with water, his blue veins made an even darker blue by the woad.

"Such a spirit should take her time," he murmured. "The energies leak."

She gave him a lingering look of gratitude. "I was unkind to you, old man," she said, and Alaysha knew she heard Yuri's voice humming beneath the graciousness of the words.

Theron hung his head as though he was sharing a memory with the woman. If he wanted to respond to Yusmine, his feet and the woad traced over them took the words from him and stole his attention. Yusmine reached for his hand when he said nothing.

"You will see her again, old man." The hands that were Yenic's moved to cup Theron's face. "She is only waiting, no more."

The shaman gave a subtle nod. Alaysha could swear she saw tears in his eyes. "Trapped," he said. "As we all are." His shoulders shook and in moments, he'd fallen into Yusmine's embrace, with Yuri's voice shushing his tears. It was as much as Alaysha could stand. She tried to wait until the shaman had gathered himself, but it seemed to take longer than Gael could stand to wait for.

"Trapped?" he demanded and Yusmine regarded him over Theron's shoulder.

"Yes," Yusmine said. "There is much to explain, but only as much as I myself understand it." Yusmine stretched and yawned, easing the shaman away. "Forgive me; moving this body when nothing fits is exhausting." She pulled away from Theron and eased him back on his haunches where he wiped at his eyes with his sleeve.

Alaysha wanted more, she wanted to hear everything. Most of all, she wanted to know one thing.

"So you're not my father?" She said.

Yusmine cocked her head. "I am. I am very much your father. But your father was not me, not really. He was only those things, those very base things, that I could remember when I was re-fleshed here in the way that your Savage world fleshes: born of a woman through pain and blood. The physical forgets how to connect to the spirit. And in the moment that we are formed, and born squalling forth, it's as though we had never lived before. Your flesh makes us forget." She sounded sad.

"But he knew what he was doing, my father. He knew he was asking me to –"

"To kill?" The woman guessed and the words made Alaysha cringe. "Indeed, I do remember that. While Yuri would not have remembered my purpose, I do remember all the things he did. I might not be pleased by them, But neither can I change them. The man who was Yuri knew only the things he was compelled to do, even if they came from some deep memory that he couldn't process."

"And what of Yenic?" Alaysha realized her hands were twisting together as she asked the question, but she needed to hear the answer. She didn't dare look at Gael as it came.

"Is Yenic this body?" Yusmine looked down at her arms, testing the movements of her fingers, and letting her hands sway back and forth in front of her. "The goddess gave us all this body to share," the woman answered.

"Can you feel him? Can I talk to him?" A flutter moved within Alaysha's chest as she asked it, not sure what she wanted the answer to be.

"It's not as easy as that," Yusmine said. Yuri and I are one spirit who was fleshed into two different bodies at two different times; Yenic…he is not part of me. Just part of this body. Perhaps sometime they can be separated. Perhaps if we can gain our own flesh," Yusmine let the words trail off, shrugging with a feminine lift that looked odd moving through Yenic's body; Alaysha had to bite back the tears. "But we are all of Etlantium," she said were cheerfully. "And so when the war is won, we will all have ourselves again.

"But why aren't you asking the goddess these things? She knows far more than I do. I'm only the Oracle. My job, my tasks are done. Long done these generations past." She looked about her as though she still couldn't quite believe she had returned to The Savage World.

"What tasks?"

"My job during my first fleshing in your Savage world was to set up the sacred oil and write the sacred texts so that when Liliah finally found her power, we could ungod her twin."

"Ungod?"

Yusmine confirmed it with a nod more gracious than Yenic could have managed. "It took generations and many fleshings here for her twin to come at the same time as she did. But he didn't know which of his court was her the last time. It was a time of much blood, that, and when he realized that I knew who she was, he took the flesh from me." This time she chuckled. "But he didn't take my flesh in time. I managed to bury the oils and hide the texts from him and he could do nothing except suffer death himself when his entire tribe rose against him." Yusmine crossed her arms thoughtfully. "It's fortunate he was born as one of your mortal men, and not as a temptress."

"You're saying this sisket was Liliah's twin? The God who would kill her?"

"More than that, they are two sides of the same spirit. To merely kill her, would leave him painfully out of balance. He needs to ungod her, take her power for himself and weaken her so that he can return to Etlantium and leave her here to wither."

Alaysha's head swam. "He took your life back then?"

Yusmine shifted on the bench. "He took my life, and many others. His own sister was a temptress of flame, and when he took the life of his own daughter, that was when his city turned against him. She was well loved, the little one."

"They murdered him for it," Alaysha guessed.

"Yes. And then his sister went mad. The witches were scattered; they would have undoubtedly lost their way, lost their knowledge of themselves. These were the early generations, you have to understand, after Liliah had fled Etlantium to this Savage Garden. He didn't know how to put the pieces of her puzzle together. He didn't even realize who he was, that he was the great half god of Etlantium come to the garden of his sister's making. As I said, your flesh makes us forget."

Alaysha thought she understood, finally. "But a witch has a long memory," she murmured. "When he finally came as one of the goddess's temptresses, he could finally remember who he was."

"If I'm here now, then that is so," Yusmine admitted. "Liliah as well. She will remember what she is. But those generations ago… Well, he would have taken the lives in vain, based only on some compulsion from a deep-seated memory that he didn't understand. Yusmine gave Alaysha careful study. "Much as I would have done in ignorance as your father."

That made Alaysha squirm. "So they both know they are here together, and both of them need to ungod the other in order to return to this Etlantium."

"An easy task when spoken with words. Not so much with deeds."

"No," Alaysha agreed. Being reborn generation after generation, hoping the next time would be into the body of one of Liliah's temptresses. It was a complex puzzle indeed. "But now they're both here, and the time has come."

Yusmine sighed. "It has come. And if you are a witch of some power, you'll understand what it will take to win the war."

"Blood," Alaysha guessed.

"Lots of it."

CHAPTER 5

Alaysha could hear the subtle creaking of Gael's leathers as he shifted uncomfortably where he stood. No doubt he would worry that the blood necessary would be her own. She turned to him and made some excuse about Theron needing to break his fast; she could hear his belly grumbling from across the lodging. It wasn't true, but it would certainly grant her an audience alone with the woman. When they had left, Alaysha turned to the woman who once had been Yenic.

"You said lots of blood," Alaysha prompted; she reached for the copper bowl filled with ash. She stared down into it, waiting for the woman to explain. Yusmine's fingers met hers as she leaned forward to grasp the other edge. Alaysha let her eyes cross the bowl and waited for some flicker of recognition, some humming to course through her fingers, reminding her that the body the woman resided in was Yenic, and that they had a bond many seasons old.

Instead, the crystalline honey of Yusmine's gaze went to the black contents within the copper. "You have collected many seeds?"

"All that I could find."

The woman made Yenic's lips twitch in thought. "That's good. The goddess will need those."

"And the blood?"

"Those who would wish to return to Etlantium, those who have been reduced to the seeds of their soul, and those who are breathing, all of them require it. The magic Liliah will need to ungod her brother requires it."

The woman leaned back, easing the bowl out of Alaysha's hands. She dipped her index finger in, rubbed it thoughtfully against her thumb. "Some of those seeds have undoubtedly been lost, collected already by Helle as he found them. He'll use those as hostages to strengthen his own power."

Alaysha squinted at Yusmine suspiciously, believing she had an idea just exactly where all of the blood would come from and she didn't like it. Not one bit.

"But the little goddess is thrice empowered," she argued. "The death of her grandmother and mother would have lent her power unlike any other witch, even Aislin. Surely that would be enough." Alaysha didn't like the way the soot filled in each crevice of Yusmine's fingertips and she took the bowl away and set it back on the floor. "Surely you won't need all of the blood shed if she's more powerful than Helle. More powerful than any of us."

"More powerful than all but you," Yusmine said. "I did one thing as your father that was worth my having to suffer this flesh. That much I grant."

Alaysha jerked to her feet. She might have known that the spirit that drove Yuri would be callous in the end, no matter that it was feminine. "You can't ask of them what you plan to ask."

Either Yusmine chose to ignore the statement or she didn't have an answer. Alaysha's arms crept around her torso, feeling the suppleness of old leather. Her fingers touched upon minute holes where threadings had been before, tying chips of Garnet to the tunic, the hopes of her nohma to find a normal sense of union with another. She faced Yusmine.

"If Liliah can bring back my father, can she bring back others?"

Yusmine cocked her head thoughtfully. "But she didn't bring back your father, Alaysha, not as you knew him. If she brought back others, they would not be as you knew them either. They would be… Different."

"Because they would be the true spirits of Etlantium," Alaysha guessed. "Not the people who loved me here." She thought of her nohma, of her mother. She had a brief image of her twin sister in her father's parapet room, of the final recognition in her sister's eyes as she let herself be sacrificed to Aislin's fire. What would it matter if she didn't know them, so long as they had a chance to live again.

"You didn't answer the question. Can she bring them back?"

"If the seeds are in our possession, they can be re-fleshed, yes, but under one condition." Yusmine's amber eyes were wary.

"They would need bodies," Alaysha guessed.

"Indeed. But all of that doesn't matter. Even if they returned somehow to this flesh, they still belong to Etlantium, and Liliah has need of them."

Alaysha thought of all those she loved who would be part of this Etlantium Yusmine spoke of, of the blood they would have to shed. Lots of it, the woman had said. That meant only one thing to Alaysha. "Surely she doesn't have need of all of them," she said.

"Surely not, but would they want to remain in this Savage world to be born of your flesh squalling and in pain their entire lives, only to die and never to return. You would be asking them to give up more than you know. More than you think I'm asking of them."

"So it can be done. They don't have to choose Etlantium."

"We have a choice, yes." Yusmine was guarded in her response, even her posture went rigid.

"And your texts and your sacred oil, all of these things are necessary as well."

"We need to gather your seeds, yes. And return for those things I left that can bring Liliah to success."

"And where will we wage this battle?"

Yusmine crossed one leg over the other and gave her a look that reminded Alaysha so much of Yuri, that she shivered. "Where do you think the battle will be waged, Witch?"

"In Sarum," Alaysha guessed. She should have known. She thought back to her little cave in the mountain that Theron called sacred. In her mind's eye, she traveled the tunnels again, finding the Crystal skull cave, the pit that Edulph had been thrown into. She remembered the night she and Gael had found comfort with each other, leaving Aedus in a small room just off a stone alcove where dozens of amphorae collected dust and cobwebs. "In the tunnels," she heard herself say. "That's where you hid them."

Yusmine gave a slow, sly nod as though these revelations were something Alaysha had been part of all along. "The tunnels shift. Part of Liliah's magic. It's where she came to this world, where she birthed the original temptresses. It's where she gave them her power so that she could lay weak and untended: blood, bone, breath--"

"And being," Alaysha finished.

"Yes, and being." Yusmine sounded pleased. "That last bit is the spark of life," Yusmine said. "With what little power she had left she granted the temptresses each a means of safety."

Alaysha tried to imagine the little goddess lying cold and shivering in the depths of the mountain, funneling her energy down into four living vessels she'd crafted to hold her magic. She thought of how vulnerable the girl would be, indeed, how vulnerable those vessels – now women – would be should their powers be discovered. Despite their strength, they would need more.

"Arms of protection," she murmured.

This time, Yusmine nodded. "She expected Helle would not be able to target her if her power was split into so many bodies. She lost her spirit flesh and became as you see yourself. A vessel of mortal skin. She fully expected Helle to follow her and thus lose himself the same way she did. And that was the exquisite beauty of her plan."

"But that would mean they would both be lost here," Alaysha said and Yusmine's face brightened.

"Ah, but she granted herself a means of escape. When she gave her power over to your skin, she would have died in your Savage world, yet she left the temptresses with the understanding that they could weave a spell of fleshing that would grant her rebirth here, and rebirth and rebirth and rebirth until the time would come when Helle either lost himself or she was able to face him."

"And now she is able," Alaysha said. Except she wasn't, was she? Except the little goddess was young and untried. Except the little goddess had a healthy body, but a very weak mind. Powerful she might be, but Aislin had all the cunning of a woman grown, a woman who had memory of her entire godhood at her disposal. How much the little goddess understood and how much power she could wield was still in question.

Yusmine stretched her legs in front of her, inspecting the hard muscles of Yenic's thighs. "She will need all of Etlantium if she is to be refleshed to Etlantium," she said. "And that means all the magic and power that rests in all of the fallen temptresses from the beginning of Liliah's escape until now. It means we must find the seeds of those temptresses you have collected; in them is the strongest power, and we will need the blood of those of Etlantium who still live."

"Their blood," Alaysha heard the dread in her own tone. She thought of Theron and Gael and Saxa, of Aedus. She couldn't ask it of them, and she wouldn't. "They will have to have the choice," Alaysha said grimly.

"They will have a choice," Yusmine said with a peculiar look on her face. "Most of them."

"Most?" Alaysha wasn't following her. Was it possible that some of them will be sacrificed anyway? She felt a hard ball coil in her belly.

"Those who are bound to the temptresses will be needed in the battle and in the fleshing so they will not have the choice. We need to keep them in your Savage flesh to perform the rituals."

A spark of hope ignited within Alaysha's chest. Not having a choice in this case was positive. "So Gael, Cai? Neither of them will be able to offer themselves?" She made a mental note to get Theron to mark Aedus as Liliah's blood witch, to mark Saxon as her Arm of Protection once they found him. That would only leave Saxa and Bronwyn. Alaysha's mind raced to see if there were others she could save as well. Her stomach suddenly began to unclump.

"Their blood must not be spilled," Yusmine was saying. "The blood witches as well. All serve the purpose of the ritual until the ritual is complete.

"But no doubt they will want to return to Etlantium when Hel is ungodded," she went on. "Those who served the goddess will need to be re-fleshed in her image if they are to return home. For the goddess to perform that magic, she will need a special kind of blood."

"The blood of the witches she created," Alaysha guessed. She imagined that the last of the ritual would require her own blood, the blood of the Theron's Earth witch, and of Aislin's. She swallowed down hard, thinking that this war could mean the end of her own life as well. Not too long ago, she'd have been happy to let it go. Living the life of a weapon, taking lives at another's bidding, finding herself used and manipulated without hope of ever finding peace.

"You're not wrong," Yusmine said carefully. "The witches, all of the blood witches, their Arms, they will undoubtedly want to return as well, and so that one small sacrifice should they want it, will be a tiny thing. So you're not wrong, but you're not right either."

"But you said..." Alaysha said warily. "A special kind of blood."

"Indeed. Very special," Yusmine's crystalline eyes held a strange glint that made Alaysha's hands tremble as she lifted one to push the hair from her face.

"No," Alaysha said, realizing what the woman was really getting at. "The most special would be the witch who is also a goddess. Her blood. What you're saying is that in order to return to her Etlantium, the little goddess must die."

CHAPTER 6

Alaysha stumbled from the tent, her mind reeling with the truths she'd extracted from Yusmine, her vision blurred with a strange wetness she didn't understand. Why would she weep for the little goddess when the prospect of her own death set like a boiled sun on the horizon. In all this time, she'd never thought that the truths she'd been seeking would end in such bloodshed. She'd expected the people she'd come to love to be safe. She'd entered this troublesome quarrel hesitantly, not caring herself what direction the road took her only that she could allow herself to feel the emotion her father had taken a lifetime to train out of her. The deities were indeed cruel to grant her that only to see she felt pain for it. If she'd only remained complacent, she would never be in this spot at all.

If these loved ones were truly of Etlantium and truly would want to return, what right did she have to rob them of that choice? And yet, she wanted to rob them of it. She thought of her nohma and of Aedus. She thought of Gael and Saxa and the as yet unrecovered Saxon. They would deserve the choice, but the way her stomach churned, the way her legs trembled at the thought of losing them to such a ritual sacrifice, the way the bile rose in her throat… All of those things told her she was not willing to give them up to such foolishness just so they could return to a world Alaysha wasn't even sure truly existed. She might not doubt her own power or the power of the others: she'd witnessed those with her own eyes, felt the magic move. But Etlantium? Who was to say it wasn't just one more painful realm.

Indeed, she'd been used all of her life as a tool for others. She imagined that all of the witches were the same. They'd spent their lives in hiding, keeping to themselves so that no man could manipulate them into using their power. Surely Aislin wouldn't let life continue on as though she wasn't a god in the flesh with a sister of equal power sharing the same plane, threatening his existence. No, Aislin would come for her. And she would come for the other witches, Alaysha included. But she'd need all of them to complete the ritual; otherwise, it was mere death and rebirth. Alaysha thought she could live with that.

Gael was crouched next to the fire as the flap fell behind her, his broad hands working to make the flames lift higher to crisp the skin of the spitted hare. Theron was busy retracing patterns on his feet with his index finger dipping it into a pot of woad and drawing lines up his instep. She turned away when she saw them, swiping at her cheeks with the palms of her hands and letting the fingers draw the rest of the water collecting in her tear ducts. She wondered how much they might have heard and then decided that it didn't matter. She would deny all of it if she had to. If the others had a choice, then so did she. And her choice was to walk away.

"Done?' Gael asked her, standing from where he was crouched and wiping his hands clean of splinters of wood and dirt onto his breeks.

"Not done," said Alaysha. "So very far from done." She felt guilty and tried to avoid his eyes.

Half a dozen steps and no more and Gael was close enough to lift her chin with his fingers. She might have met his gaze, then, but she could only do so by chewing fiercely on the inside of her cheek. He squinted down at her, his gray green eyes carefully guarded, his brow a measured and level line across it. "The sun will be setting soon."

She pulled her bottom lip into her mouth, finding a bit of peeling skin and capturing it with her teeth.

"A torturous day for all of us."

"Yes," she whispered. She took his hands in hers and eased them away from her face, taking a step backwards and moving towards the fire. She knew she'd never be able to fool him into thinking nothing was wrong, but she couldn't stand the careful measure of his gaze. She hugged herself as she stared down into the flames.

She could hear him behind her, moving closer, felt his hands on hers as his arms encircled her waist. "Yenic?"

Alaysha bristled at the name, but she supposed it was better than Gael calling him Yuri. "Yusmine," she said, stressing the correction, "was looking exhausted."

She wouldn't tell him, not yet. She had to sort it all out in her mind first.

"I left her to rest," she said. "Perhaps Theron will bring her some of the roasted hare Bodicca has turning over the fire." She looked askance at the shaman, who now remained quiet and contemplative. He was looking at her with a thoughtful gaze, one that unnerved her. "You can both stay here tonight, Theron. Gael is right, the sun will set soon and we've yet to eat and rest from all that's happened."

He wiped his finger on the bottom of his cassock and stood. She could see his glance flick towards the lodging and thought perhaps he might have heard more than she wanted him to. "This witch will not sleep here?" He asked her.

Alaysha had to think about it. She was sick with information and she needed to lie down, get away. In the heights of the huge redwoods was out of the question; her head spun just thinking about climbing those stairs and everything within her was trembling enough to make her want to vomit. "I'll sleep with Barruch," she answered. "It won't be the first night we slept under the stars together."

The scent of roasted hare grew stronger and Bodicca strode across the compound, mixing something in a large hammered copper bowl with a thick wooden spoon. Undoubtedly, she'd gone foraging in other places besides the woods. Without a word, the old warrior settled close to the fire, spreading a thick, doughy paste over hot rocks and drizzling honey she'd undoubtedly found on the same forage onto the slowly rising dough. She looked up sharply as Alaysha padded near.

"How is the Emir?" A pained look of concern set uneasily on the woman's face.

"It isn't the Emir," Alaysha told her, not sure where to begin and not sure how much she wanted to divulge.

"But I heard him."

"As did we all," Alaysha said, sighing. "But it's not as we thought."

Gael settled onto a fallen tree that someone had thoughtfully gathered close to the cook fire, one of three that created impromptu seating, and stretched his boots toward the fire. "It's not like anything we could have thought," he confessed, and Alaysha was wont to tell him he had no idea how far off they'd been, but she held her tongue.

Bodicca gave her a curious look. And Alaysha shook her head, thinking that if she changed the subject, it would have to go away.

"The meal smells delicious." Is what she said.

The exiled Enyalian grinned proudly. "It didn't take long to find the honey. The spices were another story."

She had already pulled the rabbit from its spit and was quartering it, breaking off the now risen bread from the hot rocks and scraping meat from the carcass onto the cooked dough. The aroma made Alaysha's stomach gurgle. Once Bodicca tested the other two, and spread fragments of meat onto those, she passed one to Alaysha and then leaned back, her right elbow resting against one of the dead and fallen trees that served as seats around the cook fire.

"Yuri loved roasted hare," the warrior said with a reminiscent tone that made Alaysha feel as though she succeeded in deflecting the conversation. "Ever since our young days in the woods, he would beg me to make wild rabbit with roasted honey, fired over open flame." She eased her eyes closed as though remembering, her eyelids fluttering lightly. "The first rabbit I caught for him, he gave to me. He said such a brave one deserved the first bite. That was our first night away from the village, moons after I'd cast for him and the bone witch bought our lives with the promise of killing the infant."

There was a long moment while Bodicca obviously relived those days, and Alaysha imagined what it must've been like for a young girl not even blooded by the moon to cast for a young man there in the Enyalian village. She had to know the risk she was taking, that if another decided to fight for him, that she might die instead of saving him. Instead, the girl had accomplished the near impossible: she'd managed to extract a young man from a village where men were killed before they could escape, sacrificed in a blood ritual that would insure the procreation and continuance of a perfect Enyalian line.

She waited for the warrior to open her eyes, and when she did they bore into Alaysha. "I spent many long nights and days with him, witch. I know him. That was Yuri in Yenic's body. You can't tell me otherwise."

It was, yes, but how to explain to Bodicca that it also wasn't. Deflection had worked before. Perhaps it would again if she ignored the underlying question in the woman's statement. "Tell me more about my father."

Bodicca bore into her with a look that would have made Alaysha squirm if she wasn't so exhausted already. She sighed, as though she was indulging a young child, but she went on. "I think the most important thing you would want to hear would be that he could be kind. He saved his brother. When my people would have killed him, with his own mother would have let him die, Yuri saved him. And others too.

"We crept back to the village, together he and I, leaving the babe with Corrin. We knew of all the men, boys, and yes, sometimes old women who had lost their use, we knew they would be committed to the fires within the next season.

"You've noticed there are no old in Enyalia," she quirked her brow at Alaysha and waited for her to nod. "It's a hard place."

Alaysha didn't need to be reminded. She suppressed a shiver as the woman continued.

"Living in such a hard village, walking about, training, eating, even sleeping, knowing that you are doing so with freedom only because you're a woman. Realizing that many others who wear skin, just as you do, who walk on two legs, can carry a sword, must eat and sleep and drink the same as you, knowing their days will end in flame..." The old warrior dug a bone from inside her cheeks with two fingers and flicked it aside. It landed in a patch of dried grass, a broken, splintered thing stripped of its meat.

"It bothered you," Alaysha guessed and the woman offered her a fleeting lopsided grin.

"It was nothing to me, but it gnawed at Yuri." She shrugged. "I'm just telling you how hard my people are."

"But you're not." Alaysha could almost hear the note of scorn in her own voice. She was beginning to feel the effects of the entire day and she was losing patience with trying to process information in any kind of empathetic manner.

In response, Bodicca shook her head. "I am what you see, that's all. My duty was to the Emir. My duty was to the people we saved from that village. From a death as certain as time. If he wanted it – anything – I would give it to him and think no more on it."

"And the people you conquered later? The people that Yuri had me kill for?" It was an accusation Alaysha would've wanted to deliver to Yuri, and would have if she'd not been so overwhelmed. Now, however, the anger was beginning to rise and she had no one left to take it out on.

The woman's mouth moved into a crooked line. "You don't have a command, witch. You don't know how heavy those things can lay on a brow. You don't know the way of it. The history of it. We stole the throwaways from the Enyalia; no more than that. Perhaps a few nursing women who could feed the young babe. Young boys who would grow in their short season to feed the fires of the quarter solstice. Old women who would have passed their use. They came to us one by one through the night. And we crept them out of the village and through the woods and when we had to fight, we thought, we would. But we hid, mostly. Because you saw how fierce, how unstoppable the Enyalia can be.

"The Emir knew that battles weren't always won by force. He used his wisdom to bring us all the way across the burnt lands, though we were large in number. We found Theron's witch. His temptress, he always called her. And we delivered to her a son of her lover's own blood. Though he was born of a woman he hated, Yuri wanted him to live."

Left the son and took the shaman you mean; Alaysha wasn't to be fooled. She'd heard the story back in Enyalia, when she was as much a captive as Yenic and Theron before him. She knew how determined the Enyalia were to keep their culture pure in their own eyes, but she knew more than that. She knew exactly how the great Yuri saved his brother. "He murdered her, his own mother."

The woman's face went cold. "Not murder. Mercy. She was dying. He gave her a chance to die with her dignity. A chance to die with her sword in her hand."

"And in turn, he murdered my mother. My grandmother. He subjected me to torture. I was an outcast in my own city. I lived like a tool, not like a daughter. And I killed for him in turn." It sickened her to say those words, and she treated them as an accusation, not as an admission.

Bodicca took a bite of her meat and chewed reflectively. "What Yuri did, what he asked of me, I can't say his reasoning behind those orders. I only know I followed them. But I tell you this: he followed the tale of the witches like a dog would chew on a favored bone. He tore at it over the flames at night, what could a person do if they had that much power within their grasp: what could be done to a person if that much power was unleashed?" The woman shifted against the fallen tree and wiped her hands in some moss she pulled from the rotting bark. "He was a survivor if nothing else. Don't ask me what he thought, I couldn't tell you. I can tell you he saved as many people as you killed.

"You would have me feel guilty," Alaysha said.

The woman shook her head. "I would have you understand how well I know the man." The woman stood, wiping her hands together. "Now tell me, where is my Emir?"

"He's gone," Alaysha said, lifting her hands at her sides in a helpless gesture she hoped Bodicca would recognize as genuine.

"You've done something with him, something while I was occupied to your menial tasks. Cooking for you. Setting the cook fire. You took advantage of that and the Emir's vulnerable state." While the words warned Alaysha that the warrior in Bodicca was rising, the tone betrayed no emotion. She knew this would be when the woman was at her most dangerous.

Gael stood to face her, as sure a block as an army of a thousand men. "The Emir is gone. That Yuri you knew, you know no longer. He's as gone as Yenic."

Bodicca pulled a blade from her belt and danced away from Gael. "I hope you're prepared to back that up with your life, man."

CHAPTER 7

It was almost ludicrous, the way Bodicca splayed her feet and dared Gael with her posture. It was almost ludicrous, and it was most definitely the last straw. After all they'd been through, after Yenic's death and rebirth, after Bodicca's own flight from Sarum with Yenic in tow, after near-death, near starvation, near dying of thirst, battles they fought and won, the spontaneous combustion of a slew of highland villagers. It was preposterous that Bodicca would take up arms against them. It was so absurd, that even in Alaysha's exhaustion, something told her that there had to be more to it. That Bodicca would not square off against them for any reason except one. A slow realization dawned upon Alaysha and she reached out to still the woman's knife hand, testing the woman's resolve.

"Bodicca, think about it." She pleaded. "If it was Yuri in Yenic's body, why would we harm him?"

Bodicca's grimaced. "Harm? I don't think you would merely harm him," she said to Alaysha. "I think you would kill him."

Gael had pulled his own sword and was glowering at Bodicca. "Harm him or kill," he said. "It doesn't matter," he said to Alaysha. "If the woman begs for death then let it be so." He was ready as always, Alaysha noticed. Sword already drawn, muscle tensed to launch or spring. She had to take control and quickly. She stepped between them. Her head had begun to hurt.

"Kill him?" she said, the weariness sounding in her voice. "After all of this?"

"You hate him," Bodicca said.

An answer to that accusation wouldn't leave Alaysha's tongue. When she didn't speak, the woman shook her head like a dog trying to rid its ears of water. "You won't have me stand down until I see the Emir." Dogged determination to match the speech patterns, Alaysha supposed. The woman had never been tactically imaginative.

Alaysha sighed heavily. "Go then," she told her. "Go inside with Theron and see what you can find in there." She waved the woman in and collapsed heavily onto the tree trunk. She patted the spot next to her and Gael settled down.

She looked at him. That same strange charge again wavered through the air. She felt it settle at the base of her spine. She wanted to touch him, she realized. She wanted to feel their skin connect. Perhaps it was the sense of comfort he gave. Perhaps it was something else. All she knew was that she was bone tired and the thought of giving into something seemed as alluring as a warm bath after a day of soiling oneself in battle. Even as she thought it, she noticed his hand went beneath his armpit, stroking absently the spot where she'd marked him.

"Does it hurt?" she asked.

He seemed to only notice what he was doing when she asked him about it. "Not hurt," he told her. "Something else."

"I feel it too," she admitted. She eased herself closer so that her thigh touched his. The spark again, and this time she let it run up her entire leg to the small of her back. It felt good to succumb. Life was too perilous to be fighting all the time, and yet she knew there were more battles to come. She considered her choice for a moment, the one that told her she should walk away, let go all of the issues that were not hers in the first place.

"What should we do?" she asked him.

It took him a long time to answer. "We have the little witch," he said to her. "We need another."

"The other witch," she said. "You would have us return to Enyalia?" It was on the tip of her tongue to tell him what she learned from Yusmine, but she found she couldn't speak of it.

He scraped at the earth with the heel of his boot. "If the witch we seek is there, I'm afraid we have no choice." He gave her careful study. She wasn't sure what she saw within those gray green eyes, but she was certain it was some kind of decision.

"What?" She asked him.

"You will not go."

Despite her decision to not get involved, she wasn't sure she enjoyed being told what she could do. "You can't tell me that."

"We'll send Cai."

"They'll burn her back raw with melted boar grease. You know this." Alaysha reminded him and he shrugged in response. She thought she was exhausted, but an awakening anger that he could think so little of it his co-Arm sent renewed energy into her.

"You can't think she'll go willingly. It would mean her death." If the woman did survive the stripping of her skin from melted boar's fat, then she'd surely die before she returned. She was strong, yes, but even Bodicca had barely made it and only a chance meeting with Theron was able to put her on the road to recovery.

"Do we have a choice?"

And there it was, the heart of the matter after all. "We do have the choice. All of us. And I will not let any of us believe we have to sacrifice ourselves for a cause no one believes in."

He hung his head. "Perhaps we wouldn't do it for a cause," he said.

"What of Isolde," she said. "If I remember correctly, she swore to Cai that she would dispose of the bone witch." She gave a thought to the old woman back in the Enyalian village who would have had her dead, who had ordered Theron's death a generation ago, and of his and Alkaia's son born to her at their quarter solstice. The woman who conspired to kill Alaysha even if she won the casting for Yenic. She could see again the woman's tangle of hair and bones sticking from without, the chalk on her face. The tattaued hands.

"We can't be certain she's gone yet," Alaysha said. "And we can't take the chance that she still lives and wields any power in the village."

"But how would we dream of getting the clay witch out?"

Alaysha licked her lips, daring to wonder if she could plant the seed. "Perhaps we don't need to."

Gael squeezed her knee as though he thought she was being foolish. "Of course we do; we can't think to beat Aislin without her."

"So you believe we should fight?"

"What is a warrior marked for if not to fight for the proper thing?"

Indeed. Alaysha would have agreed, except she wasn't sure what the right thing was.

"You don't trust Cai?" Gael asked, mistaking her silence and she looked at him, unsure how to explain her doubts, that what she wanted to do more than anything was to extract them from all of this trouble.

"It's not that."

"She won't let herself get burned, Alaysha," Gael said, his voice tinged with concern and with something else that Alaysha struggled to understand in the light of who they were speaking of. "She's smarter than that. Far more cunning. And they respect her there. You saw how Isolde obeyed her even though she was no longer Komandiri." He squirmed uncomfortably, perhaps hating the sound of himself defending her. "There are many things that I think that woman is, but foolish is not one of them."

It was a grudging respect that Alaysha heard in his tone, she realized, and she knew how much it would cost him to say so. He'd suffered at Enyalia hands, forced to service half a dozen Enyalia warriors against his will. Such powerlessness over your own body would have done terrible things to a man's psyche, let alone a warrior trained to kill without compunction. And that's what they were, she knew, what Yuri had made of them, warriors devoid of empathy and compassion. She thought perhaps they had more in common with the Enyalia than she wanted to admit. Even so, it pained her to think of the torment he'd endured, that had so affected him that she'd had no other choice but to save him from it.

"I don't trust Enyalia," he said. " But Cai is not Enyalian anymore. Whether I like it or not, she's bound with me to you. She came to you willingly, as I did." This time when Gael squeezed, he let his hand travel to the middle of her thigh, the tips of his fingers reaching in toward the tender flesh inside her legs. The flutter at the back of her throat made her realize her weariness was making her complacent. She eased as gently as she could away from Gael and faced him, crossing her ankles as a means of barricading herself, and she wondered in the moment she did so if it was him she didn't trust or herself.

She spoke before she could give it too much thought. "Even still, we would be putting her at risk, asking her to betray her homeland."

"Where is the betrayal," Gael asked. "She's only robbing them of two women who don't belong there."

"Two?"

"The clay witch and Thera." He said the second name as though he'd bitten into a lemon and didn't like the taste.

Alaysha was confused. "Why her?"

Gael shrugged. "She would have treated the clay witch. She would know things."

Alaysha sighed, not wanting to give in. He must have thought she would refuse because he said, "she won't be alone, Alaysha. We'll send Bodicca as well."

He wasn't listening. And if he was listening, he didn't care. "Do you know what they'll do to them, Bodicca and Cai, if they return to Enyalia?" Alaysha demanded of him.

"I have some knowledge of the cruelty of the Enyalia, yes," he said softly.

"Do you remember Bodicca's back? What they did to it, to her, as reward for her returning when they exiled her?"

He seemed to ignore that. Instead he inclined his head towards the woods as though it held secrets she needed to know.

"Do you really believe what she told you about her and Yuri's escape. You can't honestly think that your father had not planned some sort of escape long before the bone witch allowed them to leave unmolested so long as they trailed and murdered Alkaia and her son. Yuri couldn't have known that Bodicca would win her casting for him, or even that they would allow her to throw down for him in the first place. He would have planned an escape just in case. And surely he would have told her. There's routes from the Enyalian village," he said. "And there's ways in. There has to be. Ways in and out that the sentries don't know of, perhaps that Yuri created himself. There's no way that they simply waited in the woods until people crept from the village to join their cause. He would have set it up ahead of time."

Alaysha scratched a spot behind her ear that had suddenly grown itchy. Her father had never been one to leave things to chance. He'd even planned on taking the man he eventually called Corrin, the one who in his turn trained all of Sarum's warriors. A man who, like the women he'd been born from, felt no emotion.

"Perhaps you're right," Alaysha chewed the bottom of her lip thoughtfully. "He was never one to go unprepared. I doubt he was any different in his youth."

Gael mumbled something that sounded like a curse then said, "So then, although she might not tell us, Bodicca would know of a way in. It could well be that she and Cai could return to Enyalia unmolested and leave with both Thera and the clay witch in their grasp and none of the village be the wiser." He beamed at her.

A witch was not a woman who would come along without provocation, she'd be cautious, Alaysha knew, owing to her years of enforced manipulation. Perhaps showing her face might help lend credence to their claims. Then at least, if she didn't fight for Liliah, she could offer another witch some safety, and a choice. It was a reasonable compromise that Alaysha could easily live with.

"They might need me," Alaysha murmured more to herself than him.

Gael reacted to her words by leaning toward her and slipping his finger beneath her chin, tilting her face toward him.

"Somebody has to stay behind and watch Edulph and the little goddess." His gray green eyes met hers and the tingle at the base of her spine snaked up towards her neck. "And then someone has to stay behind to wring his filthy secret from him." This last was said with a bitter edge, and Alaysha remembered that the man still held Saxon and promised to trade.

"So I'm the first, and you're the second?" She said, and he took a step closer so that he was towering over her like a broad cloak about to go round her.

"Both of us here together," he said, his voice a rasp of emotion. "Acting as one. You were in my heart before, witch, but now with this mark of yours you are in my blood too."

She swallowed. She felt it as well. Yenic had warned her of the strength of the bond between a witch and her Arm of protection, he'd hinted that it was even enough to make mother and son long for each other. She hadn't truly believed it until she began to feel it for herself. But she couldn't admit that, not now when Yenic was still lost to them beneath Yusmine's consciousness. It wouldn't be fair to him. She could acknowledge the current moving between herself and Gael, but she must not act on it.

"We'll work together," she said. "And we will find him, Gael." She reached out and circled his wrist with her hand, meaning to offer him comfort. But it seemed all he noticed was that she'd not spoken to the feelings he'd so baldy confessed, and he stepped away, creating a space between them that felt like a chasm. For the moment, she was relieved. She had too many conflicting emotions running rampant through her. So many years of smothering them, letting them sit in the dark recesses of her memory, and now she had so many to deal with all at once. She didn't trust her feet to tiptoe through them without trampling.

His voice was a complete return to business. "No one can trust Edulph, and I mean to make sure he keeps his promise." He took several steps towards the lodging, seeming to want to enter but instead pacing in front of it. He was deciding something, she was certain of it.

Chapter 8

The night promised to be a hard, long one. Rather than stay with Theron and Yusmine in her own lodging, Alaysha opted to sleep with Barruch under the stars. She'd pulled her thatch mat out from its bundle that she'd stuffed in the corner of her hut and strode out to the hastily erected post where Barruch was tied. The Highland folks had no beasts of burden, no horses, no strange beasts like the Enyalia did. Fortunately, Barruch was obedient, if not spoiled. She regarded him in the creeping darkness for long moments, his baleful eye returning her gaze with something Alaysha would've called hurt.

"No peaches here, old man," she told him and he whickered noisily back at her. She thought she heard a chiding note within. These last sun cycles he'd had to content himself with sour grass and the occasional dried piece of fruit. Despite traveling with her and her companions some distance safely, despite near death in the burnt lands and flight from Enyalia, he'd yet to be rewarded and he let her know it. She'd set to brushing him down with gentle purpose, cleaning his hooves and bringing him fresh water before she spread her mat next to him and lay face up to contemplate the stars with the shadow canopy of tree leaves about them both.

Here and there she heard a scuttling in the underbrush, probably squirrels or raccoons foraging. She told herself there was nothing more dangerous in the undergrowth then a few rodents. After all that had happened, Alaysha wanted to believe she could be safe even for a short time. She knew Edulph and Liliah and Aedus would be safe with Cai and she knew Yusmine was in good hands with Theron. She needed a respite from all the activity, all the frenzied goings-on that she hadn't yet been able to process.

Alaysha wasn't sure what she'd expected from Bodicca once the warrior realized the man she'd loved in life enough to fight for, had returned as a woman in a man's body, but it certainly wasn't what had happened. With a bland alacrity, demonstrated so far as Alaysha could see, only by the emotionless Enyalia, the old warrior seemed that much more loyal to Yuri. She'd exited the lodging with a determined look on her face. The woman bent to retrieve the last leg of roasted hare that she'd left beside the fire, bit from the end, chewed, and stated that the Emir had indeed returned, but truly in the form that he should have taken in the first place.

Then the long-exiled Enyalian set up her guard outside the Lodge with her feet splayed and her hands in constant readiness to grab either her dagger from her hip or her sword from her back. Her face brooked no invitation to question. She wasn't sure how to convince Bodicca that retrieving the clay witch was as important as keeping her Emir safe.

She said as much to Barruch who kept his counsel except to flick his tail at her now and then. She had misgivings about any of the decisions she was making, and the darkness made them seem even more dreadful.

Gael found her there; she could smell him as he came upon her in the darkness, all smokey from the fire with fragrant spices clinging to his hair. But the natural smell beneath all that, of him, was stronger: of leather and horseflesh and something beneath it all that was his smell and his alone.

"There's something I need to say to you, Alaysha," he said.

"It must be something terrible if you're using my name," she said and noted that the hulking shadow of him moved closer. He rarely called her by name; always, it was witch, said so endearingly that she never took offense.

The sense of him so close now disconcerted her. The thrumming in her ears, the way her blood heated her skin. It was the bond, she told herself. Yenic had tried to warn her how strong it could be. She'd tried to ignore it and found she could only brush it lightly aside. "Tell me what's wrong," she said.

"Just this," he murmured and the shadow where he stood shifted as he closed the distance between them. She felt his thumb on her chin, toying with it as it trembled beneath his touch. His palm slipped behind her head, cupping her neck as his mouth claimed hers. She found her tongue dancing with his, a frenzied movement so rhythmless she could only blame it on the squirreling of her stomach and the way her chest fluttered within as though sparrows had taken residence. She felt her breast rising as though the wings inside had given her flight.

It was all she could do to press her palms against his chest and push away, to gain just enough space that she could breathe again, calm the flutterings in her stomach.

"You shouldn't have-- Yenic –"

"Is gone, Alaysha." He still had hold of her except somehow his hands were on the small of her back, his hips pressed against hers. She could feel how hard he was; it was a rigid unrelenting pressure insisting she join him.

"Not truly gone," she said of Yenic, thinking she should twist away, break Gael's hold on her so that she could think clearly. "I shouldn't be doing this." It was an admission that sounded hollow even to her own ears.

"If you had truly given him your heart, witch, you wouldn't be," he murmured. "You never would have."

Never would have, meaning not betrayed the bond with Gael twice now. But it hadn't been that simple, not either time, and he knew that.

"I belong to him." Even as she said it, she wondered if it was still true. She remembered her grief when Yenic died, the way she'd felt the bond disappear, dissolve into nothing. She remembered the feeling of abandonment, a feeling she should have gotten used to over the seasons, but that still gave her so much pain.

"You belonged to him," Gael said, emphasizing the past tense as he corrected her. "Indeed, you gave him your maiden's blood, I know," he said, and she found herself wincing at the words, knowing they weren't quite true. Gael seemed not to notice as he went on. "You gave him your bond long before that. I understand those things. I respected them. But you also gave me your body."

She had. Back in Enyalia when the warriors took from him what they needed of him and planned to rid themselves of him later. When he'd become a ghost of himself afterwards, tormenting himself with the betrayal of his body. He'd been a walking sword, then, no more than that. And she couldn't stand it. She'd had to heal him.

"I did it to save you," she admitted.

"And you did, but you wanted me too, witch. I know you did. I have ten seasons on you; I'm no stranger to women. I know when one wants me."

She did want him; she couldn't deny her body's response. It hadn't just been about saving him, or about the brew that Theron had given them, all three of them, to drive the magic of the tattaus, to ensnare them all in a bond that would never break until one of them died. So many bonds. Yenic had taken his life rather than let the bond with his mother continue to cause Alaysha pain. She couldn't dishonor that act this way. No matter how badly she wanted to feel Gael's hands on her, to feel his skin beneath her own. She'd been given a taste of obsession with Cai, she understood lust. But love should be more. She owed Yenic that.

"It's not right. Not fair to Yenic."

He chuckled darkly in the shadows and reached up with one hand to stroke her hair. "I swore to you I'd never mention our first night together. I told myself that once with you would be enough for me, that I could live my entire life with just that one memory. Out of fairness to your bond with Yenic, I offered that, and I wouldn't have you break it."

His other hand rose to meet its partner, and the fingers of both tangled behind the nape of her neck, kneading the muscles there. He kissed her again, lightly on the corner of her mouth, whispering each time his lips broke away from hers. "I wouldn't ask you to break a bond, but it *is* broken, witch. You feel it. I know you do. And even if somehow Yenic can find his way back, will you ever be able to separate him from Yuri? Ever? They are bound more tightly than you or he could ever be."

He shifted and Alaysha felt him plant his feet outside hers, holding her there between the thickness of his legs. "I have no bonds save the one you marked me with, and I'm restless with it. All I want to do is kill for your sake or take you in fever. I can think of barely anything else."

The magic, she thought. The night she'd marked him and joined him to her power, she'd created the double-edged sword that bled them both and now she had to wield it somehow without harming them all. She wanted to explain it to him, that it was only the magic that tied them. "You're no better than Cai," is what she heard herself say and cringed at the croak of desire she heard.

"I think you'll find I'm far better than Cai," he said, abandoning the muscles in her neck to move his callused hands to the outside of her thigh. She felt the delicious roughness of his palm travel her skin, easing her tunic higher on her hips, grasping her leg and hooking it onto his waist. His hands snaked beneath the leather, cupping her from behind, seeking the slickness between her thighs. A moan sounded in her ears and she wasn't sure if it was hers or if his lips against her throat had somehow let go his hunger.

"Your bond with him is broken, witch," he murmured. "Confess it. Let it go. Let him go. Come to me."

Before she could untangle the protests from her mind, to give them voice, his finger slid inside her, frictionless, and she heard herself gasp in pleasure. She realized how badly she wanted him there; she couldn't stop her hips from climbing his waist, urging him deeper. She thought she heard him chuckle and bit down onto his mouth to keep the sound from shaming her into pulling away. He tasted of honey and cinnamon and some strange spice Bodicca had undoubtedly used to baste the rabbits they'd eaten. She rocked against him, not sure what she wanted, only knowing her body had every intention of using his in the most primal way it could. She would take that from him, his punishment for making her feel this way, for planting the doubts and sowing such terrible desire. She should have felt shame or guilt, but he was devouring it with each masterful slip of his tongue, each stroke of his fingers into her core.

He pulled at the neckline of her tunic, tearing it away from her chest, filling his mouth with the hard pebble of her nipple, teasing it with his teeth. She was barely aware that she was moaning each time he pulled at it, sucking it in and releasing it; she only knew that each time he drew it in, she felt something within herself stretch just beyond her flesh, yearning to join with his.

He responded to her needs before she even knew what they were. No stranger to women, he'd said, and she believed it. When his fingers left her, wet and hot, to grip her hips, she knew she had let it go too far. He'd somehow undone his breeches and lifted her higher, letting her slip down, unguided and unhindered, onto him. She felt her womb grasp at his member, pulling him in even further. With an agonizing leisure, he lifted her and released, rocking her up and down with such sure care that it seemed to take an eon to travel the length of him and back. Each time, she felt lighter than the time before. She was weightless in his hands, a fevered thing riding a wave that drove to shore relentlessly but so slowly she found herself thinking it would never end, that she would never find completion.

Without warning, she was clinging to him, the darkness shattering behind her eyelids as she squeezed them shut so fiercely she had to bite her lip to keep from crying out. She tasted blood and for a second thought that when he kissed her he would taste it too.

Her head fell to his chest, exhausted, but ready to let him ride his own wave, to give him that at least.

Instead she felt his hands shift ever so slightly, enough to ease her to her feet. He began pulling at her tunic, smoothing it down over her thighs.

Blind and groping in the darkness, bewildered, she said, "But you didn't –"

"And I won't," he murmured. "Not till I have all of you. It's your heart I'm after, witch, not just your body." He kissed her again, this time chastely on the cheek. "Come to me when you want more than just mine."

CHAPTER 9

When morning came, Alaysha groaned herself to her side. She'd slept on her back all night and her throat was raw from inhaling harsh air. Her muscles ached, strained and tired as she was. Barruch stood still next her, his left hind leg bent; he'd trampled in a pile of his own dung during the night, and she could swear it was his fastidious way of telling her he wanted it cleaned. She tended to him quietly, occasionally humming, enjoying the sound of birds chirping in the trees. The Highland village seemed to just be yawning awake. Several young boys trod their way through the underbrush, collecting wood for the fires. Gathering in squirrels and hares and wild onions. She wasn't ready to face Gael. Her face flamed just thinking about him, and her fingers went to her stomach absently. He wanted her heart he'd said, but she wasn't sure she had a free one to give. With a sigh she pushed the night's memory aside and forced herself to think instead of the task at hand.

She certainly wasn't ready to face Bodicca either, to tell her she had to return to the village she'd exiled herself from so many years ago. The same village that left her back bloody and weeping with pus. The woman still held onto a few scabs where it healed. Though she never complained about it, Alaysha could often see her scratching when she thought no one was looking. How much of her injury she thought she deserved or how much she hated the women for, Alaysha would never know. Bodicca was as frugal with her speech as she was with her emotions. As for Cai, she wasn't sure that the ex-Komandiri would willingly return to the village with a woman she considered a traitor. Certainly, they'd found some sort of uneasy truce, but years of believing a thing could not be undone so easily.

And then there was Yenic turned Yusmine. The woman who, if she was to be believed, was the feminine spirit of Yuri. Alaysha shook her head. So many things she wanted to ask her father, and yet the quiet dignity of this woman made her hesitate to do so. Why not ask the goddess, the woman had asked. Indeed, they hadn't yet told her that the goddess was a simple child. One whose mind power was as short as her magical power was long. Assuming there was a battle to be waged, how would they ever do so when the goddess herself had little control over the way her mind worked.

It was almost ironic; Alaysha seemed to have finally found control of her own power, only to discover that the witch that was as powerful if not more powerful than she was, had no control over her thoughts. Navigating around the girl and her thinking, would be as difficult as navigating their way to Saxon through Edulph. And yet the girl was the key there. She knew this. If Edulph truly loved his daughter as he said, and wasn't just using her to manipulate the power, then they could use that emotion to force him to reveal the boy's whereabouts.

But one thing niggled at her. Why would Edulph take Saxa's son in the first place? The boy held no special power. Except for the fact that he was Yuri's son, he had no special use. At least none that would coerce a man like

Edulph to abduct him. There had to be more behind the story than he was admitting.

Cai found her still brushing Barruch's coat long after the campfires had been lit and the smell of roasted boar belly took to the air. Barruch himself had grown restless and kept avoiding Alaysha's hand as she ran it down his flank.

"The beast has had enough," Cai told her.

Alaysha looked at her hands and realized she'd been brushing the same spot over and over. She patted Barruch's rump lightly; no wonder he was so restless. "Sorry, old man," she told him and turned to face Cai.

The woman wore her fiery hair in one large plait down the side of her shoulder. Alaysha noticed the soft leather of her halter had turned black just around her armpit.

"How does it feel?" She asked the Enyalian.

The woman's shrug seemed to indicate that she'd forgotten she'd been marked at all. She lifted her arm to peer beneath. "I think it's a good thing we practiced on me," she said. "Not all of this went into my skin." She grinned at Alaysha and a small responsive flutter moved within her belly.

"I don't think I did that bad a job," Alaysha told her, trying to disguise her reaction.

The Enyalian shrugged again. "It's no matter. The man came second. That's all I care."

"The man has a name," Alaysha scolded her but the Enyalian seemed impassive.

"So many of your men have names; I can't remember them all."

"You do so remember."

The woman flashed a coy grin, one that didn't suit her features. "Do I?" Cai reached out to Barruch's nose and with her thumb, scrubbed at the white spot there.

Alaysha sighed. "Will you ever give in?"

"I would give in willingly," Cai crossed her arms and inclined one red brow just enough to indicate to Alaysha exactly where her inclinations were.

"You know what I mean," Alaysha said.

"I do." The Enyalian stuck a plump red tongue into the corner of her mouth, thinking. "I wish I could give you what you wanted."

It was about as far as Alaysha was going to get, she knew. "I'm sure you don't mean him any disrespect," she said and held up her hand in surrender when she heard the woman snort. She opted to abandon the argument, knowing that part of her was only pressing the point because she didn't want to move into the real part of the conversation, the one where she asked the Enyalian to risk her back.

"I need something from you," Alaysha said bluntly. When the water was cold, best to just dive right in.

To her credit, the Enyalian didn't react. "You want me to return to my sword sisters," she said blandly.

"You've seen Gael," Alaysha guessed.

"The man found me. Yes."

"And you agreed?"

"No, I did not agree. Leave you here with the man? Who will protect you?"

"I think Gael is quite capable –"

"The man is capable," the Enyalian agreed. "But he is not of Enyalia."

Alaysha ignored that. "We think Bodicca might know a safe way in."

"And you want me to return with her because you think I can keep my sword sisters from burning her back again." Cai reached for the pouch that always seemed to be handy on her belt. She dug in to extract a handful of almonds and a few pieces of dried fruit. "I have no command there anymore, little maga. My sword sisters will burn my back as quickly as they would burn Bodicca's. When I walked away, I foreswore any right to return but on pain of reward."

"I know," Alaysha couldn't help hanging her head. She'd known exactly what she was asking, and part of her wanted the woman to refuse. In some way she was relieved. "You're telling me this because you refuse?"

"I tell you this so you will understand exactly what it means for me to return."

Alaysha protested. "I do understand –"

"No, you don't. You think I'm afraid of the pain. I'm not. What I'm saying is I understand the consequences, and yet I'm going anyway. For you."

It made Alaysha's stomach feel even sicker; knowing someone would risk her own body because she asked her to. It was enough to humble a woman. "It's still your choice," she said.

The woman lifted her hands to the sides, palms up, helpless. The circlet on her bicep chattered. "And what choice does a witch's Arm have?" She asked. Strangely enough, the intent of the helpless gesture made the woman look as powerless as a bull on full rampage. The pouch in her hand, the way she chewed the few nuts she'd popped into her mouth, would make a regular woman seem nonchalant, but for an Enyalian of Cai's size, they only serve to remind Alaysha of her time in the burnt lands when Cai had offered her a similar handful of nuts. She'd made it seem like Alaysha had a choice, then. That she could come along with them peacefully when in truth, there had been no choice at all.

"I want you to always have a choice," Alaysha said, meaning it.

"So that's why you tapped your mark onto me," Cai said slyly.

"You begged it of me," Alaysha reminded her.

The woman shrugged. "I would beg it of you again," she said, "because you wouldn't let me demand it of you. I had no choice, little maga. Love takes away such luxury."

"It's not love," Alaysha mumbled. "I don't know what it is, but you don't love me."

Cai passed a handful of food over to Alaysha. She waited until Alaysha picked out three choice nuts and a piece of Apple. "Believe it or not, it changes nothing. I am sworn to protect you. At risk of my own life, bodily harm, past even the loyalty of my sword sisters. I'm joined to you through your mark. So you're shaman says and so I agreed to. And now I feel that truth deep in my belly. Tingling up my spine."

The woman stepped closer. "What I felt for you before, little maga is nothing to what I feel now."

Cai ran her palm down over Alaysha's hair, smoothing it against her neck. Alaysha could smell the apple on her fingers, the fragrance transferred to her hair so that when she moved the smell twisted into her palette.

"I can't stop thinking about us," the warrior said. "I want you again."

Alaysha's feet were frozen to the ground. Again, she thought. She didn't think she had it in her to defend herself against another onslaught of lust and obsession. She'd been foolish the night before. Foolish and wanton and ludicrously insensitive. She unwisely thought that the night she and Gael and Cai had spent together after she'd marked them, might be forgotten. Swept away as a peculiar, even if it was enjoyable, experience. She'd felt transported by the kykeon brew that Theron had given them. She remembered the way her arms felt like warm water, moving over the skin of her lovers. She remembered again the rush of heat she felt from toe to scalp, the way their hands made her flesh respond to them.

Like the way it had responded to Gael earlier, Alaysha's body responded again to Cai's. Her eyes eased closed of their own volition, as the woman's fingers left her hair and whispered down her neck. The warrior's touch at first was gentle, and Alaysha let those fingers roam wherever her skin was bare of clothing, but when Cai pulled her forward roughly, both hands at the small of her back, pulling their hips together, Alaysha found the wits to struggle out of Cai's grasp. She broke away, and watched as the Enyalian's face broke into a good-humored, if not chagrined expression.

Russet brows lifted almost in disbelief before the woman took careful inventory of the circlet around her bicep. "The man got to you before I did," she guessed. She rearranged the circlet so that two of the teeth, black ones that appeared to be mates from a rotted mouth, disappeared beneath her triceps.

Alaysha crossed her arms over her chest. "It's not that," she stammered, trying to worm her way out of the lie. "It's…"

"You prefer a dog with two legs to a woman of strength," Cai responded pragmatically. There was nothing in her voice to indicate to Alaysha that she was hurt. Rather, she sounded resigned. Then she placed her hands on her hips matter-of-factly. "Unless it's that you prefer the two of us together." A sly tone of intimacy slipped into the woman's tone and Alaysha wasn't surprised when she said, "If that's the way of it, I won't disagree."

Fortunately, Barruch seemed to have grown tired of the conversation. With the scent of apples in the air, he had grown less patient. He whickered and slapped Alaysha on the back with his tail. It was fortunate timing, Alaysha thought.

"Will you take Barruch when you return?"

Cai huffed thoughtfully. If she was upset about the sudden change of topic, she gave no indication. "I suppose the beast will do. Since were not crossing the burnt lands, I won't require the same stamina I would ask of Enyalia beasts." She touched Barruch, running her palm along his flank. "He will sit two?"

"He can, but the question is will he." Alaysha grinned at Barruch. He had a way of keeping his own mind.

"He will bend to a woman like any man should." Cai slapped the tender part of Barruch's rump, making him complain. She offered him a piece of dried apple from her pouch by way of apology. He sniffed at it haughtily, then turned his head. Alaysha couldn't help feeling a certain pride.

"Give it to me," she said, extending her hand and when Cai's russet brow raised in an equally haughty arch, Alaysha found herself explaining. "He's difficult," she told the Enyalian. "He feels like he's been neglected."

"Indeed, no doubt he has." Cai took to circling the horse, probing his ribs, running her hands down his legs. "You've tacked him well, but his muscle mass grows too lean. Otherwise, I see no evidence of neglect."

"I didn't mean physical neglect."

This confused the warrior. "What other kind of neglect could there be?"

It was one more frustrating thing about the Enyalia: so unused to compassion and emotion that they didn't seem to have words for certain things. Father, brother, were only two of the ones Alaysha had discovered had no existence in the Enyalian culture. They didn't even name the boys they gave birth to or the men they raided for, those men they used to procreate and then put to the flame with their throats cut. Alaysha realized explaining might be more trouble than it was worth.

"You think you will be able to retrieve both of them?" Alaysha asked instead.

"I have my doubts about the clay witch. We don't even know she is in Enyalia."

"She is," Alaysha said. "I know it."

The woman lifted a broad shoulder in deference. "It will be as you say, I'm sure. But if I return with only one, we best make certain the littlest one doesn't do something foolish."

Alaysha sighed. "I admit I have no idea how to explain it all to her."

"If she's as she says she is, she'll understand. She wept for your small man, brought him back. She understands some things."

Alaysha cringed at mention of Yenic. "She didn't exactly bring Yenic back," she had to admit. "She brought back my father because his seeds were in my pouch."

"Even still, if she can breathe life into a body, and take breath from a body, she must understand certain things; otherwise everyone around her would be constantly dying and living again." As Cai moved back around the horse, she came close to Alaysha again. The air hummed between them and she met Alaysha's eyes with daring.

"It seems my wooing was for naught," the woman said. "So if you won't let me take you again, then best we gather up the sullen old warrior so the two of us can set off on your errand."

Alaysha couldn't help but chuckle. "That was what passes for wooing in Enyalia?"

"Others have called me irresistible." Cai looked affronted. "Few warriors of Enyalia understand how to let themselves show vulnerability, let alone expose it to another. When one of our stock women sees it, they're often unprepared for resistance."

Besides the surprise of hearing that Cai believed she'd shown vulnerability, was the outright shock that she understood the word. "That isn't a word I would have thought to hear you use," Alaysha admitted.

"Bodicca taught it to me. She explained that it's like leaving a gaping hole for an enemy to exploit during battle." The woman adjusted her belt, testing the contents of her pouch, making sure her hemp rope was secure. When she looked at Alaysha again, it was with a directness that surprised her.

"Apparently, this love notion must be a battle as well. You should know I never lose a fight."

CHAPTER 10

Bodicca was where they'd left her the night before. Alaysha wondered if the old warrior had even slept; she stood in the same position with feet splayed in the dirt and arms across her chest. The only evidence to suggest the woman had moved from her spot at all was the milky broth bubbling over a lazy cook fire. It smelled of cloves and onions and barley. Several duck eggs were boiling in a copper pot. Alaysha also noticed a hare skinned and gutted, lying across a board scattered with various herbs. A gourd filled with wild honey sat nearby. Alaysha had no doubt the woman had ordered one of the Highland boys to gather her specifics. She also had no doubt that Yuri's best warrior was hoping to court his memory through his stomach. It was as sound a plan as any.

"I hope it works, Bodicca," Alaysha told her, dragging in a great gulp of honey scented air. "Did you sleep?" Alaysha looked around her. While some of the Highland village had begun to stir, with boys running in and out of the woods, collecting and foraging, the sun still hadn't gained much warmth. Just over the treetops, she could see the dawn was still just a blush in the canopy. The heat of the sun through all this foliage wouldn't reach the heart of the village for hours yet.

"Did you at least eat," Alaysha asked again when Bodicca didn't answer.

The warrior regarded her with a critical eye. "The Emir always breaks his fast first."

"The Emir no longer rules," Alaysha reminded her. "The Emir is a woman in my bondsman's body." Alaysha wondered at the stubbornness of the Enyalia. First Cai, and now Bodicca. She began to think that men were far less complex a thing to understand.

She turned to where Cai was sniffing at the broth. "Shall you tell her, or shall I?" Alaysha asked.

Cai straightened to her full, imposing height and faced Bodicca. Alaysha found herself wondering which one of the leaders in her life Bodicca would feel the most loyalty to. The woman inside who needed a guard about as much as Yuri needed to feel compassion. Or to the woman in front of her, sworn Komandiri to the Enyalia, Bodicca's sword sister from her childhood homeland. It was no secret that the woman felt as though she'd finally been allowed to return home, their flight in the woods when Cai called her sister, a person would have to be blind not to notice the pleasure that stole across the hardened warrior's face at those words. Alaysha hoped that the battle within the warrior would be fought quickly.

Cai approached her in measured strides. "I have need of you, sword sister," Cai said.

Bodicca made no move to indicate she was intrigued. In the face of the stoic expression, Cai continued undaunted. "We have business in our homeland. Much unfinished business."

That got Bodicca's attention. While she didn't speak, she at least regarded Cai levelly.

The ex-Komandiri of the Enyalia placed her broad, freckled hand on Bodicca's shoulder. "The little maga would have us return to fetch two witches she says are needed. But I would have us return for another purpose."

That took Alaysha by surprise, but she chewed her lip to keep from questioning her Arm in front of Bodicca. She trusted Cai, didn't she? She'd marked her simply because she did. She let the woman continue.

"The land is without a Komandiri, Bodicca; you know this."

Bodicca said nothing, her long face a purposeful mask.

"You know what will happen if there is a lot of contest."

Finally, Bodicca nodded but she said nothing.

"We can't let that happen, sister. Our numbers are too few as it is. We've already taken the lives of many of our sisters. We have to rebuild what we destroyed." She wrapped her arms around the old warrior's shoulders then. Alaysha realized that loyal to her Arm's oath the Enyalian might be, but the land she once ruled would not be far from her thoughts as long as she lived.

"You planned to go anyway," Alaysha said.

The Enyalian offered a sheepish grin, a strange expression for her. "Rather I had hoped that I could do the two things with the one task."

"But your backs… Will they –"

"Of course they will. They will have to."

"What about the secret paths, the ones that must be there. The ones that Bodicca--"

Cai interrupted with a shake of her head. "I will not sneak into my own land. I may be exiled, but I respect their right to do so. I will return and bear their justice, I will find a way to release the two women you need, and if we live," she jerked her chin at Bodicca. "*If* we live, then Isolde can take my place as Komandiri, the land will be safe, and I can return to you. To do my duty here." She winked at Alaysha naughtily.

"It would be nice if I had a fair welcome back."

That made Alaysha squirm, but she couldn't let Cai see that; she'd never stop the teasing reminders of the night she'd marked two Arms--and savored their bodies as well when the magic took her. "Good," Alaysha said, her face burning. "You'll be on your way, then."

Cai nodded.

"Where is Gael?" Alaysha said, looking about for her other Arm.

Cai gave her a strange look. "You sent him to deal with Edulph," she said.

To deal with Edulph. Alaysha began to search frantically then because she'd given no such request to the man. She felt Cai's hand on her shoulder; Alaysha looked up at her, uneasiness making her stomach quiver.

"Off that way," the warrior pointed toward one of the large redwoods wooden stairs that disappeared high above Alaysha's vision. There'd be a lodging there, somewhere in those heights, complete with a leather flap door and several hissing stone braziers to roast small game.

Where before she'd felt anxious, now she felt dizzy with panic.

"What's wrong?" The warrior asked.

"Nothing," Alaysha said, lying. "Nothing at all if what we want is Edulph's painful demise."

CHAPTER 11

The first of the steps wasn't so bad. Alaysha told herself they were just steps within the castle. Nothing more, nothing less. They could be trodden upon and trusted as though she'd walked them a thousand times. By the time she reached step ten, she'd convinced herself that it was true; if only her body would listen to her mind. It wasn't so easily convinced. The stairs were carved straight out of the trunk and wound up the tree. She would have had to select such a one to house the brutish man, she thought bitterly. She could easily have selected one of the other trees with separate wooden steps and hemp rope to hold onto. But no, she'd decided that the little goddess and her father would be far safer in the biggest, most difficult-to-climb tree.

"Is something wrong, little maga?" Cai's voice prodded her from behind. She would have put a hand to her hammering heart if both of them hadn't been holding on to the tree so resolutely.

"Nothing." She stammered. "I'm fine."

"You started out fine," the warrior said. "But the way your butt clenches and unclenches as you stand there frozen, tells me a different story. Not that I don't enjoy looking at it; it's shaped very much like a bowl of baker's dough," the warrior added.

This time Alaysha did feel the warrior's fingers prodding into her thigh. "Move on," Cai said.

"You should have gone first," Alaysha admitted. "You could have been up there by now."

She could almost hear the woman nodding as she agreed. "Indeed, little maga, I'm but I'm a lowly Arm," Cai said. "I do as I'm told."

Yes, Alaysha had bid her to come behind. Not so much an order, really, but merely a comment as she had taken off for the tree without thinking. Follow me, she'd said to the warrior. She'd undoubtedly need the woman's strength to pull Gael off of Edulph. A dozen imagined scenarios ran through her mind: not the least of which, had Gael's hands around the little traitor's neck. Should that happen, the rest of them would be as good as dead. The little goddess would surely take her vengeance.

"Are you going to move?" Cai said from behind her.

Alaysha inhaled deeply, counting as she did so. Surely when she got to ten, she'd be able to move again. Fifteen passed and still she remained tight to the tree, her arms gone round more so that she was almost hugging it.

"There's plenty of width for two," Cai said as if to embolden her,

Alaysha eased her head so that she was facing Cai, her cheek pressed against the bark. Cai hopped up one step, jumped backwards, and did an ungainly, two-step on the one in between. "See?" the warrior said. "Plenty of space. Now move."

Alaysha could easily imagine Cai coming forward to help her into her arms and carrying her the rest of the way up. She tilted her head to see upwards and saw that the rest of the way up was an entirely long way. She imagined herself in Cai's arms, and she wasn't sure if she felt relief or even more fear.

"This wasn't a good idea," she mumbled to herself and Cai must have heard her because she craned her neck behind her to look back down the trunk and then tilted her head upwards to peer off into the branches above them.

"Too late to think about that now, little maga. Your goddess is up there and so is that vile man. Well," Cai said thoughtfully, a finger to her full lips. "I should distinguish between the vile men for you since there are *two* of them up there. I meant to say the vile man that is her father. The other vile man…"

"Could you stop saying that?"

"You don't care for the word man?"

"I don't care to have them described as vile," Alaysha said, peevish.

"Oh, of course. I forgot how much you love your men." Cai shrugged sheepishly. "I suppose vile *is* a bit too strong for the large one; since that one may well be my only hope of having you again." The woman eyed her without any trace of lust, though that could mean anything; Cai was very good at keeping her emotions from her face. If anything, Alaysha noted the woman looked slightly uncomfortable. No. Not uncomfortable. Could it be humor that put that strange crooked line on the woman's face, Alaysha wasn't sure.

"You're enjoying this," Alaysha said, realizing it even as she spoke the words.

"I would enjoy the image more if it didn't have to include that *foul* man," Cai said. "And believe me, I've thought about it often. It brings me much pleasure." She gave Alaysha a careful, if not assessing study. "But at the moment, I'm really only trying to get you up the tree."

She began to climb quickly, devouring the distance between them with her long legs. Alaysha had the disconcerting image of the two of them together on one step, of the woman grabbing her and forcing her to move. Of pulling her the rest of the way up. What air she had been managing to drag in up until that point, began to expire in her chest. She gasped, gulping down whatever bit she could pull into her open mouth. She felt her heart racing. If she were to move, it would have to be now, on her own terms, or be swept into the woman's arms and carried like a doll. Even with the threat of hanging limp in someone's arms, powerless, she knew she couldn't do it. The bark bit into her belly even more sharply as she pressed against the trunk.

In the end, Alaysha was too paralyzed to move, and her eyes must have sent a beseeching message to Cai that she didn't want to be carried because Cai brushed past her, giving her a gentle touch on the small of her back as she went by. Alaysha ended up having to wait because no matter how hard she tried, she could not force her legs to do her bidding. She clung to the side of the trunk, pressing her back into it each time a breeze swept over her skin. Even though the Enyalian skirted the steps masterfully and was out of sight before Alaysha could drag in four breaths, the tree itself was broad and high. She hoped Cai would be able to get to Gael before any harm came to Edulph, and in turn before any harm came to the rest of them through Liliah.

The wait was agonizing.

It was Aedus who met her first. The girl came sauntering around the corner of the trunk as though the stairs were no more frightening than a few steps in the Emir's Castle. Alaysha noted the girl had washed, stripped herself of the twigs and branches that she'd stuffed into her hair as a disguise. Even her hair was clean. She looked so much older in that moment. Not like the frightened girl she'd met so many moons ago who had to scavenge for food and keep hidden from her master. She was taller, Alaysha noticed. With a scrubbed face and clean hair, the ferret-like features disappeared. Alaysha wondered if they'd ever been there or if they had been merely illusions cast by smudges of dirt beneath her cheekbones or the hollows of her skin. She looked almost healthy. The girl stopped three treads away from Alaysha. She sat, twirling her hair. Such a girlish thing to do, that Alaysha found herself wondering how old the girl was. How many seasons she truly had.

"We're all fine," the girl said to her in answer to a question Alaysha hadn't voiced but certainly thought. She wondered how much Cai had said when she'd gained the lodging above.

"Everyone?" She wasn't sure whether she wanted to know whether Gael had hurt Edulph or whether Liliah had hurt Gael or whether nothing had happened at all. Such a terrible thing to be trapped by your own cowardice.

The girl looked up from where she'd come. "Everyone." She repeated. ""Although I'm not sure if my niece will survive the tickling she's getting."

"Tickling?"

Aedus nodded. "That big woman is giving her a terrible fit of giggles."

"You mean Cai?" The girl couldn't be speaking about anyone else, but it was a shock to hear this and to imagine Cai doing anything remotely playful. Aedus scraped at the bark of the tree. "My niece wanted a piggyback ride down the tree, and the big woman – Cai, you say – told her she would only agree to it when the goddess could sit through the spider dance." Aedus chuckled. "She's losing."

Alaysha could barely believe her ears. "Gael? And Edulph?" She almost hated to ask.

Aedus lifted a spare shoulder. "Talking."

"Talking?" Alaysha wanted to be sure. "That's all."

Aedus was peeling a bit of bark away, inspecting it for mite holes. "I can't hear what they're saying, but neither one of them sounds happy."

"I don't imagine," Alaysha said. She eased herself down onto the tread and leaned against the trunk, looking up at Aedus. "I think your brother will have to give up Saxon." It was a test, this admission. Alaysha wasn't sure how much the girl knew. There'd been a time in the burnt lands when they've been separated, when Edulph had managed to wrest himself from the Enyalia. She waited to see how the girl would react.

True to expectations, Aedus looked surprised. "You think he knows where Saxa's boy is?"

"I know he does." On her hands and knees, Alaysha began to climb the three treads that separated them. It wasn't as bad as walking, and in fact she found herself quite able to ascend without feeling as though her heart was going to burst through her chest. Even the sound of her heartbeat in her ears dissipated. "He told me he was the one who abducted him." She pushed close to Aedus, when she'd gained the same tread, and the girl scooted toward the trunk to make room.

"I don't understand why," the girl said. "Even your father assumed it was Aislin who had him. She didn't? Are you sure the fire witch doesn't have Saxon?" The pleading note in the girl's voice sounded genuine. It would be just another blow to the girl's trust to know that her brother had abducted the infant.

"All I know," Alaysha continued. "Is that Edulph says he will take us to him."

"What if he's lying?" The girl struck at the core of the problem. She'd seen how cunning her brother could be.

"He's buying his daughter back with Saxon. I doubt he would take the chance. Plus, we'll have the little goddess. If he doesn't bring us to Saxon, he can't guarantee no harm will come to Liliah."

No sooner had she said it, than Alaysha regretted the words. The look on Aedus's face revealed exactly what the cost of that statement was. Alaysha had forgotten how much the girl had come to love her niece, and even though her words had been meant to reinforce how much she believed Edulph would comply, all it seemed they served to do was make Aedus fear for the little goddess.

"We'd never harm her," she blurted out, trying to calm Aedus's fears. "You do know that, don't you?"

The nod came slowly, and the wary eyes, so often used to discern the right of things around her, to warn her of danger, narrowed in suspicion. Alaysha reached out to touch Aedus's cheek, brushing her knuckles down the soft skin. "You can't believe I would harm her, Aedus. She's of your blood. She's too important to us."

"Then where would the danger be for Edulph? If he doesn't worry about her safety, why would he bother to give you the boy?"

That made her squirm. The girl was crafty, as crafty as her brother. Luckily, the girl was on her side. "He wants her back and taking us to Saxon is the price."

"I see," the girl murmured, but something in her tone sent a small bee into Alaysha's breastbone. "So she will stay safely here while you go for him?"

Alaysha hugged her. "As safe as you can make her, Aedus. I trust no one else with such a task." She heard boots above her, sounding on wood and realized the man and Cai were making their way down the stairs. "You'll do that for me, won't you?" She smoothed an errant lock behind Aedus's ear. "You'll keep her safe while we are gone?"

The girl held Alaysha's eyes steadily. "I will," she promised.

"What will you do?" Gael said as he drew close. Alaysha noted that his neck was flushed. He'd been trying to keep his temper, obviously, and when his eyes met Alaysha's, she could tell she was right. She could see him swallowing it down. By the time he got close enough to Alaysha, he'd managed to pull a mask of stoicism back over his features.

"Aedus is charged with keeping the little goddess happy as well as safe," she said, aiming the sentence for Edulph, who was a short distance behind Gael, flanked himself by Cai who stood at least three shoulders taller and was scowling at the back of his head. "Is she well this morning?" Alaysha scooted down one tread below Aedus and pressed herself into the tree trunk. The others were coming down far too fast for her liking.

Gael bent to scoop Aedus into his arms. "She's asking for you," he told the girl, and Alaysha could see that he was deliberately acting lighthearted, almost as though he very much needed to pretend everything was okay. "I was told to tickle you the entire way back up to see if you can stand against the spider dance." He hoisted the girl over his shoulder playfully, but the tension and Aedus's body made Alaysha wonder what was running through the girl's mind.

"She can walk," Alaysha told him. "Let her be."

Gael must have understood Alaysha's unspoken concerns. He dropped Aedus to her feet and pressed her back gently with three of his fingers. "Go on, then," he told her. "But make sure you blame someone other than me when she sees you're not dancing with the spider."

Aedus slipped past Edulph and Cai and disappeared around the broad trunk, her steps sounding quietly. When she'd gone past the hearing, Alaysha pulled her knees closer to her chin and leaned her head against the trunk. Things would just be okay if she could sit here. She just needed to sit here for long enough. Some fool had asked a question, though. And that question meant she had to stand again.

"We should leave right away," she said in answer, but couldn't for the life of her lift her body up into a stand. She avoided Edulph's gaze as he watched her so closely that she could swear his eyes were forming words. "I'm fine," she said out loud as though the answer. "If you think I'm scared, then you'd be a fool." She reached up for Gael's outstretched hand, thankful that he'd realize her words were pure bravado.

"I'd think you are a fool if you weren't afraid," Edulph said and was stumbling from the shove Cai gave him from behind as she said,

"No one cares what you think, man," Cai said.

Alaysha only had time to formulate a protest of Cai's generic use of the word man when she felt Edulph slam into her, dislodging her hand from Gael's. She lurched forward, stumbling off the beaten wooden steps, and swam in the air for one single heartbeat. Her arms flapped ineffectually, her hands scrabbling for purchase and finding none. She knew then the only sound that would come out of her throat would be the exhale of her lungs when her body struck ground.

CHAPTER 12

There was a foolish, joyous moment when she thought she was flying when she expected the ground to thud against her rib cage, knocking the wind out of her and sending sharp pains of bone splintering through her body, she felt instead a whisper of breeze playing with her neck and joining with her fingers like a lover curling her hand into his. It's like swimming, she thought. The buoyancy of flight making her giddy until she saw the sober expressions of her companions on the tree staircase. Gael was first to lose his expression of sheer astonishment and leaned out over the tree, reaching for her as though he thought she would fall at any second. She knew better than to grapple for his grasping hand. She knew the moment she took it, she would lose her height and pull him down with her, thudding to the forest floor.

The joyous moment was gone and in came sharp reality. She wasn't falling, no, but something like a bubble of air floated her in the stratosphere with a great, but perilous care. She knew if she moved she would slip off to her death, and if she reached for help, she'd pull that help down with her. *It's the girl, the little goddess.* The thought startled her. It was an intense knowledge so thorough it rippled through her body. Without straining too much, she craned her neck upwards past the three on the steps: Gael with his frantic scrambling to reach her, Cai leaning backwards, holding onto Gael's hips so he could stretch further, and Edulph – yes Edulph, even-- with his arms crossed, offering nothing in the way of help or compassion. Past those three Alaysha peered up into the depths of the Redwood to where both Aedus and Liliah stood, caught almost mid-stride as they threaded their way down the tree trunk. Liliah looked almost as frightened as Aedus did.

There was a heart-stopping moment when Alaysha believed the girl would let her go; the current of air shivered and plummeted as Liliah realized she held Alaysha in a draft of breath. Alaysha didn't have time to plead with her before the girl's face grew determined, the realization of what was happening finally cresting across her brow. Another draft moved beneath Alaysha's body, then, and another one slithered in from the other direction. Together they wound into a solid seat that whimpered bit by bit like a starved pup hoping for a morsel, easing off so that it floated down, down as softly as a feather fallen from an eagle until Alaysha's bare toes just about touched the forest floor. When the humus brushed against her heel, she let go her own breath and let herself fall the rest of the way until she knelt on her hands and knees, gasping from the fear of such near brush of death, heart pounding again in her ears.

They all came at her at once, but it was to Liliah that Alaysha turned. The close bob of curls bounced about the girl's ears as she jumped from the tree onto solid ground. She darted towards Alaysha, and then stopped short next to her father.

"What did you do?" Alaysha asked her.

Suddenly shy, the girl turned her face into Edulph's leg.

"It's okay, Liliah," Alaysha said, easing to one knee, and then discovering her landing had been a soft one and that she wasn't hurt, onto her two feet. She took careful steps towards the young goddess. "What did you do, Liliah?"

The child peeked out from behind Edulph's breeches. "You not fall," she said.

Alaysha stretched her arms out towards the little girl. "I didn't fall," she agreed. "Did you do that for me?"

The girl waggled her head up and down, sticking her finger into her mouth, and chewing. It came out wet and slimy. "Me don't like falling."

Suspicion crept up Alaysha's spine. "Did you fall before?" She glared at Edulph. "Stay back," Alaysha told Gael as he took steps towards the young goddess.

"If he –" the warrior grumbled.

"If he did, the girl will tell us." Alaysha knelt onto one knee, close enough to the young girl now that she could almost touch her. "Liliah," she said. "Did you fall before? Did someone push you?"

The young goddess shook her head. Alaysha sent a warning look towards Edulph who didn't so much as flinch. "Who fell, then?" She asked.

Now that she was this close to the girl, Alaysha could see how young the child really was. What she'd thought was a toddler about two seasons old, couldn't truly have been much more than a season and a half. That the girl had words was surprising enough. Perhaps she had been wrong thinking the girl was simple. Perhaps she was just very young.

"Who fell, Liliah?"

The girl tugged on Edulph's leg. She peered up at Edulph as though looking for permission.

"Never mind your father," Alaysha told her. "It's okay. You can tell us. Who fell?"

"No one."

"Did someone push you?"

Again, the girl shook her head. "Mommy falled."

This time it was Edulph who looked confused. Confused and shocked. His glance darted down to his daughter and his eyes narrowed in suspicion. "Your mommy?" He knelt and gathered the girl into his arms. He met the girl's eyes with his own. "Tell me, Liliah. Did this woman push your Mommy?" He glared at Alaysha.

How had this turned on her? Alaysha's tried an indignant protest. "I didn't –"

Edulph ignored her, interrupting her with a finger to his lips before turning again to Liliah. "Did she, Liliah? Did this woman push your mommy?"

Liliah turned those brilliant eyes to Alaysha and Alaysha's heart nearly stopped in her chest. She could feel her bowels quivering.

"Not hurt," Liliah murmured.

"Who, then?" Edulph asked. "Did someone here??"

The girl hung her head and began to whimper; Edulph gathered her into his arms, glaring at Alaysha over her shoulder.

It was a good act, this distraction. Alaysha could imagine Edulph's brain working overtime, trying to lay the blame back on to Alaysha, when Alaysha knew she had not killed the girl's mother. She couldn't have. When the grandmother died, it had been Alaysha who had killed her in the mud village; she would've also had to take the mother's life at the same time in order for this child to be so powerful. But there had been no one else unaccounted for in the village. She should have seen it before. The other Crones had made sure their daughters were safely away when Alaysha came. They lured her through Yuri into the village and sacrificed themselves in order for their daughters to remain safe.

She stood with renewed purpose and faced Edulph. "You can't fool me, Edulph," she said. "You lied to me when you told me Aislin said I killed her mother." She took a step toward him, not certain what she would do when she reached him. She wanted to wrest the girl from his grasp, push her safely behind her where Cai or Gael would gather her safely into their arms and whisk her away. She wanted to throttle Edulph. She wanted to take every ounce of his fluid.

"You did it," she said in a voice so low she barely heard herself. "You pushed her mother out of one of these blessed trees. And she remembers, she remembers because she is a witch and we have long memories."

When she thought he would protest, he pushed his daughter behind him protectively. "Stay away from her," he said.

"It's not her I want," she told him. She felt Cai next to her then. She imagined the woman flexing her arms, she could hear the rattling of the teeth that circled her biceps. Gael moved to her left. The three of them faced Edulph.

"We leave tomorrow. You'll use today to gather the things you need, to bring us to Saxon. Then tomorrow at first light you will lead us to the boy. She will stay here." Alaysha nodded at Liliah. "Aedus will look after her."

Edulph had the grace to nod quietly, but his face didn't lose its surly expression. His brow still furrowed angrily, and his hands were still behind him, holding onto Liliah's shoulders. Aedus took her place next to the little goddess and urged her away from Edulph. She gave Alaysha one lingering look that Alaysha could not comprehend. Aedus seemed uncertain, flustered.

To her credit, Aedus did not show anything to Liliah but playful attentiveness. Within a few moments, she began a game of pat-a-cake with the young goddess, and the child was giggling happily. Alaysha tried not to look at her. Tried not to imagine what it must have been like to be a newborn infant, seeing your mother plummet to her death. She had suffered her own tragedy at birth, but had blocked it out in order to survive the trauma. It was only later that she discovered her father had taken her mother's life within the first few hours of her own. She'd been left with only her nohma then, suckled on cloth soaked in goat's milk. She'd survived, yes. But there was no way for her to thrive.

She found her gaze wandering to the child's pink cheeks. This child had thrived however. But then, if there had been no mother's milk, how had the girl survived? She eyed Edulph thoughtfully. ""You have a lot to explain," she said to him. Alaysha flicked her gaze to Cai. "I imagine the Enyalia have a host of inventive ways to make a man explain."

Cai chuckled softly. "We've never had much use for a man or his words. And so we've never needed to invent creative ways to make one speak. We only use death."

The giggling had stopped and Alaysha peered over at Aedus and Liliah. Both were looking at her with owlish eyes. She turned her attention back Edulph. "Have no fear, Edulph," she said. "We still have plenty use for you."

She wanted to say more, she wanted to say how she'd learned many things at the hands of Corrin and his brutality. She wanted to tell him of the nights that she'd wept from pain and fear. The things that she had come to understand could make a person grow inflexible and lose all ability to feel in the face of cruelty.

She was about to voice all that when a shout met the air. Someone was running towards them and turned to see Theron, his robe pulled up to his knees as he sprinted with his blue veined legs. "Come," he was shouting. "Come. Oh come come come."

"She has taken him," Theron said. "Taken *her*, this shaman means. The woman has taken her."

Gael was closing the distance between the shaman and Alaysha even as Alaysha began to dart forward. He was breathing heavily, hunched over, trying to catch his breath. He looked up at them, his face flushed from running. Alaysha noticed that he had traced the lines of blue woad on his face and down his neck. She wondered what he'd been doing while they'd been busy.

"Who took her? And who is her?" She asked the shaman.

"Bodicca," he gasped. Alaysha could tell he was having a hard time gathering enough air to speak. She waited patiently. "The old warrior took him, I mean she took her," he struggled to say. "Bodicca took Yusmine."

Bodicca took Yusmine? It didn't make any sense. Why would the warrior steal Yusmine away, what use could the old warrior possibly have for Yenic's body or the woman within it?

Then it dawned on Alaysha. "It's Yuri, she's after."

Cai had come up from behind them and Alaysha looked at her. "You told Bodicca they would be needing a new Komandiri in Enyalia."

The large warrior nodded. "And since Yuri is now alive and well as a woman…"

"No, still a man." Alaysha lifted her hands helplessly. Enyalia would never accept a man as a Komandiri. Bad enough they would reinjure the woman's newly healed back, but they would do even worse to Yenic, not understanding that it was a woman who had taken over his body. And Yenic was in there somewhere. Even Yusmine had said so. They had to find a way to get him back. In one piece.

"How could she be so foolish? It's a man's body they'll see."

"With a woman's mind," Cai said patiently. That's all Bodicca will see. That's all she does see. It makes no sense to you and I." She shrugged. "But do you think she loves Yuri less now that he's in Yenic's body? All she knows is that he has finally returned, and with a woman's spirit as he was meant to have. She believes he can finally take his rightful place."

"As the leader of his mother's people." Alaysha cursed. The Yuri she knew as her father might be able to strategize his way out of this mess, but the woman within – did she have the same cunning, the same ruthless methods…

"Come back to me, little maga." Cai touched her on the wrist. "We have no time to lose. We must get them both back."

Alaysha nodded silently, knowing in her heart that the best plan was the same plan. "Go," she told the warrior. She had to trust that Cai could do this for her. There was no one better suited, and with her loyalties already divided between Yenic, the little goddess, and Saxon who was somewhere still held captive, she knew she had no choice but to let the woman go off alone. She held Cai's gaze with her own. "Do what you have to, to get him back."

"And Bodicca?"

Alaysha studied her toes, feeling the slow boil of anger in the middle of her chest.

"Bodicca is expendable."

CHAPTER 13

The river was swollen with old rain. In Sarum, they would have called the season flood tide for that time after the heavens wept in relief to see the earth coming alive again and the time just after the harvest when the burden of fruit and vegetable was so heavy on the vines and trees that they went dormant, trying to regain their energy. Alaysha noticed the beavers had constructed a dwelling of the thin saplings that surrounded the lazy river. The waters bloated on one side and then on the other, making crossing relatively easy. They only went up to their knees. Though the heat was nowhere near what it could be in the season to come after, Alaysha was glad to feel the liquid against her skin. Her bare feet allowed her sure footing while Gael and Adolf struggled in their boots to find purchase on the slimy rocks beneath.

She looked askance at Edulph as he slipped on yet another rock. She had her doubts that he truly knew where Gael's nephew was. She couldn't imagine who would be loyal enough to Edulph to harbor a boy related to the large bulk of man following along close on Edulph's heels. That bulk was even now walking far more gracefully across the river then Edulph was. Gael had taken off his leathers and tunic, stripped himself of his breeks, so that he wore nothing but his small clothes to cross. His sword, he'd slung across his back as though he were still dressed, and it made for an amusing sight to see the warrior picking his way across the river all but naked except for boots and sword and small clothes. Alaysha didn't care if her leathers got wet. She had no compunction about stripping it off after she passed through the river. Flesh was merely that, vulnerable, yes, but better to protect it with leathers in case she slipped in the river. Skin could be vulnerable to rocks if she fell and so she left her leather tunic on as she crossed thinking that if it got wet and cumbersome when she reached the other side, she'd simply pull it off and go naked. For a moment she thought of the many times she done so as she battled for her father. It only seemed fair to her that she be vulnerable as she took the lives and fluid of those he'd condemned to death.

Unbidden, thoughts of Yenic poked at the dark spots in her mind where she'd hidden them. He'd come to her after her last battle, ordered by her father to kill an entire village that later turned out to be nothing more than peaceful villagers. The last of her clan, Yenic told her then. Even that had been a sort of lie. He told her that only the two of them remained, when within Sarum an offshoot of that line, Gael and his sister and yes even the shaman Theron as well, lived their lives as chattel within the city. Aedus's line too. Had he known about them? Had he been aware that so many of the witches' families still lived? Alaysha wanted to believe he'd been as manipulated as she was in the end. And now here they were: she and Gael crossing a river to find Yuri's own son, stolen by an offshoot of the original tribe.

She readusted the pouch she'd tied to her back. Usually, she hefted all of her belongings onto Barruch's saddle: her thatch sleeping mat, her furs and skins, her pouch with food and utensils and tinder for the fire. Her sword was always on her person, her dagger tied to her calf. But she felt more weary, carrying all these things on her own and it made her think of Barruch and the haughty way he had of blowing air through his mouth when she undid his wrappings and released him from his burden. Indeed, she felt he must have believed himself a pack horse or mule. These things were heavy. So heavy she questioned her wits to have taken them the first place.

She told herself it was because she had no idea how long they would be traveling. Edulph had given no indication of how many days and nights it would take to reach Saxon. He refused to divulge any more than the direction they were to travel. Gael had indulged him only at her behest. And was looking very much like he regretted every moment of his convincing.

"Should we make camp on the other bank?" Alaysha turned to Edulph, where he struggled across, his arms outstretched for balance.

"We'll make camp," he agreed. "And then we will wait."

Alaysha climbed on the bank, pulling at her tunic at the same time. Several torrents had washed onto her hips as she crossed, and soaked the leather up as far as her breastbone. The leather would be half supple when wet, but would stick to her skin mercilessly as it dried, become nearly impliable. She had furs wrapped in her bundle on her back that would be undoubtedly more dry. And those furs would be warmer when the sun set and the flood tide nights grew chilly.

She dropped her pack and bundle as well as her leather tunic onto the bank and eased herself down to her elbows, then wrapped her knees under her chin as she watched the other two trying to find the bank.

She tried not to reveal her anxiety as she thought of Edulph's words. They'd be found. So he had people coming, then. She wondered if Gael had caught on to the hidden meaning in those words. She hadn't forgotten the horde of brutal men who had traveled with him during the time he'd taken his own sister's finger, shoved it into the mouth of one of his decapitated generals and sent it with Yenic to find her in the dark.

He'd been cocky, then. So arrogant that Alaysha had actually feared him for a time. She remembered that he'd been cunning enough to abduct her own half-sister just in case Alaysha wouldn't do his bidding with Aedus in danger alone. He'd been smart enough to keep those she cared about close to her, so that she could bring her power down to bear upon him and his migrant soldiers. In the end, it had been his own sister who had bested him. Painting him with the dreamer's worm and sending him mad temporarily.

But he'd been mad far too long, she speculated. What had it been that had managed to steal his sanity in the woods after he escaped from her father's clutches? He'd played the madman for a long time, that was for sure. Fooling even Aislin into believing he was too far gone to remember anything about the witch he'd gone to seek. He'd fooled them all. And when he'd found a chance in the burnt lands against the Enyalia, he'd somehow discovered a way to kill some of their best and maim others. This was no vulnerable, beaten man acting as a father to a cherished child. This was a man to be feared if not for his strength and brutality, then certainly for his cunning. She would do well to remember that. Even knowing Gael was quick to hand, by Edulph's own admission, he didn't rely on strength, but on wits to win his battles.

At least his daughter, the little goddess was safe in the Highland village, and guarded by Aedus and Theron. Alaysha trusted the small girl who had been with her since the beginning of the strange journey. While all others had given her dubious trust, Aedus had remained loyal throughout. And she loved the girl. That was plain to see. So all Alaysha had to do was best whatever plan Edulph had, gather up Saxon, and return home.

She had to struggle out of her tunic, but once she did she felt better. Made of soft calfskin, bleached and tanned by her own nohma back when she was just a young girl. At one time, Alaysha knew that it had chips of Garnet for courage sewn into it, but it had been worn instead as everyday wear rather than the wedding leather it had been meant to be. It was soft now as her own skin, but when it grew wet, it stuck to her, and when it dried, it needed to be worked to regain suppleness. She always chose to wear it instead of flaxspun or linen. It reminded her of her nohma, and of the guarded happiness of her early youth. She stretched out into the grass, so that her toes pointed towards the river. Edulph and Gael were still splashing midway, but Gael had overtaken Edulph and was taking longer, more sure-footed strides the closer he got to the bank. When he gained dry land, Alaysha could see the hunger in his eyes at her recumbent form and rethought her nudity.

Pulling the wet tunic down over her shoulders proved to be as difficult if not more so than taking it off. He knelt beside her, laying his hands on hers as he helped pull it down over her chest and smooth it over her legs.

"Thank you," she told him, suddenly shy. His palm lingered over her thigh. Although his hands were cold from the river, she felt flushed all the same.

"The gratitude should be mine," he said to her. He withdrew his hand but his eyes stayed on her leg. She recalled how rough and calloused those palms were, how delicious they could make her feel as they smoothed out her skin. She was about to grab his wrist when Edulph came splashing ashore.

"You needn't have dressed again for me, witch," he said and flopped down next to her. He nodded at Gael. "But I'd appreciate it if *you* would dress," he said.

Alaysha noticed that Edulph was breathing heavily from exertion. He leaned back so that his head rested on his open hands as he stared at the sky, spent for the moment like the rest of them. His stomach bellowed in and out each intake of his breath.

"You're out of shape, Edulph," she said, grinning. She wasn't sure why that pleased her, except it showed some weakness in him.

"Torture takes a lot out of a man," he said in answer.

Gael eased away and found a spot between him and Alaysha. "What now, Edulph?" He asked; while his question was directed to Edulph, his eyes remained on Alaysha's hips. She thought she could read what he was thinking and the tingle crept up her spine.

Oblivious, Edulph sighed heavily. "Now we wait."

The wait brought on dusk, and then darker night. Gael lit a small fire, but it crackled lazily for want of good dry kindling and fuel. They'd had to feed it with what wet wood and damp leaves they could find from the forest floor. Alaysha pulled bits of dried Apple and near moldy dates from her pouch and offered them around. She thought of testing the river for fish, but imagined that night might bring different kinds of foragers to the river, ones more dangerous than they. She heard wolves howling in the distance, and a snuffling in the scrub brush that she thought might be too big for a mere raccoon. She hoped it wasn't a bear.

All they had to do was wait. With Gael, now back in his full leathers, lying next to her, covering them both with his cloak and with Alaysha using her furs as a pillow, she fell asleep without meaning to.

They came during the night. Alaysha woke to a palm stretched across her mouth, lips met her ear whispering to her to stay quiet. She heard the rustling in the underbrush, crackling twigs breaking. A shadow moved across the fire then another. She felt Gael's body grow tense against her own and marveled at the way he could pretend to lay asleep while how ever many men prowled about their fire. She would have expected him to have leapt to his feet far earlier, swinging his sword and dancing to the tune of death. He had far more patience than she'd ever given him credit for. Beneath the cloak, she felt Gael press a dagger into her hand and her fingers closed around it as she swallowed down hard. He tapped her four times on the forearm.

Four men, she understood. Four men were nothing to the two of them, so long as they could gain their feet. She found herself wondering why they hadn't yet attacked, why Gael had fallen asleep in the first place. It was uncharacteristic for him to close his eyes, and then she realized that he hadn't gone to sleep. He planned to let Edulph think he was unguarded. All the better to bring the shadows into the firelight. She listened, straining her ears to hear whether Edulph was lying next to them, or whether he had risen in the dark to meet his fellows. Gael's hand slipped suddenly away from her mouth and ran back down beneath the cloak to touch her on her hip. With an easy gentleness, he rolled her slowly to her side, giving her the purchase to leap to her feet should she need to. Yet she found there was no need because in the next instant, Gael was on his feet, his arms spread to protect her, his feet splayed facing the fire. Alaysha rolled to her own feet and turned to face them. She was at his side in moments. Her dagger was in her sword hand, to thrust or throw. She strained her eyes into the darkness but it was her ears that told the story.

A perverse chuckling rolled across the fire.

"Show yourself, Edulph," she commanded him.

He met her with further humor. "Look around you, witch. You're surrounded."

Shadows lengthened as they moved out from the trees, and as they grew closer to the firelight, they shortened into forms no higher than Alaysha's chest.

"Children," Alaysha said in wonder.

"Meet your threat, witch," Edulph said, laughing. "Come closer, children. Come closer."

Three boys and one girl edged closer to the flame, stretching their hands towards the fire as though they were chilly. One of them, the tallest, rubbed his hands one over the other and then turned to point his backside towards the heat. All of them were naked, painted Alaysha could now see in mud and chalk. The girl had twigs in her hair and owlish eyes that blinked out across the fire at Alaysha.

"Why children?" She asked Edulph.

He shrugged. "Did you think I meant to harm you? You who promised to keep my daughter safe so long as I brought you to the boy."

He pulled the girl closer by her elbow, and made her face Alaysha. "This one sat right next to your bedding place, did you not see her?" His voice was full of good humor, but it didn't fool Alaysha. It was mockery he offered her, not good-natured humor.

"Where's my nephew?" Gael commanded, impatient. "I tire of this foolishness."

Edulph's mouth moved into a crooked line of reproach: even in the meager firelight, Alaysha could see him gloating. "You will play the games I wish if you want your nephew back."

A sword makes no sound when it's pulled from its leather, and before Alaysha knew it, Gael had stretched his out and pointed it at Edulph. "We did not agree on games," Gael said. "We agreed to follow you here and collect him. You agreed to give him up."

"And you'd like for me to do so?" Edulph asked innocently.

"I do,"

"Then you will have to admit that I need to protect myself at the same time." Edulph took a step towards the sword, so that the tip pressed into his chest. "These children are the next step of the journey. I meant you no harm or threat. It's you who saw threats in the face of innocence."

"Who are they?" Alaysha asked.

"Our guides," Edulph said. "We'll leave when the sun rises."

The sun was far from peeling its eyelid open but Alaysha had a hard time finding sleep nonetheless. Edulph snored lightly on his side of the fire, but she and Gael sat with their knees beneath their chins, staring off at the strange children.

Watching the children on their side of the fire, their eyes glowing strangely in the light. They reminded her of wolves, the way they sat tense and unmoving. Three of them held onto long staffs that were no more than twisted branches curling around each other.

They put Alaysha in mind of children from her father's first conquest. Those children had the same look: they were gaunt, hungry looking, with an almost feral way about them. Even still, there was something else beneath the surface of their skin, perhaps in their posture, or their mannerisms, that spoke to some sort of deeply ingrained civility. Those people of the first conquest had accepted chattelhood much the same as Edulph's own people did. They were resigned, accepting. But always there had been the air about them that they were better than their Lords and they wore their haughtiness like many men wore cloaks.

These children were much the same. When the sun rose they broke their fast quietly on nuts and berries, parceling out between them some dried fish and drinking from water skins that were as pale as human skin. Alaysha could swear she even saw freckles on the water skin of one of the boys, perhaps even a large liver spot.

It was disconcerting; the more she looked, the more certain she grew that those water skins had been made of men flayed. She eyed Edulph carefully, wondering if he had noticed or if he suspected that the children who would be his guides had tanned human skin. The fool showed no indication that he believed such. Alaysha turned to Gael and touched him briefly on the elbow. "What do you make of that?" She whispered.

Gael bent to put on his boots, more Alaysha thought to speak without being heard than to show haste of getting dressed. His voice was muffled, but his message plain. "I have my doubts that Edulph would entrust such a valuable trophy to children."

"I don't trust him either," Alaysha said. In truth, trust had never entered the equation. It was necessary to follow Edulph; that was all. But she had begun to worry that Edulph had something sinister planned for the both of them. She had her doubts they were heading toward Saxon at all.

"We'll keep him in front of us, him and the children." She tucked her hair behind her ear, flinging aside the errant strands that had come loose and tangled in her fingers. She didn't need to tell Gael she thought there was something queer about the whole affair. She could feel his own uncertainty, in the air, connecting to her very tissues. She chewed her lip thoughtfully. When the first of the children headed off into the dankness of the forest, tapping in front of him with his quarterstaff, the others followed in a fanned out formation, doing the same. The fourth and final: the girl, walked in a zigzag pattern much like a rabbit losing a hound.

Edulph sent Alaysha a crooked smile. "The last leg of the journey, now," he said. "I only hope that by the time we find your brother, you will have lost your desire for my death."

Alaysha said nothing, merely exchanged a meaningful look with Gael. A living Edulph was far more risk than a happy, but deceased Edulph.

She let Gael move in front of her and watched as he strolled into the forest behind Edulph. With a kind of reluctant dread, she followed them.

Many hours and leagues later, the thickness of forest turned into a boggy wetland that Edulph called the muck lands. She could still see the children far ahead, their staffs poking into the dirt, sometimes nearly drowning beneath the bog and being pulled up again by their holders. When this happened, the girl who was zigzagging like a rabbit moved off towards the side, seeming to know without being told that the leaders would be doing the same. Inevitably they would all shuffle to the left or the right with the rabbit girl.

The muck lands was a sea of sucking black Earth topped by a pillow of lime green moss. Frogs croaked in the distance and the incessant whine of mosquitoes drilled into Alaysha's ear. Here and there trees reached for the sky with limbs that wore sleeves of heavy moss, dangling to the ground in curtains. One misstep and Alaysha feared her bare feet would bury themselves so deep she'd not be able to pull them back out again. The children ahead of them beat their paths with a sure footed grace only offered them on the heels of constant tap tapping of their quarterstaffs. Once, Alaysha thought she saw a snake slithering through the sponge to the right of her feet, but it was gone so fast she doubted she'd seen it. In its wake, the moss laid over on each side, showing a seam of mucky brown water. If it was a swimming serpent, it had seemed a little wide and long for her taste.

Twice Alaysha's bare feet sunk into the sponge. When she pulled her foot out again, it made a sucking sound and she thought she pulled a muscle in her thigh from the effort. At least she noticed Gael was having just as hard a time as she was. With his height and weight, he sank deeper and had to work harder to pull his feet free. None of the children turned back to see if they were still following. Even Edulph seemed more interested in keeping his feet from sticking than he did in knowing whether or not Alaysha and Gael followed.

She noticed there were precious few animals in the muck lands. What birds she saw were hawks soaring high above them headed for the thickness of the Woodlands beyond. She was swatting two different places with both hands when she heard the shout. So intent had she been on her own feet and on the mosquitoes that she hadn't noticed how far ahead everyone had got.

The cry for help made her stop short. She felt herself sinking into the moss. Ahead of her, Gael had taken to high-stepping his way through, his body in all earnestness, seeming to be trying to run forward. She had to strain her way forward, and only when Gael fell forward and clamoured at the muck, did she see Edulph ahead of him waist deep in the bog. Waist deep, and going down fast.

Gael was up again before Alaysha could react.

The girl turned and hollered a warning. "Lie down," she shouted. Gael didn't listen. He was busy stomping toward Edulph, his boots disappearing beneath the moss even as the girl shouted at him to stop moving. Either Gael didn't understand or he didn't think she was talking to him. He forged ahead, heedless that his boots were sinking deeper into the moss the faster he ran. Even Alaysha could see that he was having a hard time yanking his feet back out of the sucking muck.

"I said lie down," the girl shouted again. The boys in the column ahead had stopped; each of them rested on their quarterstaffs, but beneath their armpits, they seemed to have found some sort of hard packed ground. Alaysha scanned the area to see that Edulph had gone far a field of where the boys had tapped clear. Off toward the left, almost as though intentionally. That couldn't be. Surely he was smart enough to follow where the boys had tapped clear. A niggle of suspicion crept up her spine.

"Lie down," Alaysha shouted at Gael. For good measure, she yelled his name and he turned. "Down."

This time, Gael listened. When he pulled his feet free, he lay flat, sprawled across the moss with his arms outstretched and his legs splayed. The toes of his boots buried themselves into the sponge. Alaysha could tell that even though he was fine, the bog was doing its best to swallow him whole. Edulph had gone as far as his chest. Strangely, he wasn't struggling. Rather, he stretched his arms out over the moss that engulfed him but even at this distance, Alaysha could see his eyes were brimming with fear. The girl reached for a knife she had tied to her leg. Creeping sideways, she entered a small stand of trees and climbed it deftly. When she returned, it was with a thick green vine coiled over her wrists and trailing behind her.

"Grab this," she shouted to Gael and threw the coil toward him. "Wrap it around his wrist."

A thought struck Alaysha. She found herself stumbling forward. "Don't," she yelled at him. "Don't do it."

Gael sent her a questioning look. Alaysha ignored it. She felt her knees scrabble across the moss, hand over hand; she pulled herself forward until she was close enough to feel that she could touch his boot. "Hold it, but don't throw it."

He craned to look back at her. "Why not?"

"Saxon," was all she said.

"Without him, we won't get Saxon."

She stretched forward, reaching for the line that Gael had. "Give it to me," she said.

He flicked it towards her and she caught it with her right hand. With her left, she pulled closer so that she was lying parallel to Gael. She could feel the bog seeping into her leather tunic. It smelled of death. She wondered if somewhere below, the muck lands were full of brimstone.

"What about Saxon?" Gael asked.

Ignoring the question, Alaysha turned her attention to where Edulph was steadily sinking. He was nearly to his neck, and rather than his arms being outstretched on the bog, they had almost taken the air. He began to wave at them frantically.

"Where is Saxon?" She shouted at him. "Tell me now."

"I have to show you," he said.

"No, you don't." Alaysha shook the vine in the air. "Tell us and we'll haul you out."

"Alaysha," Gael said, touching her on the shoulder. "You can't do that. What if he won't tell you? What if we lose him?"

There was a dread in Gael's voice she'd never heard before. Even so, she continued.

"Tell us, Edulph. Or I'll let you sink."

She felt Gael's fingers digging into her forearm. "Don't, Alaysha. Please don't."

He's nothing," she told Gael. "You know he's nothing. He doesn't deserve to live anyway."

"And you're the woman to make that decision?"

She wasn't sure she liked the look in Gael's eyes. "Someone has to make that decision."

Worse than the look in his eyes, was the sound in her own voice. It sounded cold and hard and it reminded her of her father's voice when he gave an order he wanted obeyed. She told herself it didn't matter. All that mattered was getting Saxon back. All that mattered, all that should have mattered, was that she keep her people safe. What was the life of one cruel man to the lives of innocents?

"If not me, then who?" She asked Gael. "Who do you think would make these hard decisions? You?"

"It's not a hard decision, it's a rash one."

She threaded a distasteful moue onto her mouth to tell him how much she hated to correct him. "If we don't use him, we lose Saxon."

"You sound like your father."

She turned away and shook the vine in the air, aiming it toward the man in the muck. "Tell me, Edulph. What's your decision?"

Edulph struggled, aiming his voice to the heavens. "I told you; I need to show you."

For a hundred heartbeats, Alaysha waited, hoping Edulph would finally break down. It was Gael who tore the vine from her hands and scrambled forward, pulling himself with his hands in the muck until he was close enough to throw the vine. Edulph reached for it and wrapped it around his wrist; a gulping, sucking sound emerged from the bowels of the bog as Gael pulled him backwards to relative safety, Gael's face a sheen of sweat from the effort.

Alaysha reached for Gael with a timid hand, thinking she could explain that it had been a threat only, that she'd not meant to let Edulph die before they'd found Saxon. He jerked away, gently enough that she couldn't mistake his meaning that although he wasn't disgusted with her, he was at least disappointed.

It was nightfall before the children stopped their niggardly pace. The oldest of the boys gathered wood and a few berries while the youngest produced a nest of duck eggs that they boiled and peeled as they sat around a crackling fire; for a long time, no one spoke. Alaysha caught herself studying Edulph as he chewed noisily, popping small round globes into his mouth and then extracting the seeds with a filthy black nail.

Gael neither spoke to her, nor attempted to touch her. She felt entirely miserable as she ate her meagre fare, stealing glances at him across the fire.

They reached their destination long before midmorning. Gael had woke them all before the sun had chased the shadows of night away. Alaysha didn't mind. It had been an uncomfortable night. She'd been cold and had dreamt badly, chasing at demonic smoke and shadows most of the night. She even woke with aching knees as though she'd been running.

The village was fenced in with what looked like tanned human flesh. Intermittent posts of hemlock were strung with frames of stretched bits of unbroken flesh sewn together with smaller parts. Here and there, gaps in the fencing revealed small parts of the village within: adobe brick buildings, several large cook fires, a few children milling about. Alaysha caught Gael's eye and thought she read within it the same anxiety she felt within her own. At first glance, there didn't appear to be any fortifications set outside to protect the people within. That didn't mean there were no booby-traps. The Enyalia had a habit of deflecting attention from one trap by using another, more obvious one. With that in mind, she inspected the perimeter closely, knowing Gael was doing the same. There were no telltale vines reaching into the tree tops, nor were there sharpened poles stuck base first into the dirt. For all intents and purposes, the inhabitants appeared to think that the leathered fence would be dismaying enough to visitors that no one would think to enter and molest them.

She quailed at the sight of the gate as the girl used the butt of her quarterstaff to push it open. Made of what appeared to Alaysha to be bleached thigh bones and forearms and painted with unadulterated pitch stuck with several bugs and detritus.

If Alaysha was anxious at the leathered fence that surrounded the village, she was even more dismayed by what she saw within. Two tall posts rested within the gates, each one sporting very small shrivelled heads tied to the gates by their hair. Some of the shrunken heads wore long black braids coiled about their foreheads and slung over the pegs that held them, some were white-haired faces whose leather strings wrapped around the locks of hair in such intricate and complex patterns, that they would have been beautiful if woven into living hair. Several had their lips sewn together and sported bits of bone that pierced through the bottom in hooks that pointed toward Alaysha like claws. Dread settled into her belly as she realized that the same pattern of posts was repeated all along the inside of the fencing, standing sentry about three paces away from each other, all sporting their own myriad of blackened faces. She couldn't help a shudder when she saw the breadth of the village, thinking of how many people would have had to die to decorate those posts.

For a second Alaysha worried that Saxon wouldn't be in the village at all, at least not alive.

She turned to Gael. "Pray to the deities we find him quickly."

He was so close beside her that she could feel the heat coming off him, and smell the perspiration of a hard day's walk.

"Best to pray to the deities that I find him at all," he said, echoing her thoughts.

Alaysha eyed Edulph as he came along behind them, ambling mindfully clear of Gael's reach. "Where?" She asked him.

He pointed to a hut built of mud brick and thatch. Outside its door, several scrawny dogs fought over a deer's head. The woman beside them, oblivious to the squabbling and bent over a large bubbling cauldron, looked sickeningly familiar.

"Greetha," Alaysha said, thinking even as she said it that it wasn't right. The only female in Edulph's motley band had been stouter, with a longer face.

Edulph shook his head. "No. Greetha's elder sister. Their priestess."

Any questions Alaysha wanted to ask were left frozen in her throat as a long piercing wail tore through the air. It was obviously a child's cry, shrill and agonized.

Gael was already sprinting towards the hut, his sword drawn from his back and pumping back and forth in his hand as he ran. Alaysha was behind him, not caring whether Edulph followed or not. Another screech sounded, a pained thing that clawed at the air and curdled Alaysha's breath as she dragged in lungfuls of oxygen, trying desperately to fuel the muscles in her legs. She was panting when she drew up next to Gael, who was kicking at one of the dogs as he tried to get past them to the hovel, working to fling it off his leg where the teeth had buried into the leather.

"Get this thing off me, Crone," he was shouting at the woman. The sound of the cry had wound down to a sob but the sound of that pitiful whimper assaulted Alaysha's ears just the same.

The second of the dogs had joined the attack and both now had Gael's breek's legs deep into the backs of their mouths, shaking at the leather, growling through lips peeled back far enough over long canines to show the blackened teeth at the rear. The woman stepped in front of the doorway, barring Alaysha as she moved to enter. The horrific smell of the bubbling cauldron wafted toward her, and involuntarily, Alaysha's hand waved across her nose.

"What's that stink?" Alaysha asked, fighting back the thoughts that whatever could be happening to Saxon at this moment could well have something to do with the stink inside that pot.

"Old woman," she said. "Where is he?"

Another bloodcurdling scream rent the air. Alaysha squeezed her eyes closed, trying to hone in on its origin from inside the hut. The dogs grew more insistent; the second worked itself below Gael's knee, leaving the bottom of his other leg to the first. Alaysha thought she heard leather tear before one of them yelped as Gael landed a burly fist against one of their rib cages. The old woman leapt forward, trying to wrangle them far enough from Gale's sword that a sudden, frustrated strike would settle the matter once and for all. Still, the screaming didn't stop. Instead, it rose in pitch. Definitely a pained cry.

"Gael," Alaysha said. "Kill the dogs."

At that, the old woman lifted her face to Alaysha's. The wrinkles in her face went so deep, Alaysha could swear they were cut into her face. She opened her mouth wide to show her a gaping maul of toothless cavern. The woman had no tongue. Whatever remnant she had of it was a mere stump that waggled at her as though it was trying to form words.

"Do you understand, old woman? He is going to kill those dogs if you don't pull them off."

Gael needed no more encouragement. With the mongrels still clinging to his legs, growling and bucking backwards now, Gael hoisted his sword above his head and brought it down in one fluid motion that sent one head skittering across the ground. It did nothing to quell the sound of the infant's cries but it intensified the chaos. Before Alaysha could enter the lodging, the woman had reached for a ladle hanging on a tripod next to the fire. She dipped it in the bubbling broth, obviously planning to fling it at Gael. With one more deft swing, he took the head of her second mongrel and danced away in a spray of blood that covered him from torso to shins. The woman flung the contents of the label toward him, missing him by inches to spread steaming on the humus. Alaysha took that moment to grab for the crone's hands and pull them behind her back, wrists held together. She was old, but she was wiry. It took all Alaysha had to keep the woman from wresting herself free.

Gael stepped forward. His gray green eyes were dark with fury. While his face didn't reveal anything but controlled calm, his voice ground out like so much gravel beneath a heel. "He'd best be unharmed, old woman." His sword might have been sheathed, but there was an edge in his voice.

By now a crowd began to gather. The children who had brought them stood in front of a quarter hundred men and women in a menacing line with equally menacing obsidian tipped spears. Their weapons were poised, their faces just as implacable as Gael's.

Mercifully, the screaming had stopped. Alaysha couldn't even detect the barest of a whimper; she wasn't sure what it might mean: a respite from pain or had someone smothered out the boy's life. Even the crone relaxed in her grip. For a moment she thought she could leave Gael to deal with the village, while she rushed to Saxon's aid, but they'd drawn so much attention she knew it wouldn't be prudent.

It was the girl who came forward.

"Her face didn't look so young now Alaysha really looked at her. She might have been Aedus's age, perhaps a season or two older. And she had Greetha's distinct facial features now she really looked.

"You shed the blood of our gods," she said nodding toward Gael.

"Your gods?" Alaysha said, confused. They'd been nothing but mongrels. Alaysha let go of the Crone's wrists and the old woman fell to her knees next to the dogs, her fingers scrabbling across their fur, digging in as she bowed forward, her forehead touching the humus with her arms stretched in front of her.

"Our priestess would have gladly helped you," the girl said. Alaysha's attention turned again to the woman. Somehow the Crone had got a small obsidian blade in her hand, and in two strokes, had gutted one of the mongrels, letting its intestines spill onto the ground. Her fingers moved in and out of the gelatinous mess, until she'd dug far enough inside that she somehow nicked at the heart and pulled it, bloody, from the carcass. With a glower at Gael and Alaysha, the old woman scooped up the mess and carried it, hanging limply from her arms and dragging across the ground into her hut.

Alaysha had to swallow down the nausea that crept up her throat. She did her best to face the rest of the village. Each of them had taken stations, beginning to circle her and Gael. The girl was the only one in the center. She reached down to the dirt where pools of the dog's blood had begun to clot. She stuck her hands in, then ran her fingers down her cheeks. Several others crept forward and repeated the motion, then stepped back, awaiting something. A test perhaps, a trap?

Alaysha felt Gael's back pressed into hers, the backs of his boots digging into her heels. "No sudden movements, witch," he warned. She felt Gael moving slowly, pressing her towards the hut, out of reach of the mob.

"None." She agreed. "A trap, do you think?"

A movement to her left caught her attention, and she flicked her gaze toward it, making sure it wasn't attack. But it was just loose hair on a pole, catching the wind and waving at them. The cauldron burped and a fresh wave of stink wrinkled Alaysha's nose. Unwilling, her gaze wandered to the cauldron, and she heard herself groan out loud.

Three heads burbled within, their eyes staring straight up at Alaysha, their hair floating in the liquid like maidengrass in a lazy river. "Sweet deities," she murmured and looked back to capture the girl's stony gaze. Alaysha stepped away from Gael carefully, watching the girl, pinning her eyes to the spot between her nose.

"What are you doing?" he demanded, whispering.

In response, Alaysha bent her knee next to the pool of blood and stuck her fingers in. She felt the greasey blend of old earth and fresh blood streak her cheeks as she trailed her fingers from beneath her eyes to her jaw.

"Until we know whether Saxon is here, we need to show some healthy fear," she explained without looking back at him. Even as she stood again, she heard the girl chuckle softly and the air seemed to return to the lungs of the mob. They inhaled in seeming unison.

"Why are you laughing?" She asked the girl.

The girl shrugged. "Our gods look like shit on your face."

"Those aren't gods," Alaysha told her. "Those are mongrels."

It was then that Edulph decided to break through the crowd, striding forward in that arrogant way he had. The moustache on his lips moved like a caterpillar on the forage. It undulated over his skin as his lips twitched in a dark humour.

"Anything is a god to them that gives them reason to take another head." He indicated the posts lining the outside walls. "Greetha's daughter," he said, pointing to the girl. The girl let her spear rest butt first on the ground.

Almost as if sensing it to be some sort of signal, the rest of the crowd did too.

"Greetha's people are skin lovers. They think there's power in an enemy's flesh." He shrugged deferentially and offered a weak, but humorless smile. "And there must be some truth to it; the fences seem to keep a good many of them that bay."

"Except for you," Alaysha said bitterly.

"And you," Edulph countered. "You have something in common with them, it seems."

"That is?"

He nodded to indicate the heads. "They think our essence lies within and can be trapped there." He tapped his temple next to his left eye.

Gael closed the distance between himself and Edulph before Alaysha had the chance to realize what he was doing. He faced the man, towering over him, leaving her to face the most of the crowd alone.

"You better hope he's alive," Gael growled. "And you better hope that screaming wasn't him."

Edulph sent a questioning look toward the girl. And for a heartbeat, Alaysha thought the child would point towards one of the posts. She could almost imagine the silver hair just long enough to reach the bottoms of Saxon's ears, tied up into a leather-strained ponytail, hanging from a peg on one of those timbers. But when Greetha's daughter pointed instead to the old woman's hut, Alaysha wasn't sure whether she felt relief or further dread.

"You brought us into a trap," Alaysha said to him.

He shook his head. "No I didn't. He's in there. You can trust her."

"Like we can trust you?"

"I brought you here, didn't I? And they didn't attack you." The tip of his tongue ran over the bottom of his lip. "If one of them wanted to do you harm, you would have been harmed by now."

Gael snorted and Edulph gave him a patronizing look. "Don't underestimate them," he said.

The girl was shuffling forward when another scream rent the air. Alaysha felt Gael's fingers biting into her elbow and then she was being pulled into the gloom of the hut. It took long moments before her eyes adjusted, but she didn't need vision to know where the source waited: the shrieking was enough to guide them. A fresh wave of screaming rose and fell, then teetered off into a whimpering cry.

"Saxon," Alaysha said, sprinting toward the sound. She'd forgotten the old woman in her haste, forgotten that she had been carrying slithery streams of entrails and blood into the lodging with her. Alaysha slipped on a disgusting mash of long digested food and new shit. The mix of it squelched between her toes, and sent her face first into the earth floor. She brought her palms alongside her head and pushed herself up, her vision adjusting finally to the dark.

Several tiny faces grinned at her as they hung from their pegs on the wall. One of them had eyes cloudy and milk white and Alaysha's mind went ridiculously to Aislin in that moment. How one of her eyes had begun to grow milky. She had enough time to get to her knees before the old woman knelt in front of her, her black eyes level with Alaysha's. The stink coming from her mouth, level with her nose.

She thought it would be Gael's hands that gripped her and helped her to her feet, but it was the crone who did so. She had several oil lamps lit in niches along the wall, flooding light onto Saxon's bed.

Gael was next to her in an instant. Before Alaysha could reach for him, Gael had scooped him from the bedding of furs. He'd grown, Alaysha realized. She'd assumed from the piteous cries and screams of pain that Saxon would be drawn and puny. But he was plump and hale, more robust than she'd ever seen him in Sarum. He was being cared for, obviously. Gael rocked the boy gently, crooning to him. It did nothing to mollify him or stop the whimpering.

The old woman placed greasy hands on the babe's fat arms. She lifted the right one so his chubby fist was pointing towards the ceiling. Perplexed, Gael aimed Saxon so that his tiny rib cage was pointing towards the light. The old woman pressed a bony finger into the baby's armpit. She grunted. When neither of them responded, she made a noise of impatience and lifted a small oil lamp from the niche closest to the boy's bed and moved it closer to his skin. The light wavered in the draft and found its strength again. It was brief, but when the play of light moved across Saxon's skin, Alaysha knew what it was the woman was pointing to.

There were marks there, tattaus so fresh that the skin around the marks was crimson and furious looking. No wonder he'd been crying.

"They marked him, Gael," Alaysha whispered. "Just like I marked you." She could hear the relief in her voice. "That's it, that's all. His skin hurts from the tattauing."

Even as she said it, Saxon's little body tensed and he let out another shriek of pain. The light that still played over his rib cage, revealed to Alaysha that the soreness around his marks had grown redder. They began to bubble and blister in front of them, and as they popped and receded and bubbled to the surface again, Saxon wailed to the ceiling in renewed agony. Gael pulled him even closer, nuzzling the boy's face into his neck. Alaysha thought she heard Gael whimper too.

Alaysha clenched her bottom lip with her teeth. This was no regular tattau and no regular inking pain. Her memory went speeding down the long tunnels of her memory searching for just the right room. Not simple marks at all. A witch's tattau. A tattau that she knew very intimately because she'd seen it on another rib cage another lifetime ago when she thought she'd managed to find some peace and acceptance. Yenic's marks. Yenic's rib cage.

And that meant that the marks on Saxon's flesh had to be Aislin's.

CHAPTER 14

It seemed like hours before Saxon stopped crying. Each time he shrieked, Alaysha felt as if a knife was slicing through her chest. Even Gael, that stoic warrior, suffered plainly each time Saxon writhed in his arms. The crone came then with a palm full of stinking grease and smeared it over Saxon's tattaus. She made a sound that could have been a matronly clucking sound meant to calm the boy, but Alaysha couldn't tell whether the woman felt responsible for the pain he was feeling or whether she simply couldn't stand to see the baby cry. After long agonizing moments, he fell into a restless sleep in Gael's arms as the warrior paced back and forth in the hut. They'd sought each other's eyes each time the boy had screeched, like helpless parents suffering with their child and powerless to relieve his suffering. Alaysha had never felt so weak and beneath the helplessness that gnawed at her, there broiled a steady flame of anger. Once the boy settled she thought she could breathe again, but they were hard drafts, poised on the knowledge that the searing pain could come again at any moment. She herself strode back and forth in the hovel, hard on Gael's heels until he swung to face her.

"You're doing him no good here." He pleaded. "Go find out what they did to him."

Alaysha nodded in answer and scurried out of the lodging. She was surprised to see Edulph still standing near the cauldron, staring down into it morosely. She drew near enough to peer inside as she took her place next to him. This close she could tell that what she'd first thought were full heads, were only just masks of flesh, obviously peeled off the bone and set to bubble inside this fetid liquid. She couldn't help a shudder.

"Those heads I sent you when I'd captured Yenic were Greetha's idea," Edulph said as he stared into the grisly soup. "Her people believe there is magic in heads." He took the long handled spoon and dipped it inside pot, twirling it in and around the bubbling liquid, making the faces swim grotesquely. "Her people believe there is a certain power in them." He lifted his gaze to the edges of the village, where the posts lined around the human skin fences.

"Some of them are enemies, some of them ancestors." Almost absently, he clumped the handle of the wooden spoon against the rim of the pot. "You have to admit there's a certain kind of charm to them. A certain craft." He took the ladle of the spoon and pointed it at one of the faces within the low boiling water. "Once that gentleman is finished, he'll look as close to himself as any head can look. He'll look to be sleeping, yes, and he'll be much, much smaller, but each feature will be carefully manipulated back into the semblance of the man he was. When he's done boiling, the priestess inside will dump in hot round stones to sear the skin on the inside. She'll work his mask for days and days with rocks and sand until he's complete."

He lifted his eyes to Alaysha and must have sensed her revulsion because his expression became almost pleading. "That's why I turned to them," he explained. "I thought they might have the skill to craft the marks."

Alaysha tried very hard not to let him see her anger. "But you used Aislin's symbols, Edulph."

"Not Aislin's." He lifted his hands in a helpless gesture. "I didn't know that. I didn't know the marks could be different at all."

Something niggled at her and she recalled the short time in the wilderness before he'd tried to use her to capture Sarum. Alaysha found herself remembering just how long he would have had Yenic in his care before he'd sent them off with his grisly treasures to find Alaysha and deliver the ultimatum. Yenic: The only witch's Arm Edulph would have known.

"You copied Yenic's."

"Not then." Edulph pulled at his moustache with his bottom teeth nervously. "I had no idea then what they were or why I would have needed them. It was only after I left Sarum and fled to the Highlands. When I found Liliah, I realized she would need an Arm as well. I drew the marks from Yenic's skin from memory as best I could. After I brought the boy here."

"Thinking that they could duplicate them for you."

He nodded.

Alaysha gave him wary study. "When did you know something was wrong? Is this why you brought us here?"

He shook his head. "Nothing was wrong. I swear it." He pointed the spoon at the door of the priestess's home. "You've seen him. He's hearty and hale. Plump and well fed. Greetha's daughter and that cronc of a priestess dote on him."

"Something must have changed," Alaysha said, thinking. "If he's not been this way the whole time," she murmured more to herself and him. She was angry at Edulph, yes, but she was more concerned with Saxon. If Edulph had had these people trace Yenic's marks onto Saxon's body, tattaued them in with soot, it was very possible that they'd just been mere marks. Without the ashes from a true witch, the marks would have no power. Or would they? Alaysha simply wasn't sure. Perhaps the marks themselves contained some magic, but that without the witch's soot, the magic would go bad. Perhaps then it would harm the owner of the tattau. Surely when Yenic was alive, there had been no reason those marks on Saxon's side meant anything more than simply scraped and scarred skin.

"It was Yenic's death," she said, realizing it as she said it. "It must be. When he died he broke his bond with his mother. But she would have had no way of knowing it. Each time she reached out, the bond would have failed."

"Or it would have deflected." Edulph mumbled.

"And so when she reached out for Yenic, her magic found Saxon instead."

"Except it's is not a true mark," Edulph said, guessing. "Is it?"

Alaysha shook her head. "I'm afraid not," She told him. "There's more to the magic than simply making the marks, Edulph." She said. "So much more than that." She remembered the kykeon that she'd dripped her own blood into and the flush of Gael's skin against hers as she moved against him.

Now she understood what had gone wrong, she was more interested in finding out why. She watched Edulph closely, saw the way he chewed at his moustache, and stared down into the cauldron. He certainly acted penitent, but she knew he would stop at nothing to get what he wanted. She'd experienced it far too often to think otherwise.

"I still don't understand why you would do it," she said. "Why mark him?"

"I had to." Edulph said. "Liliah needs an Arm."

"How could you know such a thing, Edulph? How could you know about us at all?"

He drew in a long breath, seeming to consider the question before he spoke. "After I escaped your father's lead scout, Mikka found me in the burnt lands, " he said. "I was weak, exhausted. I was starving, but more than that I was dying of thirst."

It took a moment for Alaysha to realize that what he was sharing was bothering him, that the things he was talking about were painful. It took him a few moments, staring up at the sky, reflective before he continued. Alaysha tried not to move, tried not to do anything to distract him. She wanted terribly to ask him who Mikka was, but didn't dare interrupt.

"She took me back to the Highland village where she fed me, healed me, loved me," he said. "We spent a good deal of time together. No doubt you can tell what happened then," he smiled wryly and she guessed he was speaking of Liliah's birth. "By the time I made my way back, it was under the madness of Meroshi's worm and I returned to a village struggling to raise a child they couldn't trust because both the mother and grandmother were dead." He gave Alaysha a knowing glance and she felt her face warm in shame. He seemed pleased with that.

"I took one look at the tiny thing," he said. "The long blonde eyelashes that rested on her cheeks as she slept, the way her tiny head fit in my palm, and I vowed that I would do whatever I had to for her safety.

"When I stormed the Sarum again, it was in secrecy as I said. Greetha and I stole into the city and while her fellow men launched arrows in the air, catching you, catching Gael, I searched out Saxa's house and stole the boy. Greetha made it out with him and you know what happened to me. Aislin caught me." He shrugged. "Then, of course, you found me. And when we began traveling the burnt lands, I thought that perhaps everything was working as it should. My manipulations didn't have to be for nothing, that you and the shaman and that brute of a warrior would see me safely through to the Highlands."

"Until the Enyalia." Alaysha guessed.

"Until the Enyalia," he agreed. "Even then, just when I thought all was lost, and you and Gael had taken off to the village ahead of us, I believed myself dead."

"What happened? How did you get free?"

He sighed, thinking, looking off into the distance. "I'm not sure," he said. "There was a man. The earthquakes had started and this man showed up out of nowhere in the middle of the night. He shook the ground beneath the Enyalian beasts, and as the Enyalia worked to recover from the magic, he freed me."

Alaysha thought back, her heart speeding in her chest, realizing finally what he was talking about. "The earthquakes, yes. Driven by the witch in Thera's hut. But who is this man? What did he look like?"

"That's the best part," this time Edulph grinned happily as though he offered her something that could buy his freedom, and she realized then that was exactly what he was doing. He'd known she would never allow him to take Sarum or to live with his daughter, that she'd never intended to pay his price and that he'd kept this morsel until just the right time.

"He had skin like an almond shell," he said, remembering. "His eyes were blacker than black. And beneath his arm –"

"Beneath his arm, a ribbon of tattaus," Alaysha guessed. "The clay witch's Arm."

"Yes. Once again, those markings proved to have some sort of power, much as they did back when I took your Yenic, back when I –"

"When you had him beaten nearly to death," Alaysha said for him and she could hear the venom in her own voice. He must've sensed it too, because he nodded ever so subtly.

"And so you thought to mark Saxon," she said. "But why? He's just an infant. How could he protect your daughter?"

Edulph met her eyes with a brazen type of courage that surprised Alaysha. "He may be small, and young, but he has the connection to three witches in his blood."

Alaysha thought about that. Liliah was of the wind, and marked by her he would have the connection of air. As Gael's nephew, he would be blood to the clay witch as well, and as Yuri's son he would share the same blood as

Alaysha did. None of it was strong, but she imagined that the three of them combined could offer the boy some power. She'd seen Yenic channel his mother's power, seen how powerful Aislin's magic could be is it worked through him to Alaysha, funnelling into innocent people and setting them to tinder as easily as if they were dry crackling kindling.

It was truth, finally, and she realized it when she heard it. But there was more, she knew that too. "And what do you get out of all of this when all is said and done," she asked him. She knew better than to believe that he was doing all of this for the love of his daughter.

Edulph dropped the spoon onto its peg and toed the dirt. "What did I want all along?"

Alaysha thought back. "Sarum."

He nodded and for long moments neither of them spoke. It was a bald admission, one that shouldn't have surprised Alaysha, but it did. To think that all of this on his part was only so that he could play at megalomania much the same as Yuri had left a sour taste on her palette. She stared past his shoulder at the line of posts and the way the faces seemed to grin at her in taunt. One thing she hadn't counted on was the greed of man. Just knowing that she had let that little fact slipped past her after all she'd suffered at her father's hands, made her feel foolish. She'd been preoccupied, she realized, with believing she was a god. And even the shame of that hope made her uncomfortable. She was still struggling to keep from physically squirming when she realized Edulph had begun to speak again.

"When all of this is done, and my good daughter and all this witch business is finished, Sarum will need a new leader. I will be happy to fill that role."

It was such a simple desire in light of all they'd been through, that Alaysha almost laughed at him except that she'd begun to suspect the complexity of his plan. "You never meant to rescue your people from Sarum, did you?"

He shook his head. "No. It was a ruse."

"You were always after Saxon," she guessed and was rewarded with a brief nod.

"Deflection, distraction. Always the better route when you're dealing with enemies more powerful than you."

Indeed.

Edulph swatted a fly. "If I had run storming to Sarum, demanding of your father that he deliver Saxon, do you think he would have ever given up looking for me?" He didn't wait for her to answer but kept on. "No. Liliah needed the boy if she was going to be protected. And so I had to make it look as though my intentions were different. One of your guards was to bring him out to me while the rest of the Highland village fled from Sarum in fear of their lives at the hands of Yuri's witch. It was really a delicious plan if you look at it logically. In the confusion of a city under siege, no one would notice a young boy being carted out. And in the aftermath, who would even begin to think that someone had spirited him away. He could have been taken by anyone in the aftermath. Surely it would never be the man who simply wanted to rescue his people from slavery."

He crossed his arms, almost to indicate that he believed in the finality of his plan. "But if I demanded him from your father, things would've been very different."

It was cunning, Alaysha had to admit. And it had nearly worked. In fact it would have worked if he'd never admitted to her that he held Saxon. She wondered if Yenic hadn't died and Liliah hadn't brought him back, ending with her forcing Edulph to show his hand, if they would have ever known the boy was safe.

"And so when all of this is done, you imagine that there will be no better leader for Sarum than you?"

He shrugged. "Who will be left? Your father is gone, the witches will have no remaining power. The city needs a strong arm and a willing mind to rule it.

He didn't know, Alaysha realized. He knew the barest facts about Liliah, and not the full truth.

"How much do you know of the legend, Edulph?" She asked him.

"Enough," he answered.

It was all she could do not to smear the full truth of the legend in his face. For all his cunning planning, his emotionless ruses, the end result would only serve to make his daughter's life that much more impossible. She wondered if she should tell him that the end of the witches and their power meant Liliah's death. As far as Alaysha was concerned, she didn't care whether the legend came to pass, whether the war was won, she only wanted to get home to Sarum and pass Saxa the missing son she grieved. She wanted to take the lot of them far away from Sarum and let the rest of them sort out the war. Telling Edulph the full truth would only make that impossible.

"Aedus, Edulph? What will happen to her?"

Again, he shrugged. "When you are all normal, with no powers behind you, you can both stay in my city."

Normal, Alaysha thought. She doubted there would ever be any such thing for her. No such chance for normalcy if Aislin continued to wage war with her sister, and if the war was won by Liliah there'd be nothing left to remain normal. The knowledge that she'd not told Gael the story either, kicked up dust in the back of her conscience, but she pushed that hastily aside.

"And what if we choose not to?" she asked.

"Then simply leave." He eyed her with barely concealed threat. "And I'll have no call to harm either of you."

Alaysha let the threat die in the air; she didn't feel the need to argue.

She sighed, frustrated. For a moment Alaysha almost felt sorry for him. At least until she heard the shrill sound of Saxon waking again in pain. Then, she could have cared no more for Edulph's feelings than she cared for Aislin's.

CHAPTER 15

Before she had a chance to sprint inside, Gael was at the door, clutching a squalling Saxon one hand and his sword in the other, his eyes searching frantically for a target. He found it standing behind the cauldron with his eyes wide and nervous. Gael lurched forward at Edulph, his sword arm ready to make the blade sing in the air.

"Gael, no," Alaysha shouted. "The baby." She sprinted for the warrior, grappling for the baby in his arms. Saxon was still squalling, piercing Alaysha's ears. She had him finally in her arms, a writhing, squirming, shouting thing that she had to wrestle against her chest and jumble helplessly up-and-down, trying desperately to soothe him. Edulph had ducked the swing, only because Gael's awkward movement as he divested himself of the infant had robbed him of his customary grace. When he'd realized he'd missed, Gael threw himself forward, his broad hands grasping onto Edulph's throat. He must've completely encircled the scrawny neck because next Alaysha knew, Edulph was lifted into the air to land against the adobe wall.

"I should have killed you long ago," Gael ground out.

Edulph's eyes went wider. He tried to speak. What came out was nothing more than a rasping cough. In seconds, the crone had found her way out of the hut and reached for a burning stick beneath the cauldron. She waved it at Gael even as the girl came trotting forward from somewhere, her brothers hard on her heels, each of them trailed by several burly men with spears twice as wide and long as the children's.

It seemed the tentative truce was dying with Edulph.

"Gael, let him down," Alaysha said, realizing that his people were Edulph's allies like it or not.

"Gael, it's not him who's to blame," Alaysha said. "It's Aislin. She's trying to connect."

"Aislin?" Gael stepped away from Edulph, letting the man fall the ground, his hands reaching for his throat to rub out the pain. "I don't understand," Gael said, shaking his head. "What do you mean she's trying to connect?"

"He has her mark," Alaysha explained. With her free hand, she pointed to the girl. "These people marked him with Yenic's mark. You know what that means."

"That he's her Arm," Gael said, but he didn't seem pleased that he guessed correctly. In fact, the truth so displeased him, that he turned back Edulph, a scowl on his face. Alaysha took a few steps closer, thinking to diffuse the situation into something manageable. "Not truly her Arm," she murmured. "He doesn't have the full magic. That's why his skin is burning."

Gael turned to her with a glazed look across his face. She couldn't reach into his eyes with hers. He'd put up some sort of icy block that she couldn't melt through. Alaysha reached for him with her free hand, laying her palm on his bicep. She could feel the muscles tense and let go as he clenched his hands and released.

"We'll find a way to fix it," she told him. Even as she said it, however, she felt the flutterings of panic within.

There were only two ways that she knew to fix such a thing. And both of them would involve death. Eventually, he relaxed enough that she knew he had found some sort of submission within. She noted that when he did, the rest of the village rested their weapons. Alaysha stole a look at Edulph who was sitting with his knees drawn up against the mud hut. He was digging at his moustache with his bottom teeth, rubbing the back of his neck. It was obvious to her that he'd found some way to endear himself to these people; they were ready to protect him if need be. Despite that seeming security, though, Edulph didn't look like he felt safe. She remembered his words: these people worshipped skin and found power within the heads that they crafted. Not all of them were enemies, or so he said. Some were ancestors. Perhaps some had been something else. He hadn't said what. Alaysha guessed that whatever bargain he'd made with Greetha to secure the village's cooperation might be unravelling.

She stole her first look around the village and saw past those posts of gruesome shrunken heads, of the fences stretched with human skin, past those things and underneath of those things, to the mundane tasks of any village. It was clear that they didn't worry about invaders. The grisly habit of decapitating and saving the heads of their enemies and ancestors, of flaying their backs and stretching it around the village for protection, would obviously offer them some sort of security, even if it was false. But did it truly deter invaders or had the villagers merely managed to hold their own each time against invasion. Don't underestimate them, Edulph had told her, and in that moment she believed that whether it was charmed or threat, the heads certainly did wield some power.

With relief, Alaysha noticed that Saxon's cries had ebbed away to short whimpers. He buried his face into her neck, and breathed down the back of her tunic. She could feel that he was plump and hearty. He had been looked after here, the tiny feet that dug into her belly worked impatiently to stand. She couldn't help pulling him tighter, letting his bum rest against her forearm. It was peculiar, but in all of the chaos that surrounded her, the feel of this small child against her made her feel calm. She breathed a silent sigh of gratitude that he was alive.

She felt the girl's fingers poking into her ribs and looked down into the squirrelly face. The girl reached for him and with a start, Alaysha realized she had done this many times before. "You want to hold him?"

"He will want to eat soon," the girl explained.

"How long has he been... Unwell?" Alaysha asked.

The girl screwed her lips up a moue of thought. "A couple of sunrises," she said. "We have no idea why. He just started screaming." She hefted the boy onto a thrust hip and stuffed a filthy index finger into his mouth. "His teeth are coming in. We thought at first it might be that."

"Until you saw his mark changing," Alaysha guessed.

The girl nodded. "It was the priestess who noticed it first. We've been trying to soothe it with different balms. Nothing works."

"Nothing will," Alaysha said dejectedly. She cast a look at Gael who had turned his back on Edulph and was glowering at the girl. "He's hungry," she said to him.

He said nothing, but nodded his silent assent. Together, they followed the girl across the compound to a place where she had obviously been preparing a small feast. Alaysha felt guilty when she saw it. There was a horn of warm milk for Saxon, a gourd full of some mush that might have been root vegetables. To the side, obviously for the new guests, sat husks of grilled corn and strips of what turned out to be goose breast poached in its own fat and flavored with wild onions and carrots. It might have been meagre fare compared to the Highland village with its several bread ovens and cook fires, but the food was savory and delicious after so many nights of nuts and roots.

To her relief, Saxon ate willingly and nodded off into a quiet sleep in Alaysha's arms. She caught Gael looking over her shoulder at him and offered him a timid smile. She was just as relieved to see him smile back even if it was somewhat tremulous.

"I'll bring you back in the morning," the girl said. "It's too dangerous out there in the dark," she reached for a pickled egg and chewed on it reflectively. "We should be back to the river before day's end."

Welcome though they might be for the time being, Alaysha was really pleased to know they would be leaving the village in the morning. She didn't want to tarry too long in a place where the inhabitants looked for any excuse to practice their head shrinking.

It must have been during the chaos that Edulph slipped away. One moment Alaysha noticed him leaning against the adobe building, the next he was gone. She had no illusions about finding him again. He'd divulged entirely too much information too willingly for Alaysha to believe he'd let himself be found again. She must have given herself away somehow, and after he'd spent all of his information, he'd realized he'd also exhausted his value. Perhaps that was even his intent. With Edulph, you could never be entirely sure. When she'd said as much to Gael, he'd shrugged, almost as though he'd expected as much.

"No doubt he's returned to the Highlands for his daughter," he said.

"Then we best set out at first light," she said, eyeing the land beyond the walls through gaps in the leather fencing. She wasn't entirely sure she wanted to be out in the muck lands again at all with a suffering child, but she could see no other choice. She stretched, trying to undo the knots of fatigue and worry in her back. Seeing it, the girl led them to a place where they could bed down for the night and Alaysha was never more grateful to be laying her to head down, or more afraid of facing the night.

The crickets sounded somewhere off in the dark, making the village seem less malevolent than during the day. In the cloak of darkness the grizzly shrunken heads were nothing but blobs of shadow through the open door. They'd been settled in a short mud brick building that might have been used at one time as a storehouse for grain but that was now empty. It was long and only about as high as Gael's waist but at least it was wide enough for the three of them to crawl in and stretch out on a thatch mat provided by the priestess as well as a thick pelt of soft black fur. Greetha's daughter explained that the hide had been peeled off the back of the two largest panthers she'd ever seen, beasts that were controlled by a giant whose head now hung from the priestess's bedpost. It was meant to ward off evil, she'd explained, and the hides were her most prized possession. She offered them in the hopes that the boy would eventually remember her, and return to take her head with him out of the village and out into the great beyond when she died.

Alaysha had kept her counsel at that story. She was quite certain that despite the seeming hospitality, neither she nor Gael would ever speak of this again. And they certainly wouldn't tell the story to Saxon or his mother. Best it lay forgotten like so many of her own tormenting memories.

The infant lay between them on a mattress made of goose feathers and linen. While she could see through the open door, the three walls that enclosed them smelled faintly of sweetgrass and a murkier stink of something she might have thought was brimstone.

She found sleep impossible. Almost absently, Gael's hand found her hip in the dark. The light feather strokes whispered down her thigh, awakening a warmth in her that made her feel at once guilty and ravenous. The exhaustion had beaten down her resolve and twisted everything into a macabre living night vision that seemed to go on and on. Just this once she wanted the night vision to ease into something more pleasant. To feel his hand creep behind her and press her against him. She reached for the laces in his breeches and slipped her hand inside. His member was hard; each time she squeezed it, it throbbed against her palm. When she moved closer to claim his lips with hers, she heard him chuckle beneath his breath.

"You're a fast learner, witch," he murmured. "But I've no more to teach you until I own more than just your body."

She retracted her hands as though he'd burned her. Her face flamed. Even as she twisted around in his arms, facing the other way, she could feel him hard against her and despite his protests, he remained that way until she finally fell into a fitful sleep and felt nothing but the dank fit of restless sleep.

Chapter 16

By the time the birds were up and chirping merrily as they called each other to repast, Alaysha's nerves were frayed. Saxon was in obvious distress by first light, his marks outlined in pus-filled boils rising alongside the black lines of his tattau. Several of the villagers huddled about the granary, some took to peering in and their hard-eyed gazes made Alaysha uneasy. They decided to set off despite Saxon's obvious protests of pain.

They would take their turns lugging him across the muck lands in a papoose type of pouch that the girl had put together for them. It was made it of a suspicious leather that Alaysha doubted would last the journey. Human skin wasn't as supple or as sturdy and durable as deer hide, but the girl had lined it with a type of fur that could have been from a young animal. She stretched the hides over and across a frame of sturdy tree limbs that in their turn strapped across Alaysha's shoulders and wrapped around her back to join at the bottom of the framework resting against her belly. There was a bag that sagged just enough in front for Saxon to nestle inside, and so with every piping he did in pain, and every intake of breath he dragged in to fuel his screams, Alaysha could feel the tremors to her very core. It wasn't weariness or exhaustion or even impatience that plagued her by the time they reached the river, it was the feeling of utter hopelessness and helplessness; she knew nothing she did could help the child, and she worried that each time Aislin tried to connect with him, thinking it was Yenic, she might finally grow desperate or angry enough to make the marks broil deep into the child's body.

So far, insults to the boy's skin seemed to go away and disappear when the power waned. She just wished the bouts of calm would happen more frequently. Instead, it seemed as if Aislin was contacting him more frequently than he was getting rest. And so she suffered with him each time, and each time she saw Gael's back in front of her go rigid, she knew that he too was at his breaking point.

The girl left them on the banks where they'd camped with Edulph overnight. From a pouch at her side, she extracted a tiny shrivelled head with a milky eye crossed into a black one. As she tied it around Saxon's papoose, Alaysha realized that it was from a child about Saxon's age. "It's the best our priestess can do," the girl said, swatting at the charm and watching it dangle. "It was the daughter of her staunchest enemy, a child with incredible magics; her soul will give him strength."

She left with a gentle stroke across the boy's brow and disappeared back into the woods. Alaysha looked at Gael, trying her best to pull on a mask of courage. She had the feeling it may have failed miserably. "At least he's quiet for now," she said.

Sullen and stricken, Gael nodded. She watched him ease his eyes closed and breathe deeply of the air. She licked her lips thoughtfully.

The boy might be sleeping now, and his charm may indeed give him the ability to bear the pain, but Alaysha couldn't. She knew one more bout of shrieking and she would not be able to stop herself from cringing into a ball and losing herself to the tempting hum of water in the river. She couldn't help him, she couldn't stop the pain, and she couldn't bear to hear him in such agony. She wasn't sure how Gael was managing it. She could certainly feel each muscle tense itself into a tight ball, bracing itself at each onslaught of pitiful cries. That she knew they would come again after they'd stilled, perhaps even in the next few heartbeats gnawed at her. It was the constant sense of foreboding that chewed at the back of her mind, so much that when the screams did come, it was almost a relief because then at least she knew she didn't have to wait for them anymore; all she had to do was grit her teeth and pray to the deities that it would soon stop. Anything else was fruitless. It almost seemed that worse than the evidence of the pain, was the hope in its absence that it wouldn't return.

Gael stole close to her as she was lost in thought, and she felt his hands reaching for the straps on her shoulders. "I'll take him across the river," he said. "I'm sturdier on my feet."

"No you're not," she backed away. "You have those ridiculous boots, you can't feel the stones. You'll fall." She shook her head.

He grabbed for her again, almost roughly, and she realized his energy had been depleted. He was on the brink of the same precipices she was. Waiting for the pain, hoping it wouldn't return, grinding his teeth in helplessness as it rose over the child in relentless waves.

"Give him to me, Alaysha," he demanded. She looked up into his eyes and discovered they were wet.

Tears had been streaming down his cheeks all this time and she hadn't known it.

She reached for one with her thumb and swiped it into his temple. "We'll find a way to stop it," she said. "We will."

He twisted his face away from her hand, but she found his cheek with the butt of her palm. She could feel the tension in his jaw, the hum beneath his skin that meant he was connected to her. It made her ache to know she could do nothing to help him either.

"Don't do that," he said.

"What?"

"That," he said. "Make my mark tingle."

"I didn't mean to…"

"I'm a grown man," he said. "I can stand what it does to me." He reached a hand beneath his armpit and squeezed, rubbing over the mark as though it pained him. "All the hunger I feel because of it, the mad connection that I have with you that makes me think of you day in and day out, the desire to protect you, to be with you, to offer my life for you if need be." He shook his head. "There's no ceasing to it," he mumbled. "No ceasing."

She knew he wasn't talking about himself. She knew he was thinking about Saxon. How much did the boy understand? Each time Aislin tried to connect to him and found only a powerless mark, was there an equal tingling in his skin, a longing somewhere within his tiny body that would resonate his hunger or fear. Maybe the worst of those all wrapped up into one emotion. She pressed her hand onto where she felt the boy's bottom might be. She felt the curve of his body against hers, and she thought of Saxa and her fear, wondered if the woman felt some sort of residual ache in her own womb as the child she loved rode waves of pain and release.

It was too much. She was riding the crest of pain as surely as the boy, as surely as Gael. "What you're feeling, Gael, it can't be what Saxon feels. His mark isn't infused with the right magic. It may not be infused with *any* magic."

"Some magic, obviously." He twisted away. She could see his back trembling, and then with a focused effort, he squared them off, inhaled deeply, and turned to face her. "Give him to me," he said.

He was taller, broader, far stronger, but he was not as sure footed. Alaysha knew this. She'd picked her own way across the river on the journey ahead of them with sure-footed grace, while Gael in Edulph had lagged behind. They'd made it, yes, but could he do so again without spilling the babe?

"No," she shook her head. "I'll take him."

"Alaysha, you can't possibly –"

His plea was interrupted by another shriek. The curve that fit so nicely around Alaysha's belly went rigid. Gael devoured the distance in mere steps and had Saxon out of his papoose so suddenly Alaysha didn't have time to adjust the straps. The bag tore where it was deepest. Human skin, Alaysha thought absently. Not half as sturdy as deer.

Freed of the papoose, Saxon's legs kicked her furiously at the air and Gael struggled to get him nestled against his chest. The boy planted his tiny feet into Gael's ribcage and pushed so that he was standing, his face tilted to the heavens, mouth gaped open. He screamed so hard and so loud and so long that he lost his breath three times in rapid succession. Gael's face went white and Alaysha could swear he was holding his own breath. She could see that his face was wet with fresh tears. And he didn't try to hide the sobbing he was doing as he pulled the boy close, flattening his legs against his chest.

Alaysha stood paralyzed, knowing that nothing she could do would help, fighting the urge to fall back deep inside of herself into one of the tunnels of memory that she knew she had created for just this purpose. She couldn't do this. She couldn't do this. She couldn't do any of this anymore. There had to be a way to end his suffering. What good would it do to have the boy, to bring him back to Sarum, to show him to her mother in the state that he was in. How much would it harm her when there was nothing that could be done.

She felt stones digging into her heels as she paced the river bank. She found her hands in her hair, smoothing it down, shaking, pulling it. The insides of her cheeks felt raw and bloody. She realized that she was chewing on them and only when she felt the hardness of the ground strike her bottom, did she realize she'd collapsed finally. She drug in a shuddering breath and looked toward Gael. A hawk shrieked overhead, and she realized that Saxon had stopped crying. She scrabbled forward on her hands and knees as Gael collapsed onto a large boulder. He splayed his legs and hunched forward, trembling. His green eyed gaze met Alaysha's.

"There's only two things that can keep it from coming again," she said, finally.

"I know," he sounded desolate as she felt.

"We have no way of killing Aislin," she warned.

"I know that too. Not in time to stop this from happening again."

In his exhausted state, he hadn't quite grasped her meaning. She chewed her bottom lip; it would be a kindness, really. If it were her, she would want the pain to stop. She found herself thinking back to her times in the tunnel, when Corrin had found some way to make her beg for release. And then just as stubbornly, she pushed it abruptly aside.

Alaysha drew in a bracing breath. "We have to take his pain away, Gael." She said.

He looked at her dumbfounded, realization dawning slowly in his green eyed gaze. She knew it had struck him fully when his expression hardened into chiselled stone. His shoulders tensed and he clutched the babe tighter.

"You can't be thinking that," he said.

"You said yourself we can't reach Aislin in time to relieve his suffering."

"No," he said.

"So there's only one other way to stop it."

"I said no. Have you lost your mind?" He said throwing himself to his feet. When she thought he'd lurch toward her, he lurched backwards, towards the woods. Almost as though he planned to flee. But he wouldn't, not Gael. He would face her head on and kill her if he had to. Didn't matter what the mark told him. It didn't matter how much it tingled, ached, or burned within him. This boy was his blood; it was a child. He would rage against the mark if he had to in order to keep the boy safe. Knowing it made Gael that much more dear to her.

"Gael," she said. "We can't do anything to relieve his pain except the one thing."

"I will not let you murder my nephew."

She sighed, said. "My brother."

"Then show some sisterly compassion," he said.

"Sometimes compassion means you have to harden your heart," she told him.

"Are you listening to yourself? Do you hear what you're saying? You're Yuri in Alaysha's skin. That beast doesn't reside in Yenic's body; he's in you. First Edulph in the muck lands and now this?" He shook his head in disbelief and disgust. "I can't let you do it," he said.

"Please, Gael…"

"No, Alaysha." He sounded firm, but he also sounded angry. Worse than that, he sounded as though she meant nothing to him in that moment. And it hurt, it hurt that he would believe she didn't feel compassion for her own brother, that she would hurt him willingly. That he would accuse her of making decisions the same way that Yuri did, without empathy when it was her emotion that was driving this in the first place. Couldn't he understand that?

She edged away from him into the water, let her feet trail across the surface, letting the coolness work its way up her legs to her spine, make her feel safe.

It came to her like a hornet landing and biting her neck. "There might be another way," she said, thinking out loud. And this time Gael's gaze narrowed suspiciously.

"I'm serious, Gael. We're thinking that there's no other way to break the bond than death, but what if there's a way to control the call?"

"You mean like smothering a fire?" Hope sounded in his voice for the first time in days.

"More like putting water on it," she said, grinning. Of course, why hadn't she thought of it before? Aislin's mark was tied to fire through magic, and Alaysha's magic was tied to water. When all was said and done, fire bowed to water.

"Perhaps we shouldn't hurry across the river," she said. "Perhaps what we should do is wait here for the next bout of pain," she stammered over the words, hating to say them, knowing that there would be another bout. "And then--"

"And then when it comes, we'll bathe him." Gael guessed and Alaysha nodded, sighing in relief.

They didn't have a long wait. This time instead of shrieking loudly and shrilly, Saxon let go nothing but whimpers, almost as though he was exhausted from being in pain and just wanted it to be over. For some reason, this bothered Alaysha even more. Both of them rushed the babe to the river, and with Gael cradling him in his arms, Alaysha scooped water up and over the baby's skin, letting the water sluice over him. She tried to take the warmest part on the edge of the river so as not to shock his fevered skin. When that didn't seem to help at all, she moved to the deeper, faster part of the river where it was cooler… and then deeper, and deeper. "It's not working," she said. "Gael, it's not working."

"It has to work," Gael said "It has to. We have no other choices."

For long agonizing moments, they worked at trying to get the boy some relief. Several times, whimpers turned to outright cries, and Alaysha felt the frantic beatings of fear tightening her chest. At one point, she wasn't sure if the water on her face was from the river or from her tears, and in the back of her mind, she kept hearing Yuri scolding her, telling her to be calm, that giving into her fear, giving into her emotions for the boy was hindering her from thinking. And thinking was the saviour of panic. There had to be something else. There had to be some other way.

Somewhere during the fruitless bathing, Alaysha lost herself to memory. Long ingrained as a self-preservation tactic, she found herself tunneling into her psyche, searching for relief from her own pains. She found herself again in the bathhouse with Corrin. He had taken to tying her hands above her head and bending her over a table he designed himself with manacles on its legs to hold her ankles, and a hooked clamp to chain her hands. She'd be pinned against the wooden top, him slamming into her from behind over and over until she sunk deeper into the waters of unconsciousness and let him finish. She'd find herself left there perhaps for hours afterwards, abandoned naked, sore and aching, burning from neck to buttock from bites he'd left on her skin. She'd have to wait for him to return and untie her so that she could stand, at least, with her hands hanging either above her or tied behind her back.

Once, perhaps the last time if she recollected it correctly, he'd lined up all sorts of instruments on the table within her sight but out of reach of her manacled hands. Each time he drilled into her, she'd be left wondering which one of the tools he'd decide to use, if he'd use all of them, or if she'd be lucky, and he'd only want her to imagine the threat. She could never tell with Corrin. Sometimes it was the emotional turmoil that pleased him the best. He relished it, and enjoyed every second of it to its full. Yes. During the last event, staring at those instruments of torture, she'd finally come to discover that was what it was all about. That he enjoyed her shame, that he took pleasure in her pain. That more than anything, he wanted her to squirm and fear him for what he might do, not what he did.

That time, she didn't let herself sink into the calming depths; rather, she stayed present. She urged him on, shamelessly, purposefully. She shouted his name in feigned pleasure all the while training herself to wrap steel around the bars of her consciousness. She'd not let him take his pleasure in her pain. She'd not let him steal her mind. She felt him go flaccid within her, and knew that he would untie her this time before he left. He'd need to find some other way to fulfill his perverse need conquer her. This time she knew he'd untie her, and he'd stay there with her, and he'd try something more, and so she pinned her eyes on the rusted pincers closest to her and waited patiently for his hands to grapple at her wrists, thinking he'd pull her away from the table. But she was too quick for him. She planned it just as patiently as he'd planned her assault. Secret, creeping fingers closed around the pincers, and as he yanked her around to face him, she drove the pincers into his shoulder and he staggered backwards. She faced him heaving, daring him to come at her again, then forced her breathing to still as though he meant nothing to her.

He left her. She remembered grinning as he walked away. She knew she'd broken through something, and that he could be defeated in the end. That if she kept her calm in the face of her fear and pain, calm under any emotion, that she could rule them. And that was what Yuri had wanted her to learn.

She might curse her father for the lesson, but it could serve her now.

Sluicing the water once again over Saxon fevered skin, she realized this was one of those times when she would need to rule her emotions. She swallowed down the fear, and she felt the power building within her. She let it uncoil, and her fingers tingled with the charge of the magic wanting release. She let her mind travel back to another memory, of the course of the journey through a human body, finding its way to the pores, creeping through skin to find the place just below the armpit to a black and sooty mark needed to be smothered. She found the blisters and the heat that in its fever desired fluid as much as it desired fuel.

From somewhere outside of herself she heard a voice, soft and guttural, but familiar all the same. "It's working, Alaysha," she heard. Gael's voice. Gael telling her that what she was doing was helping.

She pressed on, imagining the fire extinguishing beneath the onslaught of water. She pushed everything she had, every molecule of fluid from her own body, from the river below her, from the trees, their leaves, the moss, the fungus, everything she could pull and drain, she put into the boy. And she knew that as she was doing it, it was working. She felt his relief. She felt the searing pain let go and let her power backtrack through the pores and skin and flesh to retreat back into her own body, the river, the grass, the fungus, but even as she did so she felt a burst of fury so strong that an image formed in her mind's eye. The image had fire red hair and milk cloudy eyes and an almost inhumanly beautiful face snarling into a grimace of absolute rage.

She fell backwards into the water, sinking beneath, hearing her heart beat in the sonic underwater, through her ears. She swallowed a lung full of water. She groped blindly for the surface, trying to get her feet beneath her but feeling them give in and let go. There was no strength in her muscles; thighs that were normally strong and supple were quivering and weak. She had enough time to know that the blackness would take her, and enough time for the fleeting hope that Gael would manage to rescue her in time.

The rest was all blackness.

Chapter 17

Alaysha awoke thinking Barruch was working his wet lips over her face, demanding a peach or an equally gaseous plum, and for a moment she felt at peace. Then the anxieties of the last few hours flooded back, knotting up her chest and making her eyes fly open, her hands scrambling at the weight on her chest, thinking only that she had to bolt to her feet and face whatever enemy was to hand. When her fingers found soft flesh and her eyes met the silver fuzz of Saxon's hair, she realized that what she'd thought was Barruch's muzzle, was Saxon's wet mouth gumming her cheeks. She felt the scrape of new teeth grazing her skin and peeled him away from her, holding him back so she could look at him. She lay on her back, facing up, holding the boy by his armpits. He was gurgling happily.

She could feel a smile moving across her face as realization crept in. They'd done it. She and Gael had broken the connection. She sat up, putting the baby on her lap, and searching about for Gael. She found him leaning against a tree as he sat slumped in exhaustion but still very much aware.

"You're awake," he said.

"It seems I'm not dead," she answered smiling. It felt good to smile. Good to feel relief.

He shifted to his knees and crawled towards her, taking Saxon from her and jumbling him up and down. The boy giggled in delight.

"He's better," Alaysha said.

Gael nodded. "He slept almost as long as you did," he said. "I put him down next to you, and didn't have the heart to wake either of you."

Alaysha ran her hands down her tunic, it was damp, but not sopping wet. "After you pulled me out of the water, obviously," she said. "How long was I sleeping?"

"Sleeping? Not long. Unconscious for a good deal longer."

"Thank you." She hung her head, suddenly shy. "I must have slipped on a rock, I..." She eased her eyes closed, trying to bring back the memory; it was fleeting. Every time she thought she touched it, it evaporated like so much steam.

"It doesn't matter," Gael said. "I pulled you out in time."

Out in time, she thought. Yes. She'd gone under, slipping beneath the water, gasping for breath and pulling in water instead. "Good thing you were holding the baby," she said, distracted, still thinking. Something was there in the back of her mind, something important.

"Yeah," he said. "And I thought you were the surefooted one."

She'd told him that, yes, because it was true. It was possible she'd slipped and fallen, but she didn't think it was accurate. There was something else in there wrapped around that truth. She'd remembered her time in the tunnels with Corrin, hadn't she? Relived again some awful torture he'd inflicted on her. Yes, she recalled it now. It had something to do with one of his more cruel penchants, and how she'd finally broken under the strain of it and turned into a cold-hearted killing machine for her father. So many of those memories she'd buried, but she knew that was the worst of them. Mostly because she felt some shame beneath all of the fear, that she'd finally given up part of her humanity so willingly, so she could endure the torture mindfully, so that she could best him, finally. It had been a hard lesson, a long lesson. One that had taken years and hundreds of sessions to instill. But she'd finally learned to shut things down. And that made the difference this time. She needed to shut things down this time. For the baby's sake, she had to stop feeling her fear. That memory had allowed her to concentrate, to focus her power enough that she could help relieve the boy's suffering.

Even so, there was something else on the heels of that memory, something that made her chest tighten and her mouth go dry. If only she could reach for it--

"Alaysha?"

She looked at Gael questioningly. And he sighed, realizing she'd not heard one thing he said.

"I was telling you how beautiful it looked," he said.

"Beautiful? What?"

"You. The power. The way it extinguished the burning. It's the most amazing thing I've ever seen."

She smiled for him, still distracted, but willing to indulge him. She rarely heard him wax poetic. "What did it look like?"

"Like thousands of rainbows."

She looked at him with head cocked, trying to picture it and failing. "Strange," was all she could manage to say.

"Strange but beautiful," Gael said. He twisted away as Saxon's fingers went up his nose. He scolded the boy playfully and Saxon squealed happily.

"He seems healthy enough," Alaysha said.

"Do you think the same thing is happening to Yenic?" Gael said looking at her. "I mean, if it's happening to Saxon because of the mark, would it be happening to Yenic too?"

Alaysha shook her head. "I don't think so. If Aislin had been able to connect to Yenic, we'd have seen something before we set out with Edulph. "No," she said. "I don't think Yusmine is feeling that."

"But they would both have her mark."

"Both would have it, but one had a broken bond to go with it." Alaysha mulled it over aloud. "I mean, Yenic pretty much mutilated his mark when he pierced his lung, and when he died, I felt our bond die too." She chewed her bottom lip, peeling bits of dried skin off with her teeth as she considered it. "Of course, our bond was never tied to his mark anyway." She was thinking out loud, really, not imagining that what she was saying would have any effect on Gael. But he must've caught something of importance because he shifted suddenly to face her, putting the baby down on his lap and holding him tight there.

"What?" She asked.

"So you think she doesn't know about Yenic?" Gael said.

"She must not or she wouldn't be trying to connect to the mark." Even as Alaysha said it, parts of things began to seep back in like dirty water. She looked off over the river, thinking. She watched a hawk fly over and head towards a tree, trying her best to gain some clarity from the shifting memory.

"I saw her, Gael. At the end, when I knew that I had managed to alleviate Saxon's suffering, when I knew that I'd added enough water, I saw her. I shouldn't have been able to because my bond with Yenic is broken, but I did see her. She knows something's not right. She doesn't know Yenic died, but she knows that something is off. I think that maybe she believes I'm using my power to block hers through Yenic. And she's angry about it."

"Let her be angry."

Alaysha chuckled. "She can't touch me here. Can't touch Yenic. I should be glad of that," she said, sighing. "But I am glad it's over," she said, leaning back and letting her head rest on the backs of her forearms. She stared up into the canopy, watching the hawk scouting for food. "Now that we have Saxon, now that Yenic is gone, now that Aedus is safe. It seems to me all of this running can end."

"It can't end," Gael said and she sat up abruptly to look at him.

"What do you mean?"

He shrugged. "Have you forgotten what started this running?

"Yuri started it. Then Yenic. With their tales of witches so powerful they could destroy the very world. They're gone now. Both of them."

"But the witches still remain."

She squinted at him. "Yes. But they can control themselves and their powers."

"Liliah can't. And Aislin wants her dead. She'll want the other witches dead too. She'll want you dead."

"I have you. I have Cai. I think I'm quite safe."

He shook his head. "Never safe. Never safe enough. I don't doubt the two of us can protect you, but she'll never stop until she gets what she wants."

"I don't care what she wants."

"You don't care what she does to that little girl?"

"I never cared what Aislin wanted," she said slowly. "I cared about Saxon. I cared about Aedus. I cared that the people I loved were safe. Now they are."

"Are they? All of them?"

She faced him, crossing her legs over each other on the riverbank. "Saxa will be safe enough soon."

"What if Aislin has harmed her?"

"Gael, Aislin would've thought no more of Saxa than that she was Yuri's bedmate. She'd have no idea how important Saxa was to him and she wouldn't care even if she did. She has nothing to do with what she wants."

"We can't be sure of that. We can't be sure that Aislin doesn't think Saxa knows something about… Well, we did just discover we're related to the clay witch, but if Theron knew it, perhaps Aislin knows too. She might have –"

She watched him swallow convulsively, trying to form the words. Alaysha wouldn't believe it. Surely if Aislin had known, she would have used Saxa far earlier.

"You don't believe all of that stuff Yusmine said," she said.

He looked at her suspiciously. "What stuff?"

Too late she remembered she'd not told him of the bulk things Yusmine had admitted to her. "Nothing," she said. She tried to get up, but his hand on her arm pressed her back down. He forced her face towards him.

"What are you talking about, Alaysha?"

"Nothing."

It doesn't look like nothing," he said.

She chewed the question over for quite a while before she finally made her decision. As they sat on the banks of the river, with Saxon crawling about in the humus, picking at wildflowers, and trying to stand against the trunks of trees, she gave Gael as much detail as she dared. She explained the history as Yusmine had given it, that Liliah needed to find a way to stop her brother in order to be able to return to her home. She explained that all of the witches and all of their Arms would be needed to perform the ritual that would allow Liliah to bring her children back home. She told him about the seeds she'd collected, what they were, but she left out the sacrifice Liliah would have to make of herself. She didn't think he'd understand that, and she didn't think she even believed it.

"True or not," he said, sinking back on his hands and crossing his feet at his ankles. "I think you had best finish our tattaus just in case."

She nodded, sighing in relief. No harm in that, she thought. She did give a brief thought to what it might be like to have to go through the ceremony again, drinking the kykeon brew that Theron would undoubtedly have to concoct for them, the smoke, the ash, the heat. She felt her face flame as well just thinking about how the heat invaded more than just her psyche, and she glanced at him sideways through lowered lashes, trying to decide if he was thinking the same thing.

He was preoccupied with making a grab for Saxon, throwing him in the air, catching him again. She thought of their night in the Greetha's village. How he'd felt against her back, how the hardness of his member had kept her awake for long hours imagining how it might feel to let the tingling of their connection burn in the middle of her thighs. She thought of how much she'd wanted him to slip inside her and drive the anxiety away.

She was about to reach out to him, thinking she might dare to explain it to him, but as her fingers moved through the air toward his shoulder, he stood as though he hadn't seen her movement, and with the baby slung across his shoulder, he headed towards the river.

"It's time we get moving," he said. "I'd like to be back to the village before dark."

It might have stung if she thought he'd done it on purpose, but of course he hadn't. He simply never noticed, Alaysha told herself, heaving to her feet.

They made it as dusk was cloaking the tree line. Aedus was the one to see them first, and she shouted so loudly that Alaysha felt for the first time in her life an overwhelming sense of welcome. If it weren't for the horrible snakes of stairs disappearing into the tree tops and the wood-slatted houses she knew were hidden in the branches, she might feel at home here. She took one look at Aedus's ecstatic face, at Liliah's blonde hair flowing behind her as she ran headlong toward them and she knew that it was the people who made her feel that way. They loved her, accepted her. They were her home. She was even happy to see Theron ambling along painfully, leaning heavily on a quarterstaff for support. He was getting even older, she thought. All of this had aged him. She noticed as she got closer, that the tracings of woad on his insteps looked shaky and crooked and the ones he'd drawn on his neck were jagged.

Aedus slammed into her first, and then came Liliah, nearly knocking her off her feet. Alaysha couldn't help laughing out loud. "I'm glad to see you too," she said.

"I have bubbles," Liliah told her proudly.

"Bubbles?"

Aedus made a face. "Spit bubbles, I guess. She keeps saying that so I just humor her and blow some myself."

"Disgusting," Alaysha said, smiling indulgently at the small blonde head.

"She seems to find it amusing," Aedus said. "At least I think she does. She keeps asking for more."

"You're a good auntie."

"Where daddy?" Liliah asked and Alaysha was saved from answering when the girl noticed Saxon trying to crawl out of his hastily repaired papoose and creep up Gael's chest. She hid behind Aedus, pulling at the girl's tunic sleeve and complaining about bubbles. When Aedus tried to uncurl the girl's fingers from her waist, Liliah started to cry and squirmed into the backs of Aedus's legs. It was peculiar enough to make Alaysha, who was already exhausted, want to moan aloud in frustration, but when Saxon's ears picked up the noise, his eyes grew round and he started to whimper. Soon enough, he was wailing and Liliah was echoing it and Gael had started to curse. He plucked at Saxon and tried to wrestle him back into the papoose but the boy's legs wouldn't give way.

Alaysha wasn't sure what to do but she wanted it all to stop at once; she bent toward Aedus, with Saxon's wails still piercing her ears.

"He won't hurt you, Liliah," she said.

The girl moaned louder and Alaysha heard her own frustrated sigh. She looked to Theron with pleading eyes.

"It's not the boy," Theron said. "Oh no no."

"Then what?" Gael was trying to unstrap the papoose and hold onto a clinging and wailing Saxon at the same time.

"Take her away, Aedus," Alaysha said. "I don't know who's getting more upset."

"No need," said Theron. "Take that away." He pointed to the shrivelled head Greetha's daugher had tied to the papoose. Alaysha had the urge to slap her forehead in realization. She grabbed for Saxon and held him while Gael tucked the head deep into the bag of the papoose and then showed his hands to Liliah.

"Gone," he said.

"Mama bubble," Liliah hiccupped. She peeked out from behind Aedus and edged her way forward.

"Yes," Alaysha sighed. "Mama bubble." She had no idea what it meant and didn't much care so long as the crying stopped. She turned to Theron, who also slumped in relief.

"Are you well, shaman?"she asked.

Theron sighed heavily. "This shaman thought our goddess would infuse us with energy, not take it away."

Alaysha laughed. So it wasn't just his age he was feeling, but the effects of running around after a toddler.

"Daddy," Liliah demanded and took hold of Alaysha's hand. She pulled hard, bringing Alaysha to one knee in front of her.

Alaysha had no experience with children and she wasn't sure how she could tell the girl her father had abandoned her again. Instead, she scanned the village, holding onto Liliah's hand as the girl tugged at it impatiently. It had a different feel this time, but seeming at both times to be fuller yet not as familiar.

"Has Cai returned?"

Theron had begun to shake his head in answer when Gael pointed towards the edge of the village. "Speak of a demon and she shall appear," he said.

Alaysha hoisted the girl onto her hip, standing so she could see better. Indeed, toward the edge of the village, just breaking through the thick underbrush, Cai strode forward, leading Barruch and four others. Barruch seemed to be struggling beneath some weight, and Alaysha had to squint into the distance to make out what it was.

"Dear deities," she heard herself say.

She heard Gael behind her choking on the memory of another warrior on another mount out in the burnt lands.

"Is it what I think, Gael?" She said, wanting confirmation but knowing even as the words came out, that she didn't need to ask the question.

Cai had indeed found the clay witch, and there were others with her: Thera and a man striding along next to them. But there was no Bodicca. No Yusmine.

There was a woman on Barruch's back, however, that much Alaysha could tell. And the knowing of it made her feel sick. She knew it could only be the large warrior sent to rid Enyalia of their aging bone witch and who had obviously been punished for her failure.

And one thing and Alaysha knew was that an Enyalian punished and sick enough to agree to be slung over a mount's back like a bag of grain was an Enyalian in very bad shape.

"Theron," she said. "I think you better go meet Isolde."

CHAPTER 18

It was worse than they could have feared. The warrior Alaysha had met just weeks earlier looked drawn and small in comparison to the woman she had been and even to the Komandiri who lifted her tenderly from Barruch's back. Cai eased Isolde onto a fresh linen sheet that Aedus had run to fetch from one of the houses. Cai looked down on her comrade with barely concealed concern. After she'd spread the woman onto her stomach across the material, she squatted next to her, tucking Isolde's hair behind her ear and murmuring to her of her bravery. Alaysha did not want to look at the woman's back; she knew full well what she would see there. She had never forgotten the sight of Bodicca's skin blistered with boils that had taken weeks to heal. When she'd found them in the burnt lands, she'd been all but dead and Alaysha knew then that it was only the woman's grim determination to return to Yuri in Sarum that kept her alive. What would keep this woman alive?

No one spoke for long moments. Cai's companions stood far back, almost as though they were offering a respectful distance to the dying. It was Theron who made the first move, pushing everyone aside deftly, murmuring to himself that warriors could never be counted upon to heal, only to kill. He squatted next to Isolde and began moving his hands ever so lightly through the air across her back, sweeping down from her neck to her buttocks, barely touching, just hovering. Each time the shaman swept over the woman's thighs, he flicked his wrists as though he were ridding his hands of water.

Without being asked, Aedus ran off again and came back with a mash of what Alaysha assumed would be ghost pipe, but Theron shook his head. He didn't dare let the woman fall into sleep no matter how bad the pain was. He wasn't sure he could bring her back.

There was a long agonizing moment when Isolde took to coughing so hard and so suddenly that she bucked into Theron's palms and groaned in pain. He pulled his hands back so fast Alaysha thought she must have burned him. He stared down at his palms that were now filled with seepage from Isolde's sores.

"She was worse," Cai mumbled staring down at Isolde. "When we found her, she was much worse."

"Some thoughtful shaman has painted her back with aloe," Theron said, sniffing his hands. "Perhaps a shaman not as good as us, but good enough to keep the woman alive." He peered over Isolde's back to where Thera stood wringing her hands. She said nothing to her estranged father, only nodded and stared down at her feet. Theron's gaze flickered then to the woman next to her, whose chin quivered beneath a ribbon of black tattau, and then to the man standing next to her, a strapping almond-skinned youth as tall as Thera and as broad shouldered.

Theron's hands trembled when he saw them, Alaysha noted, and he did his best to control it. He ordered Aedus to go for water and then lifted Isolde's eyelids to peer inside. He grunted at each pupil before letting the lid slip back down. "Some thoughtful shaman has also been feeding her garlic and honey." He nodded, seeming to be happy with his diagnosis. "Enough to keep the green death from stealing her mind. A pity in some ways."

Alaysha guessed that as much pain as the woman must be in, slipping into unconsciousness might have been a blessing. "What happened?"

Cai didn't bother to look at her when she spoke. "The bone witch." There was barely disguised fury in her voice.

Alaysha didn't have to ask further to know that Isolde had failed in her attempt to assassinate Uta. How the old woman had managed to best one of Cai's most ferocious soldiers, was beyond her. She only knew the evidence of her own eyes. "Can we save her?" She addressed Theron.

"A shaman such as us is very skilled, yes yes yes. But perhaps not skilled enough to save the child." He looked at Gael without guile or coyness. "Perhaps that would make that one happy at least."

Gael swallowed convulsively at the words. Alaysha saw his Adam's apple bob up and down three times before he managed to speak. "The child?"

"The warrior is breeding," the shaman said. "Any foolish man can see that."

Alaysha watched Gael's neck turn crimson and then that crimson tide rise into his face. He stammered, trying to form words. She tried to imagine what it must be like for him to realize that one of the women who had assaulted him in Enyalia while he'd been too weak to protest, was carrying his child. She stepped closer to him, thinking to offer him some comfort, but he stepped away, and then he turned, and then he strode furiously toward Alaysha's lodging and disappeared behind the flap.

Cai snorted. "One might think that a man finds no pleasure in an Enyalian child."

Alaysha spun on her, holding her hands over Saxon's ears. "He was raped, Cai. Have you no sympathy for what your warriors did to him?"

"A child has less to do with its father than with the act that created it. Your males," she scoffed. "So foolish."

"And if it too is a male?" Alaysha dared. Saxon squirmed in her arms.

Cai gave her careful study and then her gaze fell to the boy kicking Alaysha in the belly, obviously thinking about how she should form her response. After a time, she let a grin steal across her face. "I suppose that since we are no longer Enyalia," she nodded quickly at Isolde. "That the mother might teach the little beast to hold a sword."

"If she lives," Alaysha said, fuming.

Cai quirked a russet brow and it was then that Alaysha knew the warrior had been afraid for Isolde. "She will live," Cai said.

By then Aedus had returned with a copper bowl filled with fresh water and Theron went about washing his hands and doing his best to clean the wounds where they had accumulated dirt from the ride. At one point, Thera eased her way forward, and without a word, took the cloth from him and worked at parts he couldn't reach. Theron peered at her with small black eyes and spread his palms over the woman's back again, sweeping down from neck to buttock, flicking his hands, repeating the motion. The man in the company came forward as well, creeping from his spot so silently Alaysha didn't notice he was there standing next to Isolde until he squatted down next to Thera. The clay witch came after that. Alaysha was especially interested to see how much like the young man she looked, dark and sloe-eyed and beautiful, and how much both of them looked like Theron, and she realized it was a far stranger family reunion than she could have imagined for them.

Aedus looked almost stricken to think that she had suddenly become useless, but when Liliah began chanting in a peculiar language, she took the girl's hand and led her to the staircase. "She gets like this when she's overexcited," Aedus explained and Alaysha agreed that it was best for the girl to rest away from so much goings-on. She passed the boy to Aedus, asking her to feed him and set him to nap.

It was a good excuse for Alaysha to leave Theron and his children to find some ease with each other through healing. For once, Cai seemed just as perceptive. She fell in behind Alaysha as she headed for the relative sanctity and emptiness of the tree line where Bodicca had lain Yenic after she'd found him lifeless, a victim of his own hand.

"The village has lost a few citizens," Cai said as she drew near enough to speak and Alaysha quirked her head.

"Do you think so?"

The Enyalian grunted thoughtfully. "Gained a few too."

Alaysha looked back over her shoulder. "What do you mean?"

"You didn't notice? The villagers have changed. At least a dozen new faces, but unless the dozen I don't see are hiding in their trees, they've disappeared."

"I thought it seemed different." She paused midstep, turning to the warrior. "Should we be on guard?"

"They're just villagers. Even if they aren't from here. If they were fighters or soldiers, I'd know." Cai shrugged. "Best to watch though." Cai took Alaysha's elbow and lead her to the clearing where she must have realized Alaysha was headed.

"I'm afraid to ask about Bodicca and Yusmine," she said to the warrior as they matched stride.

"No more afraid than I am of the answer," Cai said.

"They're dead, aren't they?" Her throat tightened. She'd told Cai that Bodicca was expendable, but now that the truth of it was here, her heart ached with the possibility. She wasn't sure how she felt about Yusmine. After all, it was only her bondsman body, not his spirit. Even so, she stumbled as she considered it, and Cai had to catch her by the elbow, pulling her up tall, grasping her other arm and pulling her to face her.

"It may be worse than death," Cai said.

Worse than death, surely that meant they weren't dead. Alaysha barely dared ask. "What do you mean?"

"I misunderstood how strong Bodicca's feelings were for the man who was your… father do you call it?"

Alaysha felt herself nodding stupidly, all the while thinking that there might still be hope.

"He could never be a Komandiri in Enyalia. Bodicca would know that. I should have realized she was too smart for such a notion." Cai's tone was guarded, as though she was worried about Alaysha's reaction. That would explain why she was holding her elbows in such a tight grip.

Alaysha watched Cai's face settle into determined calm. She realized the warrior was doing all she could not to reveal what she was thinking. That alone made Alaysha realize how bad it might be.

"You're telling me you think Bodicca took Yenic back to Sarum." She heard how bland it sounded, how devoid of emotion, and she realized she was echoing Cai's determination to remain calm. "You're telling me that Bodicca took who she thought was the rightful Emir to Sarum back to his city were Aislin is even now trying unsuccessfully to connect to him. You're telling me that Bodicca took Yenic back to his mother where she will discover it's not Yenic and not Yuri but Liliah's Oracle and then she will know…"

"She'll know nothing." Cai squeezed Alaysha's arms and only then did she realize the Enyalian thought she would lose Alaysha to panic. "Bodicca is strong. She might be foolish enough to bring him back, thinking he should take his rightful place, and she might know Aislin will admit them because she sees the man who is her son, but Bodicca is Enyalia and she won't let anything happen to him."

Cai's hands covered Alaysha's ears, as though she wanted to deafen her to the truth, her fingers reaching for the back of Alaysha's neck. "I'm telling you that Bodicca will never reveal the goddess's secrets. She'll never reveal us. I'm telling you that although Yenic may be lost to you, you are safe."

"No," Alaysha murmured. "What you're really telling me is that now I have no choice. It won't take long for Aislin to realize it's not Yenic, and she will kill what's left of him. I can't let that happen, Cai; Deities help me, I can't.

"Now I have to return to Sarum and what will end up happening won't be Yenic's salvation at all, because in the end, if I return I will have to watch the people I love die."

Chapter 19

She stumbled forward, heading for the tree she knew was there, falling to her hands and knees on the grass beneath, her hands spasming into the moss where Yenic had lain, her eyes squeezed shut as she tried to find her breath. She felt Cai behind her, could tell she was working at speech.

"Do you think I can't feel your worry," is what the warrior decided on. She edged forward and settled down next to Alaysha, peering up beneath Alaysha's downturned face. It was impossible to feel so sullen with the red brows furrowing up at her like that; Alaysha rolled over to her bottom.

"Gael would undoubtedly have sensed my worry, and yet he left me alone." Alaysha said petulantly.

"I'm sure by now you've noticed that I am not the man," Cai answered. "What is it that's troubling you so? Is it my sword sister?" She stretched her long limbs out in front of her, pointing the tips of her leather boots forward and then arching them backwards again, stretching feet that were obviously tired of the long trek. Alaysha could feel the hum of their connection but all it did was remind her of Yenic.

It could've been, Alaysha thought. It could've been any number of things. But what it really was, she knew, was that she had been forced finally to make an absolute commitment. And it was a commitment she did not want.

"You're suffering," Cai said. "I can feel it."

"And you don't like it," Alaysha guessed.

The woman shrugged. "I'm unused to feeling this way, yes. But I'm not immune to emotion like you think I am." She laced her fingers through Alaysha's and pulled them into her lap. "I know that your brother was suffering," she said. "I know that you feel for your man and your males, much like we would feel for our sword sisters. I know there is a woman back in your homeland who is grieving for her son. Am I using those words right?" Cai cocked her head at Alaysha and waited for her to nod. "Good. I'm trying, Alaysha. I'm trying to learn."

"I know other things too." she said. "You are still suffering from the loss of the man you thought you loved."

She quirked a brow and Alaysha couldn't help nodding in assent.

"I thought so," the woman said. ""But there's something else that I know, that I think even you don't realize. You ache for that man, I believe it, but part of the ache comes from the loss. What you had with him is gone. And you mourn it. I would feel it if it was different. There is something else swimming beneath your desires." The Enyalian moved her hand and Alaysha's with it up to her chest where Alaysha could feel the woman's heart beating. "You feel something new."

"It's not love we feel, Cai," Alaysha heard herself say, hearing the attempted deflection in her protest. Cai wasn't mollified or fooled. She waved the words away as if they were annoying mosquitoes.

"If only that was the problem that was burdening you; I could sweep away the doubts within an afternoon. Perhaps an afternoon much like this one. I'd hoped for a more welcoming homecoming, but I can't feel despondent about such a selfish thing when you're in such pain. "

Alaysha didn't have it in her to admit defeat. "You don't love, me, Cai."

"You doubt my feelings even though I let you tie me to a mark?" Cai sounded angry.

"No, it's not like that." Alaysha said. "You just can't."

"Can't what? Love a woman, or love at all?" The woman's hand fell against her lap and she let go of Alaysha's fingers. When Alaysha thought the woman would get up and leave, she eased around and faced Alaysha, her ankles crossed. "A woman can love another better than she can love a man. But I doubt that's what you're saying." Cai said. "What you're saying is that you don't believe me. Because my people are harsh and hard. Because we rid ourselves of the male vermin born to us and who would invade us, because we allow our women to die before they're old and infirm and unable to wield a sword. You think what you have seen in my village is everything there is. You think what you see of us is all there is, and so you judge it." Cai nailed her with a look.

Alaysha felt guilty then, she thought about how Cai looked as she'd peer down at her wounded comrade, how she'd whispered to her of her bravery and she felt ashamed. She'd marked this woman because she was both ferocious and loyal. It wasn't fair to displace her own guilt onto her.

"You know about Saxon?" Alaysha asked.

"Your man's nephew?" Cai said.

"Gael. It's Gael, Cai. Why won't you say his name?"

The Enyalian looked at her with what Alaysha thought would be a smirk, but then it dissolved into all seriousness. "Because I like the fire that lights your eyes when you scold me about it," Cai admitted.

Alaysha didn't know what to say to that. She picked at bits of weeds that grew around the tree, tugging them into her hands and squeezing them with anxious fingers. Then, realizing she was doing it, she crossed her arms against her chest and leaned back, looking up into the canopy of the huge redwoods. This one was too small even at its height and girth to be considered of housing value to the highlanders. Perhaps in another couple of dozen seasons they might consider it worthy of carving stairs into its trunk and nailing slats of boards together to create a safe haven in the trees where they might bring up their young and love and live.

She thought of staying here, but the thought of making her home somewhere in one of these large redwoods made her pick at the grass again until she realized she'd pulled most of it away from the earth. Thoughts of earth led her to thoughts of Thera and then to the witch she'd saved: Theron's daughter. And then thoughts of the clay witch, led her to thoughts of Liliah and then Aislin and then Yenic and then she felt as if she couldn't breathe.

"I can see you thinking," Cai said.

"I was thinking about Saxon," she lied.

Cai snorted. "Is that so? A good enough place to start, then."

Alaysha knew Cai wasn't fooled, but she did start there. She told her about the mucklands and Greetha's daughter, about the mark on Saxon's ribcage and what it had done to him.

Cai listened without interrupting. The woman's hair was unbound this afternoon, hanging down both of her shoulders and smelling of lavender and Pine. She caught Alaysha's gaze with her own and Alaysha found within a compassion that she'd forgotten the woman could possess. She was so hard all the time, always ready to stand against any enemy real or imagined. She looked softer this afternoon, more approachable. For a heartbeat, Alaysha realized that the same tingling Gael would have felt, this woman would feel too. Cai's eyes dropped to Alaysha's mouth. For one heartbeat, Alaysha thought the woman would kiss her, but the moment was gone as quickly as it came.

Alaysha squeezed the fingers of one hand with the other. She was feeling as though she would at any time bolt into the darkness of the woods when Cai's fingers wrapped into hers.

"I know there's more, little maga."

Alaysha swallowed. The rest came out in a rush. "If I were truly my father's daughter, if I'd go through with those things he taught me, to remain emotionless, to make decisions based on logic and not emotion, then things wouldn't be so hard."

"The things you speak of have to do with your young man, the one Bodicca took," Cai guessed.

"Would you rescue Bodicca?"

"An unfair question. You told me Bodicca was expendable."

"If I hadn't told you that, would you rescue her?"

"You mean even knowing that she exiled herself years ago from my people?"

Alaysha nodded.

"Bodicca is of the old order, yet she's strong and ferocious and Enyalia for all of that." There was pride in Cai's voice.

"But would you help her if she was in danger even in the face of all that?"

"I would face danger for any of my sword sisters," Cai said carefully. "But that one woman betrayed her own people, chose a man over her sisters, and it seems that despite her age she has not learned one lesson since she's been a pre-grown warrior.

"It was me and Thera who ultimately sent her away again when she returned to Enyalia with your man. I knew she was out there, suffering, perhaps even dead. I didn't seek her then."

Alaysha chuckled humorlessly. "How different we are," Alaysha said. "My father would have done the same as you. He would risk Yenic and Bodicca if it would help Sarum. He was able to make hard decisions not swayed by his emotion."

"He was of an Enyalian warrior, after all," Cai said and Alaysha realized it was true, that it explained a good deal about her father.

It took a long while for Cai to speak again, but when she did, it dredged up Alaysha's intentions.

"You'd have us recover your man and Bodicca?" Cai said. "And so you suffer over it."

It was only fair to admit it.

"Yes and deities help me, it means death for you all."

"I don't fear death, little maga. I only fear living without you."

Alaysha smiled wryly, choosing to ignore the invitation in Cai's voice. "If I return to Sarum, then you most assuredly will be living without me," Alaysha told her.

"Then don't return."

"And leave Liliah to face her brother alone? Because she will. Eventually Aislin will come for her."

"What does all of this have to do with the little goddess?"

Alaysha did her best to explain. When she was finished, Cai took her hand silently. She pulled Alaysha to her feet, and without a word, or a trace of lust, embraced her so that Alaysha felt completely enveloped and oddly safe.

They stood like that for several minutes until the humming began in Alaysha's ears. It travelled down her jaw and burned in her chin then down her throat; she knew Cai felt it too. It was the warrior who broke away with a sheepish laugh.

"It seems I can't keep any secret desires from you, little maga."

"It seems not."

"Well, I had hoped for a more welcoming homecoming," Cai admitted, cocking an inviting brow and Alaysha had to laugh as she shook her head. It felt good. She felt good.

"You've made up your mind."

Alaysha nodded and Cai smiled. "I love a good battle."

"You've said that before."

"I also said I don't lose."

CHAPTER 20

Theron brewed kykeon all afternoon and it was ready by sunset. Alaysha expected the shaman himself to bring it to her, but it was his eldest daughter, the sloe-eyed, almond skinned beauty and the somewhat hulking height of Theron's son who came through the leather flap.

Alaysha's face must have shown her confusion because Néve had to explain that he was sleeping. "Teaching me the skill took a lot out of him."

Alaysha sighed audibly and nodded them in.

Like the first time she'd seen her, the woman's beauty made Alaysha feel decidedly plain. She couldn't stop her fingers from fumbling over her hair and smoothing it down. She could feel a twist in the back of her head that most assuredly was a tangled mess. Deciding she couldn't do anything about it now, she let her hands fall to her sides where despite her best efforts, they worked at the sides of her tunic.

"Have you prepared yourself?" Néve asked, scanning the insides of the lodging with perceptive eyes. When they landed on the copper bowl of soot, Alaysha bent to retrieve it from the bench. She showed it to the clay witch almost shyly.

"Will it be enough?" She asked. She knew Theron hadn't had a lot of time to collect up ashes from her sister when Aislin had incinerated her before they fled Sarum. She was surprised actually that he'd managed to collect as much as he had.

Néve took the bowl and shook it, peering within with a scrutinous eye "It should be." She looked up at Alaysha and never letting her gaze falter, added: "but I'm given to understand you have two Arms, not one."

Alaysha looked askance at Néve's brother. "Yes, I have two."

Without offering her thoughts on the fact, Néve placed the bowl back onto the bench, setting the goblet of kykeon next to it. Alaysha's stomach squirmed watching her. She both anticipated and feared the coming ritual. And for some reason, she felt ashamed in front of this woman that she had to find two Arms rather than the accustomed one. She felt somehow inadequate and weak.

She ran a toe across the dust of the floor, watching the trail it made. "It seemed a good idea at the time," Alaysha tried to explain.

She heard Néve chuckle and looked up to see those black, almond-shaped eyes crinkled in playful mirth. "Don't worry, Alaysha, my father told me all about it. I think a woman in your circumstance would have no choice but to bond with two rather than one."

Alaysha wasn't sure why she felt as though she was about to be newly bedded with an entire village waiting to offer their approval. She noted how Néve 's brother shuffled quietly in his spot next to the leather flap, but no more than a single stride away from his sister. His stance wasn't exactly possessive, like a lover would be possessive, but it was definitely one that demonstrated by its body language that he believed she belonged to him.

"I'm finding it difficult," she admitted to the clay witch. "They're both so…" She let the rest trail off, unsure how to describe the two warriors she had marked.

To her surprise the woman nodded in understanding. "The mark is powerful, the magic within even more so." She nodded at the goblet. "The brew has its own power as well. So much of it, it takes a lifetime to understand."

"I think it would take a lifetime for me to understand any of this," Alaysha confessed.

Néve looked at her with compassion. The black, sloe-eyes could have been chunks of obsidian without pupils at all. "When you are finished, come see me. I'll explain as much as I can to you." The woman turned to leave, her brother behind her until Alaysha grabbed her by the wrist.

"Did you and your brother…"

The woman turned to her, black brows raised in mock inquiry, but Alaysha had the feeling the woman knew exactly what the question was. She waited for the woman to explain.

"The kykeon enhances what is there," she answered. She gave her brother an endearing look and touched him briefly on the hand. "Ellison and I were brought up as brother and sister. I was still a child when his brother brought him to us. A large man, almost clear blue eyes." Néve's gaze trailed to the walls as she remembered. "His hair was long and white, so different from the darkness of the baby he carried. I remember him passing the child to my father, and telling him the mother was dead. It was obvious by the way my father couldn't look at my mother that this child was his. He looked so guilty, so pained. Even in my youth, I could feel it on him. While my mother did her best to accept the babe, even naming him after her, I knew she felt the same guilt that pained my father. They never spoke of it, but it weighed on both of them."

Again, Néve reached out for her brother and clasped his hand in hers. "I was enamored of him. He's beautiful, yes? He was even as a baby. I doted on him like a mother would. I made him part of me when he was four seasons old and I gave him my mark. I might have been twice his age, but it was long before I had reached maidenhood." She looked at him, a soft expression settling on her face.

"A woman would be foolish not to see how handsome he is, but I'm not a mere woman. I am his sister, and more than that I am his witch. My mother taught me how to bond with him as a brother first and by the time I marked him, what was enhanced was that sense of protection," she said. Then she shrugged. "There are times, yes, when the kykeon stirred up something more as I marked him." She smiled a wry smile. "But I'm strong." She twisted her hand out of Ellison's grasp and laid her palm on Alaysha's shoulder. "My mother taught me to understand my emotions and to find which one was appropriate. She helped me strengthen the right one with Ellison. You're strong too. I know this. I remember you."

"It was you, wasn't it, out there in the mud village?"

The woman nodded. "I saw you and your horse. I saw you struggling with the fire witch's attempted possession of you."

"Is that what it was?" Alaysha hadn't thought of it that way before, but it could've been. She'd felt so groggy with fever.

"Indeed. And when you worked to learn to control your power, and you brought floods of water from the wide sea, I couldn't let you die. At least not without an heir." She smiled thinly, almost resentfully and Alaysha realized the woman was feeling the burden of her power and strong as she was, still harbored some resentment of the responsibilities.

"What would happen to the line without an heir?"

It surprised Alaysha enough that she grabbed Néve's arm again and twisted it so that she could see the skin of her wrist. Néve let her see the scars there, newly healed, yes, but scars all the same. Many of them crisscrossed up arms and Alaysha lost sight of them beneath her tunic sleeve.

"So much power," Alaysha said, thinking even as she said it that it would take more than the woman's innate energy to do the things she'd done at the mud village, opening the Earth, creating fissures for the water to leak into so that Alaysha and Barruch might survive.

"Yes," the woman murmured, offering in the slight nod of her head a confirmation of Alaysha's suspicions. "And so much blood. Thank heaven for Ellison." Néve gave her brother a grateful look. He bowed quickly and a flash of humble grin, full-toothed and broad put Alaysha in mind of Cai.

"Ellison saved you?"

"Indeed he did. Although I remember little of it."

Ellison spoke finally, lending a queerly high-pitched voice for his size. "I had no skill," he said. "And the only person I knew who would have any healing art was my twin."

His twin: Thera. Alaysha put the rest of it together without help. She understood that Ellison had delivered Néve to Thera, and curious undoubtedly, Thera nursed the woman back to health while Ellison kept out of sight of the Enyalia. He'd no doubt found Edulph, as Edulph had told her. The rest didn't need explaining.

"So I was right about you creating the earthquakes."

Again, Néve nodded. "None of it intentional," she said. "I wasn't quite myself. Although I'm sure Ellison was responsible for a few of them." She grinned and her face lit up with good humor. "His way of letting me know he was still alive and kicking."

She bent to retrieve the goblet then, as if dismissing the conversation, and passed it to Alaysha. "Don't forget the blood," she said. "And remember you are stronger than you think. You can foster whatever bond you wish with the kykeon and the mark, but consider the effect it has on those who receive it. They will be yours no matter what emotion you foster, or they would have never agreed to in the first place, but it's best to let them have some say in the way they will feel for the rest of their days."

She left then, her tall brother following her through the flap and Alaysha settled down onto the bench, the goblet in her hand, thinking about what the woman had said. When Gael and Cai entered a short time later, Alaysha received them with a renewed excitement and far less dread.

The large Enyalian was first, with Gael following half a stride behind. Both of them stripped down to breeches and settled crosslegged on her sleeping mat, shaking their arms as though readying themselves for a fight. Both were of a size with each other, but while one was fair and silver, muscled across the chest with sinews that bulged and flexed with each movement, the other was russet and freckled and though just as muscled, there was a softness about her that made each sinew rounder.

A surge moved through Alaysha as she looked at them. She saw that Néve had been kind enough to trace the patterns onto their skin for her, obviously thinking to make it easier. She began the ritual as she did before, and with great determination, worked long hours of painstaking care to make sure that the ribbons of tattaus would be both beautiful and crisp. Once again, the brazier burned hot and before long Alaysha was sweating; pools of perspiration collected between her breasts and at the back of her neck.

Both Cai and Gael looked drunk, their eyes glassy and their bodies pliable. There was a hum that seemed to circle the tent, enveloping them in an energy that tingled behind Alaysha's ears and down her spine. She imagined her Arms of protection sensed it too. Cai grimaced once when Alaysha's needle dug into a tender spot on her rib, but other than that, she made no protest.

At one point, Alaysha believed she had worked through the night and halfway into the next day. But she still wasn't finished. She was overheated, and at times she felt dizzy, but she squeezed her eyes shut, concentrating and focusing on getting the right energy channelling through her fingers. She took a shuddering breath at one point, feeling as though she would pass out from hunger, but she kept on.

When she finished, she drained the last of the kykeon with a longing that went beyond simple thirst and she eased her eyes closed as it ran down the back of her throat. It burned a trail of heat down her esophagus that spread out into her shoulders and down her fingertips. It moved like liquid gold down her torso and into her legs. She couldn't imagine what she had been so nervous about. It felt right, being in this tent with these two.

She took in Gael as he leaned back on his hands, his chest glistening with perspiration; she noticed a trickle of blood moving down his rib cage and she dipped into it with her finger, wiping it on her tunic. She could tell by the way his muscles had gone tense when she touched him that he wanted her. She let her fingers trail along his hip, keeping her eyes on his, the question as plain as she could make it in her eyes. She could see from hardened member that he was ready for her, that the desire he felt for her was on his mouth, in his eyes. He shuddered with it.

So evident was it that he wanted her, that when he stood and yanked his tunic from the bench, throwing it over his shoulder and striding with resolve from the tent, Alaysha could do no more than stare after his disappearing back. When the flap the thwacked closed, she fell back onto her knees in confusion and burning disappointment, seeing in her mind's eye Isolde and her swelling belly and feeling the additional sting of jealousy.

"Men are fools, little maga," Cai said, standing.

Alaysha looked up at her, noticing that she too glistened with sweat. Her red hair covered one breast, but the other was left exposed, the hard nipple straining for the air. Cai extended her hand downwards for Alaysha, wiggling her fingers in invitation, and Alaysha took it because she dearly wanted to rid herself of the hurt of rebuff. She felt as though swirls of energy swam behind her eyes, and that her legs wouldn't be able to stand without Cai's help pulling her to her feet.

She found herself responding to the woman's masterful tongue as the warrior claimed her mouth. Her body melted against Cai's, her legs turned to water. A thought did creep into her mind that she should remember something Néve had said, but it disappeared like steam in hot air.

Her eyes fluttered open to see Cai's red-eyed gaze scoring her like a piece of fruit. The woman smelled of apples, she always smelled of apples, Alaysha thought. Wholesome and spicy. But there was something else too. Beneath all of that, there was a slightly masculine scent. One that reminded Alaysha that the warrior was as hard and durable as a stone. She could pretend it was Gael, if she wanted, imagine the hard muscles were the warrior's.

Cai's eyes crinkled at the corner as she released her claim on Alaysha's lips, and the woman's voice sounded as though it came from someplace deep within a tight chest, that she had to wrestle through it to speak.

"Come, little maga," she whispered. "Let me teach you something you'll never forget."

CHAPTER 21

Alaysha couldn't remember sleeping so well. Though she woke alone, she opened her eyes to the memory of a satisfying night. Every muscle seemed more sore than before, but it was a good pain. It reminded her of her night with Cai, and not even the memory of Gael walking out on her could darken her day. She stretched lazily on her mat and listened for the sounds of the village coming to life. She knew they'd have to depart soon, perhaps even within the day, but even that didn't dampen her spirits. There was a certain thrill in being connected with someone. Being connected with two someones only doubled the sensation.

She remembered Néve's words of caution to her, and smiled to herself; the woman may be older, but what did she know about having two protectors? What did she know about having Arms who were not blood to her. If Alaysha felt safe and comforted during the first marking ceremony, she felt complete now. Even as she lay there, she could feel the denseness of the hum behind her ears. It seemed to resonate in her jawbone and settle somewhere at the base of her skull, where it radiated down her spine and through the very tips of her toes and fingers. Indeed, she felt more alive than she'd had before. Even the bond with Yenic hadn't made her feel so full. So whole.

She was still enjoying her newfound sense of peace when Aedus poked her head into the tent. "I was hoping you'd be awake," the girl said. Alaysha waved her in and Aedus found a place at the bottom of Alaysha's mat.

"I thought perhaps the little goddess might be with you," Aedus said.

Alaysha pushed herself to a sitting position. "No," she said scratching her head. "Why?"

The look on Aedus's face in response was one of careful concern, and Alaysha was instantly anxious. "You can see she isn't," Alaysha said carefully.

Aedus chewed the bottom of her lip. "I haven't seen her this morning," she admitted.

At that, Alaysha was on her feet, pulling on her tunic and reaching for her scabbard.

She strapped it on her back and was striding to the door when Aedus stopped her. "She's disappeared before," she said.

Alaysha turned. "Before?"

Aedus nodded her head. "Yes, a couple of times while you and Gael were gone."

"And how do you find her again?"

Aedus shrugged. "She finds us," she said. "Except it's been too long this time."

"Have you told the others?"

"No. Only you."

"Good," Alaysha said, striding again for the door. She lifted the flap and peered squint-eyed outside. The sun was up, perhaps had been up for many hours. She scanned the treetops to see that the sun was just touching the tallest trees to the east. Late morning, yes, not yet time for midday repast. Aedus pushed her from behind.

"She's never been gone this long," Aedus said. "Usually she finds her way back shortly after I notice she's missing."

Alaysha squinted down at the girl. "How often?"

The girl looked off into the horizon, thinking. "Maybe half a dozen times."

Alaysha scanned the village, wondering if perhaps the girl had taken it upon herself to visit one of her neighbors. "Have you checked all of the houses?"

She looked up into the treetops, hoping she didn't have to climb many of those stairs. She hadn't received an answer from Aedus before Cai came striding from her own camp just behind Alaysha's, a tangle of branches and moss and leaves that she'd made for herself deep into the heart of the woods. She smiled when she saw Alaysha.

"I slept well, little maga," she said winking. She stopped short when she realized Alaysha was too distracted to respond. "What's wrong?" She asked.

"Liliah is gone," Aedus said. "She does it a lot, but this time I haven't been able to find her."

"Does what a lot?"

Aedus lifted her hands in a helpless gesture. "Disappears."

Cai looked around her, inspecting the village with a quick and observant eye. "And does her disappearance often have something to do with the appearance of strangers?" She said no more, but headed off towards a group of young men who were hanging around the cook fire. Alaysha turned to Aedus.

"Are they new?" She pointed out the group that by now, Cai had met. The warrior towered over the tallest of them, arms crossed but not so tightly that she couldn't move for her weapon if she needed to. Indeed, her stance was carefully created to appear casual.

Aedus squinted into the distance. "I think so." She looked back at Alaysha. "I never really noticed before," Aedus said. She chewed her lip in thought. "Do you think they have something to do with one another?"

Alaysha started to walk towards the Enyalian. "I think she does," she said.

She was still a number of paces away when the large warrior drug one of the men over toward Alaysha and pushed him in front of her.

"Tell her," Cai commanded.

The man looked at his feet instead of Alaysha's face. "I have nothing to tell," he said mumbling into the ground.

"See?" Cai asked Alaysha.

"See what, Cai? The man doesn't have anything to say."

"Ask him a question, little maga."

Alaysha did her best to catch the man's eyes, but he avoided her every time she tried to make him face her. "What's your name?" She finally asked, having to give up meeting his gaze.

He toed the dirt with a worn-out boot. The man stammered for a few moments before finally giving up.

"See?" Cai demanded again.

"See what? I don't know what you're trying to tell me."

"I thought your father trained you to warriorhood, little maga. Look at his boots. Look at his clothes. He's traveled a long way. Ask him another question."

Alaysha sighed, frustrated and not a little chagrined. "Where have you come from?"

Again, the man stammered, but said nothing. Alaysha finally grew impatient and grabbed him by his chin. She forced him to face her and noticed that his eyes were cloudy, almost glazed over in confusion. She looked over to where his companions seemed to be shuffling about, mindless of where they were. They seemed to only be aware of the fire, and occasionally stretched hands over the flames and rubbed them together. One or two of them had decided to sit directly in front of it on the ground.

Aislin," Alaysha said guessing. "Has she made some connection to them somehow?"

Cai shook her head. "I don't think so, little maga. They look like they're in shock."

"Or in a trance," Aedus said, piping up.

Alaysha looked at the man again. This time she found herself remembering what Yenic had looked like when Aedus had painted the dreamer's worm on his face at Edulph's bidding. He'd gone temporarily mad, his eyes glazed, staring ahead with no expression except for fear. "Dreamer's worm is invisible by day, isn't it?"

Aedus nodded.

Alaysha scanned the village. "Where is everybody else?" She said. Usually by this time there were dozens of children running about, collecting wood, lighting fires; by now there should be women baking flatbread on heated stones and hanging wet linen in the branches to dry. Certainly there was some of that activity, but not as much as usual.

"Where's Gael?" Alaysha demanded of Cai.

"Am I your man's keeper?" The woman asked sullenly but she set off anyway, and Alaysha knew she would search him out. She turned to Aedus. "Go get Theron and Thera as well as Néve and Ellison. Something's not right. "

CHAPTER 22

Cai suggested they make a meticulous sweep of the camp, and so they worked in pairs: Néve and Ellison moved West from Liliah's tree house; Thera went with Cai who complained loudly that she didn't want to leave Alaysha with Gael; Aedus assured everyone that she could stalk the forests without being noticed by anyone; and Alaysha knew it was true so she left her on her own. She and Gael took the easterly direction. Theron wanted to attend the party, wringing his hands nervously, but Alaysha assured him that he was needed in the camp to look after Isolde and Saxon. "We can't leave them unattended, Theron," she told him, patting his shoulder. "We can't trust that these newcomers are as harmless as they seem."

The plan was to move in an ever-increasing circle towards each other, but expanding the diameter from their point outwards in the hopes that Liliah would be caught by one of them, and if not, they would eventually converge and begin the search all over again in the same directions outward.

Alaysha and Gael picked their way to the thick underbrush at the back of the camp where some old and abandoned houses rested in the trees of much older redwoods. These were worm eaten and rotting from the base, no wonder they'd been abandoned. Alaysha looked up into one of them, thinking perhaps Liliah might have found her way up into the relative solitude of an abandoned tree house. She was light enough that the rotting might not have created too much danger.

Gael noticed the direction of her gaze and shook his head. "I doubt she's up there," he said, then trudged on without so much as catching her eye. It was peculiar for him, but she said nothing about it. It may well be he had a sleepless night, that his mark, long and thick as it was, might have burned him and kept him awake.

Still, something didn't look quite right about this small clearing. The girl was small enough that she might not bend over too much grass, or crumpled too much underbrush as she walked, but Alaysha noted that it was a little bit boggy beneath her feet. The moss squelched between her toes. Gael might not notice it as quickly as she did with his boots providing a barrier, but he did notice it a few moments after she did. He looked down at his feet as they gave some in the wet humus. He lifted a foot and peered at the sole thoughtfully.

"There must be water nearby," he said scanning the area.

"A pond, perhaps," Alaysha said, thinking. She remembered the first time she and Aedus and Yenic had found the dreamer's worm. Aedus had been ecstatic. While Yenic had only considered them a source of nutrition, Aedus had found another use. She'd mashed them down and tricked Yenic into painting the mush beneath his eyes. Left too long, the substance from the worm's body leaked into the skin and either shut down the vision, or caused walking nightmarish visions.

"We'll check later," Alaysha told him. "Our first priority is Liliah."

Once again, Gael turned away from her and trudged off without meeting her eyes. She tried to connect with him, and felt a surge of anger buzz into her jaw line. "You're angry with me," she declared, realizing it.

She tried to grab his elbow, to hold him back and make him face her, but he flung her off and stepped away. And when she felt the buzz of energy slicing up her spine, almost as if it was being pulled from her, she paused midstep, scanning left and right quickly thinking that perhaps Aislin might be near, that all of this was done at her hand, and her fist went to her mouth to stop off the sudden gasp of fear.

It was in that moment that she realized the pull of power come from Gael. He was still trudging away from her, determinedly making his way through the underbrush. His back was working beneath his leather tunic, his arms swaying as he pulled aside every sapling so that he could make his way through. But just above his head, hovering like a bit of smoke was a black mist. Alaysha was glad her fist with stuffed in her mouth, so that he wouldn't hear her laughing. Unknowingly, he was using her power, or whatever he had been able to channel of her power to create a physical manifestation of his feelings. He didn't even know that the mist wetting his hair was of his own making.

She was about to stop him and explain when she heard a short cut off giggle that could be nothing other than a child's squeal of delight. Gael heard it too, obviously; he halted and swung his head back and forth, leaning down into the underbrush, seeking the source. Alaysha could tell that his hair was completely wet, and yet he didn't brush any of it out of his face. Trained to stoicism, he let the water stream down his face as he tried to peer through the thicket of leaves.

He'd caught sight of something, Alaysha could see. She followed his gaze and found not Liliah, as she'd expected, but a flash of blackened leather streaking between the tree trunks. Gael was off before Alaysha could take in a breath. If there was one person, perhaps there were more. She swung slowly in a circle, barely breathing, straining her eyes to see through the leaves, seeking movement of any kind. A flurry of birds took to the air on her left, probably in response to Gael's noisy path of pursuit, but where Alaysha was, everything had gone quiet. It was if the entire forest was straining to hear what would happen next.

She wanted terribly to lick her lips,, and she tried to tell herself that perhaps all they'd seen were the others searching for Liliah as hard as they were. But something wasn't right; she sensed it. And the strange thing was, that what she felt was more than just the hum of Gael's connection in her mark, it was more than the coursing of that energy flowing through her tissues; it was the feeling that only the use of magic left her with.

She felt foggy and groggy and in some ways ungrounded. She rooted her feet to the moss, let her power surge down through her toes and into the water beneath. She asked of it to find perspiration and the movement of oxygen through the condensation of breath. She asked it to seek out the tang of copper in blood, the taste of saliva on the tongue, the perspiration of fear.

When it connected, she felt as though she lost her breath, realized that she was sucking at the air, trying to pull in enough to breathe. She fell to her knees, clawing at her throat, but just when she thought she might send out her power, she knew that it would do no good.

What was pulling her oxygen from her was more powerful than she was, and it could only mean that power was aided by blood and fear.

It was then that she realized that what was stealing her breath was the power sent out by Liliah.

And that the girl was bleeding.

CHAPTER 23

The power cut off as quickly as it had come, and Alaysha fell to her hands, gasping for new air. She scrabbled forward, sensing that the threat had come from somewhere ahead of her, and that if the power had stopped, there was a good chance that the little goddess might not be alive.

She was on her feet, half stumbling, half running, catching at the branches that slapped her face and tore at her tunic. Twice her feet caught on half-hidden stones and once she nearly twisted her ankle, but she kept on, telling herself that physical pain would heal.

She found the girl in a pocket of ferns twice her size. Alaysha was running to her, thinking only to scoop her out and rush her back to the village, uncaring that the girl sat in a pool of blood, but registering that the girl was crying, not truly comprehending that the bodies littered around her on their backs, on their sides, even crumpled to their knees, were even still passing fresh blood from their throats or wrists or oozing from their bellies. She only registered the feel of the girl in her arms, slipping from her grasp even as she tried to gather her close, the blood on her skin a metallic tang that crept through the air.

The girl buried her face in Alaysha's neck so hard and so deep that her top teeth cut into the skin of Alaysha's shoulders. Alaysha hugged her close, spinning in place, staring down at the dozen bodies who were all strangely the same even as they were familiar faces. It took a few heartbeats for Alaysha to realize that all of their eyes were missing.

"Sweet deities," she heard herself say and then her legs went liquid and she struck the ground on her left hip, clutching the girl still, rocking her back and forth. She yelled out something that might have been a name. It might have been two.

All she knew was Gael came for her and was kneeling in front of her and wiping the hair away from her eyes. He was snapping his fingers at her and it took long breathless moments for her to hear the sound pop in her ears. Only then did the rest of the noise come back.

She was sobbing. Gael had her in his arms with the girl between them, pulling her close, trying to swallow her with his embrace.

"You're okay, Alaysha," he said. "You're okay." He repeated it over and over until Alaysha's sobs turned to whimpers and then she managed to smother them altogether. She heard noises from behind her and realized it was the others,. She pulled away from Gael, careful not to let her eyes rest on the forms of those people around her. She forced her gaze to stay on Gael's face. She told herself nothing else existed except his silver brows, his green eyes, the rough stubble of his chin where he hadn't shaved in days. The girl in her arms squirmed and before she realized it, someone had taken Liliah from her.

She heard herself protest.

"It's okay," Gael said. "Néve has her."

"What happened?" Alaysha swallowed three times before the bile would stay down.

It was the child's voice that cut the tension. But it didn't make sense.

"They gave me bubbles," Liliah said. She whimpered in Néve's arms and then Alaysha heard her take shuddering breaths, the last exhausting throes of fear.

Alaysha was still staring at Gael's face, but a booted foot stole into her periphery. The owner knelt next to her and she saw from the corner of her eye, that he ran his hands through the ferns and the grass. She wouldn't take her eyes off Gael.

Mercifully, Gael locked eyes with Alaysha. "Are you okay?" He asked.

She wasn't sure, but she nodded feebly. He helped her to stand and his arm went around her shoulders like a warm cloak. She shuddered beneath, grateful for the warmth.

"Come," he said, leading her away and following behind Néve, who was carrying Liliah. They met up with Cai and Aedus who both looked stricken as they peered past Alaysha into the small copse of ferns.

Alaysha knew that they saw the carnage, but she said nothing. Instead, she sank down on the nearest fallen tree she could find, leaving Gael to stand next to her as she inhaled and exhaled purposefully and mindfully. When she thought she had regained her control, she peered up at him. "The person you were chasing, do you think he did that?"

He sounded guarded when he spoke, "I don't know who it was. I didn't catch him, but I think those people did that to themselves."

"Themselves?" That was Cai's voice, disbelieving, doubtful.

"Ellison will scout it out," Néve said, motioning toward the clearing with her chin. She was still clutching the girl, but by now the little goddess had begun reaching for Aedus and she relinquished the child over to her aunt.

"Obviously one of those strangers from the village," Cai said. "But why? I don't understand."

"They gave me bubbles," Liliah piped up.

"Bubbles," Aedus said, "why would they give you bubbles?"

Néve's face went white as she narrowed her eyes in thought.

"What is it?" Alaysha asked her.

"Not bubbles," Néve said. "Baubles."

"Baubles? That doesn't make any more sense than bubbles."

Néve nodded at Liliah's fist.

Alaysha's gaze followed hers and Aedus worked to open the child's fist. Inside, squished but not flattened, were two glistening round globes.

"Their eyes," Alaysha said grimacing and looking at Néve. Her face must have gone as white as the clay witch's because Cai rushed forward and pushed her head between her knees. Alaysha took three deep breaths and then mumbled that she was okay.

Cai moved to sit on the tree next to her, but she didn't leave her be.

"Liliah where did you get those?" Alaysha asked her.

Before the girl could answer, Ellison picked his way through the path to find them. He stopped wordlessly next to Néve and handed her a large leather pouch that looked strangely pale and freckled.

"I found that in the hollow of a tree nearby. Some of those bodies had been there a long time. Many of them just from today. A few paces beyond however, there was another similar grisly scene. And a few steps beyond that, another."

Néve undid the thongs that tied the leather pouch closed. She peered in and sucked in a breath of surprise. She closed the pouch again hastily and passed it back to Ellison.

"What is it?" Alaysha almost hated to ask, but she had a sneaking suspicion what was inside anyway.

Néve shuddered. "Whoever they were, they must have been from Etlantium."

CHAPTER 24

They looked on the newcomers much more warily when they re-entered the village, Liliah holding onto Aedus's hand while the rest of them followed along behind. No one spoke, obviously of the same mind that the shock would need to wear off before they could discuss what had happened. Alaysha noted that several more strange faces had appeared around the cook fire, all shuffling about aimlessly as though they had been called there like salmon to their birthplace.

She looked at Liliah with fresh eyes and for the first time since Yenic's rejuvenation, remembered Gael's warning words. We don't know what this magic can do, he'd said. They'd been so certain that the strangers had been painted with the dreamer's worm, but what if the girl had called them. What if, indeed like salmon they were seeking out their point of origin? What if, subconsciously, Liliah was bringing her children home, as Yusmine said, extracting their spirits, preparing for the final battle with her brother.

She was mulling over the possibility when Cai burst from the group towards the strangers and herded them all like goats into one big circle. She peered into each one of their eyes like the shaman would have, lifting their eyelids, examining something there within the depths. Frustrated, she pushed the last of them away and with a look of furious impotence, stormed toward the shaman's tree where he'd been treating Isolde. Alaysha imagined she'd demand much of the shaman and wished her luck in extracting any useful information.

It was then that one of the strangers noticed Liliah standing there with Aedus. Something in his face went right with recognition and he stumbled forward, aiming his feet in her direction. He only managed to take about three steps before he was airborne, floating toward her. The others followed, and Alaysha's gaze flew to the girl. Liliah's blonde curls were lifted in the air as well, as though some breeze had swept out from beneath her that no one else could feel.

She let go of Aedus's hand and her fingers were slapping into her palms as though she was impatiently calling them to her. The girl's eyes swirled with color and even as all of this was happening, Alaysha too felt some pull. Her jaw began to ache, the middle of her chin where the first of her marks had been laid tingled. She was already tasting perspiration; part of her was traveling along the paths of a body's fluid, and she realized even as it was happening, that she was sampling that man's water.

She was vaguely aware of Néve next to her until the woman's hands reached for hers and wove their fingers within her own. It was Néve's pull, very hard, on Alaysha's hand that allowed Alaysha to finally relinquish the almost insatiable thirst for water.

She heard someone call out and she realized that her companions had taken places all around her. Without thinking, the Arms had begun to barricade their witches, and only Liliah stood alone but for Aedus next to her who had gone as rapt with confusion as Liliah had gone with power. It was Theron's voice that cut the energy, but his words were not in a language Alaysha understood. His hair stood out about his head as though he was charged by lightening, the woad on his face snaked down his neck and disappeared beneath his cassock. His hands were buried in his robes.

Liliah swung her gaze to him, blank-eyed, unaware. For several long moments, the men in the air swirled about them, no more weighted on the wind than leaves in autumn, and then they fell, thudding to the ground with sickening sounds.

Liliah began to sob and her crying was one of a child's, not of a goddesses. Alaysha realized that the girl was afraid. Beneath the call to her people, something else was there, something that the girl didn't understand.

Alaysha had to remind herself that this girl, though a goddess, was also in a child's body. With a child's mind. And the mind wasn't strong.

"Aedus do something," Alaysha yelled. But it was Theron who stopped it all. One moment Liliah was standing there, pulling to her children, sobbing beneath strength of her power, and then she collapsed in a heap on the ground.

Aedus dropped to her knees, feeling for a pulse, but Alaysha turned to the trees behind her. There Theron stood with Aedus's blower. He looked both stricken and relieved at the same time.

"Good shot, shaman" she told him. And then he stumbled forward, his feeble legs making every effort to get to Liliah so he could dig his fingers beneath her neck, his ear to her mouth, checking for life.

She could see the relief on his face when he nodded at her.

"Good," she said.

"We can't wait much longer," Theron said. "We have to get her back to Sarum."

Back to Sarum, Alaysha thought. Where Bodicca had taken Yenic, where Saxa waited for her son, where the final throes of this legend of a battle would undoubtedly take the lives of all she loved. Indeed, Alaysha saw that there was no choice. She understood how compulsion worked now. She and Gael and Liliah all driven by the need to accomplish something even if they didn't understand it.

The girl was powerful. She looked at the little thing, lying limp in Aedus's arms. She sent one long lingering glance around the village and knew that it would be her last.

"Is Isolde well enough to travel?" She asked the shaman and received a curt nod in return. "Let's hope so," she said, thinking that Gael had the right to see at least the growth of his child and the woman's belly before he died. She took a look at him, studying the broad forehead, the silver brow so much like his sisters, and the full mouth that she hoped to taste at least one more time.

She sighed audibly. She looked around at the ragtag brood of ducklings she knew would have to follow her. "Be ready to go at first light."

CHAPTER 25

The Enyalia found them four days into the journey. Of course, it was Cai who noticed them first just after they'd crossed the now baked riverbed that Alaysha had drained on their journey to the Highlands. There were dozens of them, all mounted in a straight line, their lances hoisted, handles of their swords visible above their shoulders at their backs.

If Alaysha listened hard enough, she could hear the distant clattering of teeth joining together in one loud rattle as the warriors shook their circlets. Before Cai had exiled herself from her homeland, she'd worn a double band of teeth around the widest part of her thigh. Now all she had was a meager strip that stretched around her bicep. That had been only one of the things the Komandiri had given up and Alaysha watched the woman chewing the bottom of her lip in thought. For the first time since the woman had returned from her homeland, Alaysha wondered what had happened within it. She asked the woman to bring back the clay witch, and she had returned unharmed. She'd not thought to question that at the time, but now as she watched Cai's face work in anxious thought, she wondered what secrets the woman kept.

"Payment, I suppose for stealing Isolde and Thera," she put the tentative question out there, but Cai said nothing.

"I think we might be able to at least give them a good fight, except for the baggage," she went on, looking over her shoulder to where almost the contents of the entire Highland village had decided to trail along after them. It wasn't as if they could manage, they were on foot after all. The only mount carried Isolde, who was able to sit a feeble horse so long as Aedus was in front of her, holding Saxon. Thera and Ellison and Néve took their turns with an unconscious Liliah. The rest of them walked. So it wasn't difficult for the Highlanders to keep up. Even though they kept their distance, Alaysha felt the presence like a mosquito in the back of her ears.

"I don't see Uta," Alaysha said to Cai, scanning the column for the telltale gray hair wrapped up in bits of long bones. "Alaysha thought she heard Gael mumble beneath his breath a few choice nasty words about the bone witch, but she ignored him. She nudged Cai with her elbow. "Would she ride to war with the rest, or would she stay back in Enyalia?"

Without looking at her Cai gave her abrupt answer. "She's dead."

The face was perfectly composed, but Alaysha noticed the jaw working subtly; she'd come to realize the warrior had her tells; and the signs of the woman sucking on the backs of her teeth was absolutely a tell.

"How do you know she's dead? Did Isolde get to her after all? Is that why her back is burnt?" Alaysha turned to look at where Barruch was blowing impatiently, nearly heaving beneath the weight of his burden.

"She's dead I know because I killed her," Cai said.

Gael let go a whoop and reached around Alaysha to slap Cai on the back in congratulations. The Enyalian turned to him without a trace of annoyance on her face. "I will make a full circlet of your teeth for my other bicep if you touch me again, man."

She turned again, fastidiously back towards the column of Enyalia facing them in the distance.

Alaysha ventured forward, more curious now, than afraid. "I should have known they wouldn't let the insult go," Alaysha said to no one in particular. The Enyalia were fierce about protecting our homeland, never letting anyone out who entered. Sometimes they were able to stay and live a peaceful life, most times they met a horrible end. Not only had Alaysha escaped with their Komandiri and three men who are bound for the quarter solstice fire, but now Cai had stripped them of their bone witch and rescued an exiled woman.

"It's not an insult they think to repay," Cai said.

"What then?"

"They come for my death," she said.

"What did you do in there?"

"What I had to." Cai faced Alaysha then, she twisted her long russet hair into a plait and flung it behind her head to land against her shoulder blades. She pulled a knife from the belt on her waist and with her other hand, reached for the sword on her back.

"They will be more interested in me, little maga," Cai said striding away. "Take the rest of them around the East. There is a narrow pass that you can get through 2 x 2. We are too big for their beasts to manage it."

Without another word she was striding through the cracked Earth of the riverbed. Alaysha noticed movement in the ranks ahead of her and realized that the Enyalia would take Cai one by one if they had to, wear her down until she was too exhausted to lift her sword anymore.

She was still considering sending the rest of them through the pass as Cai had suggested, while she stood psyching the water from each of Cai's opponents one by one until they decided it was futile to continue when Thera came up behind her.

"She went savage when she found what they were doing to Isolde," Thera whispered. Alaysha turned to her questioningly.

Thera continued. "Uta made her suffer slowly," Thera said shrugging. "I'll spare you the details."

"And so Cai killed her," Alaysha guessed.

Thera nodded. "She killed half a dozen Enyalia before she could get to Uta."

I wouldn't doubt that she could best that many," Alaysha said.

"All at once." Thera said. "And then she made Uta suffer as badly as Isolde. Even that they might have forgiven, until she sought out each of the breeders who had taken your man, and slit their throats as if they were no more than a slab of fat."

Gael made a sound from Alaysha's side that was a noise somewhere between a chuckle and a whimper. She made to reach out to him, but he was already striding forward, pulling his sword from its scabbard, and like Cai, using his freehand to wrest free a knife from his boot. Long strides had him at the Enyalian's side, but the woman didn't so much as bother to turn in his direction; they merely stood side by side, feet splayed, daring the warriors forward.

It was enough motivation for Alaysha to order the rest of them forward. "This is the fastest way to Sarum," she said behind her. "And we won't let these bitches stop us."

She noticed Isolde gave her a feeble smile as the woman tried to stagger off Barruch, the sword in her hand too heavy.

"This fight is not for you, Isolde," she told her. "I need to keep the children safe, the shaman. Can you do that?"

Isolde lifted a weakened hand and rested it on the hilt of her sword. She slid feebly off the back of Barruch and limped painfully towards the pass.

"Just wait there, Isolde. Until we come for you."

The next Alaysha knew, she was striding forward to meet Gael and Cai in the middle of the riverbed,. She knew the others were following her. She also knew that the Enyalia had broken rank and instead of coming forward one by one as was their original intent, they were pressing forward en masse. Alaysha thought she heard Néve mumble something about "and so it happens again," but she couldn't be sure. Next the ground began to shake and Alaysha realized that the clay witch was using her power to jostle the women from their mounts.

"We could end this with Liliah's power," Ellison said.

"We'd be ending it all, then. The child has no control."

Alaysha stepped forward, focussing, urging her power forward to seek out the taste of water. She had to be discriminate; she couldn't let it loose all at once, lest she gather in the fluid of innocent and attacker alike. Gael had taken position at Cai's back, and the two shuffled together as one as several Enyalia danced about them. Alaysha selected one after the other and left them as husks so her two Arms could seek other quarry.

It was when they heard a raucous behind the Enyalia line that Alaysha broke her attention. It seemed the Enyalia--some of them--had turned back, and at first, she thought they were retreating.

"We've broken them," she shouted, but Cai swung into the torso of an attacker, dropping her to the riverbed before she answered.

"No." The Enyalian pointed to the riverbank. "Look."

A hundred boys of varying ages had set upon attack. At first, the Enyalia scored them with swords and blades as easily as if they were lazy mosquitoes at the end of summer. But then attack shifted and somehow the boys rallied, driven by vengeance and fear and that primal thing that told them they had to survive at all costs.

All at once, the combined effort made the difference. The Enyalia didn't so much as retreat as they simply broke off and disappeared, leaving the mounts of the dead huddled together on the riverbank.

"At least we have transportation for us all," Alaysha said, not quite believing they'd won.

CHAPTER 26

By the time they gained the mud village, Isolde was sitting a much stronger beast and dozens of young boys who had come to battle against the Enyalia armed with sling shots and pikes made of young saplings, either walked behind them or shared the beasts.

It had been a wearying journey, one that Alaysha hoped never to undertake again. They lost one beast early in the trek long before it had a chance to die of thirst. Cai and Gael had set about butchering the thing, and drying it in the baking sun. When they gained the Enyalian well, they'd only had to replenish a little over half of their water stores and Alaysha believed it was because everyone was mindfully rationing what they could. She told them that the well lay at least half between the ends of the burnt lands, and that they needn't ration anymore.

The boys were somber, almost distrustful companions. Each time they unmounted for the day, thinking to travel at night during the coolest time, the boys scurried to set up some sort of repast, managing meager fires, managing to parcel out dried meat and fruit in equal portions and at the same time unfurl sleeping mats and linens. Most times, they were able to erect small sanctuaries of shade built with any pikes that remained from the battle, stretching linen across and laying the mats beneath.

This would inevitably be where Alaysha would find Liliah sleeping.

They'd kept the girl drugged since they've found her gathering her gruesome seeds. Alaysha would freely admit that she felt far more relief in knowing the girl was sleeping and Theron was constantly monitoring her breathing. He and Aedus kept careful watch over the little goddess, taking turns sleeping.

Each day wore on much the same, and when they mounted again at the coming of dusk, the same boys would pack the stores onto the beasts without a word and clamber up to stare straight ahead as they journeyed.

Alaysha herself carried two boys: both of them the same ones who had attended her when she was captive in Enyalia. She knew they recognized her and she tried to speak to them more than once, only to be met with sullen silence. She kept telling herself that it was because boys were not spoken to in Enyalia unless it was to give them a command that they were expected to obey. She imagined what it must've been like to live as less than chattel, knowing you would spend your days in service only to give up your body to fire and sacrifice. She imagined the boys were even as yet trying to process the idea of their freedom. And she finally left them alone, thinking they would speak to her when they were ready.

By the time they reached the mud village and left the burnt lands far behind, a quiet dread had niggled up Alaysha's spine. She knew what would be found there. She recalled how the clay had buried the crones beneath cairns of stone too heavy to lift by hand. She knew to do so would have taken a good deal of sacrificial blood.

At first no one spoke, there was a hushed reverence as they climbed down from their beasts and stood facing the cairns. Some of Yenic's people were beneath those stones, Alaysha knew. She also knew that the clay witch's mother would be beneath one as well. She watched as Néve took her father's hand and led him to the broadest pile of stones. They both knelt before it, heads hung as Ellison strode behind them and laid his hands on their shoulders. He hadn't been the man's birth mother, but Alaysha could see that the woman's death weighed heavily on his shoulders.

Long, silent moments passed and then Néve stood, swiping tears from her cheek and hugged Theron.

The shaman's face looked pinched, and his hands trembled on Néve's back as he gripped her in a fierce embrace. Alaysha couldn't help but hang her head in shame. She had taken all of these people in death, drained them of their fluid until they were nothing but dried out husks of skin. She'd collected their seeds afterwards, as she'd collected all of her dead's seeds, then stored them in the leather pouch in her hovel.

She couldn't bear to watch the grief and turned blindly away, groping for Barruch and feeling his nose beneath her palm with a shuddering breath of relief. She wrapped her arms around his neck and buried her face into his mane.

So much had transpired since she's first been here. She remembered how it felt to stand here, nude, doing her best to show her father's supposed enemies some vulnerability as she drained them of their life's fluid. She remembered touching on Yenic's sister, her unborn child. She recalled finding the crones within the hut, the smell of sulfur reaching towards the ceiling. The smoke twirling into shapes that were almost human in their intent. She remembered the torrent, of finding the tattaus on the chins of the women she'd killed.

That had been the moment when everything changed. When she'd known she was not alone. When she had begun to let all of the memories she'd buried resurface. In some ways this journey that had begun here, held an eerie parallel to the draining journey through the burnt lands. She felt exhausted and spent. And though it seemed as though it would never end, it had indeed come back full circle.

She felt a hand on her back and knew without checking that it was Cai. Gael would be attending to Isolde, making sure the warrior was taking sustenance, perhaps drinking some water, trying to fuel and grow the babe inside. Even though she knew it was Cai, she turned and fell against the woman's chest. She buried her face in the woman's skin, gripped her tightly around the waist.

The warrior dropped light kisses on the top of her head, crooning to her. But when the warrior asked her what was wrong, Alaysha pulled away, shaking her head. There was no way she could explain it all to a woman who hadn't been through the whole journey. She couldn't explain how bereft she felt.

She was swiping the wetness from her cheeks when Ellison cleared his throat. Alaysha rubbed at her eyes frantically, trying to get all of the liquid removed, so that she could see again clearly. She gave a quick scan, counting the heads, noting with sadness the way Gael's hand was resting on Isolde 's belly.

She twisted away and faced Ellison. "What do you suggest?"

"That we exhume them."

Cai was the one who sounded shocked, but not for the reasons Alaysha thought at first. "Exhume? To what end, man?" She pointed at the broadest cairn where the clay witch rested. "We are many, and some of us are strong, but it would be foolish to waste our energy on such a fruitless task."

Ellison grinned wickedly. "Some of us are stronger than others," he said, reaching out for Néve.

Alaysha searched Néve's face. "I don't know which one she is," she said, thinking that Néve would want to exhume Liliah's grandmother.

"The witches are all laying side-by-side," Néve answered. She pointed to the cairn where her mother was. "The two next to her are of air and fire." She looked perplexed for a moment, studying the third closely, her head cocked, her eyes narrowed to slits as she considered them.

Néve and Ellison made short work of moving the stones. Alaysha was surprised to see that the air crone beneath looked the same as she had the day she'd leathered her. By sunset, they had a roaring pyre, and by morning of the next day, they had a small pile of ash and bone that the entire company whispered over reverently.

Theron agonized over the last of his stores to make the sacred kykeon, but he rationalized that Liliah was such a small thing he wouldn't need much anyway. It was the next afternoon before they had worked through the problem of getting the kykeon into Liliah's unconscious mouth, of having have wrapped her hands around the league's fingers, guiding the unconscious hand to Aedus's skin as she marked and smudged within girl's flesh.

Cai watched it all with an interested eye and when Alaysha noted that Liliah had no Arm of protection, inclined her chin toward Saxon and said. "Then they're evenly matched: the little goddess has none and that bitch in Sarum only has a child."

It was true, Alaysha realized, but looked at differently, one might imagine Aislin had an Arm who was useless, but they had a goddess who was simple.

CHAPTER 27

The oasis provided fresh water, peaches for Barruch, and plenty of fowl for them to roast over an open flame. They all went to their bedrolls with full bellies and clean bodies and while even the Enyalia boys found places up against trees, burrowed into nests of branches, Alaysha couldn't help noticing that Gael made a particularly soft bed of Evergreen boughs and the thickest of the fur cloaks that he'd been able to bring back from the mucklands.

He spread that over the branches and let Isolde settle on it, sideways, facing the fire to make sure the babe was warm. He'd curled up somewhere nearby, and leaned against the tree saying he would take first watch.

Alaysha didn't miss the fact that the post he selected was within easy reach of both Saxon and Isolde. While Alaysha felt a strange disappointment at that, Cai seemed very pleased. The arrangements afforded her the opportunity to lay her bedroll directly next to Alaysha. Twice in the night Alaysha felt the woman's hands creep over her hip. She woke once thinking someone was watching her and when she saw Gael's eyes in the flickering firelight move casually away from her and onto Isolde, she thought perhaps he had been comparing the two of them.

What better match for him really, then a woman without fear. He'd already come to accept the child she carried as his, how far would the journey be to accepting her as his help mate. It was a wise choice after all. She couldn't exactly expect him to keep a flame for her alive when it was obvious that it was a ludicrous arrangement. What man would want to be tied to a woman who also felt very connected to another woman? It had been foolish of her to mark two protectors, she realized. It had not only taken away their choice, but hers as well.

She squeezed her eyes closed, telling herself she wouldn't think about it anymore. If Gael wanted Isolde, then he was welcome to her. He deserved some happiness, after all. If she was indeed marching them to their death, then he should find some pleasure in the time he had remaining.

After that, Alaysha worked very hard to return to sleep, but it was no use. She tried to believe it was because she could hear the snores of the Enyalian boys somewhere off in the bushes. They'd opted to stay away from the fire, preferring the cloaking ability of heavy brush. If she listened hard enough, she could hear the waterfall where Yenic had first kissed her. She expected to feel sad remembering that, and she slowly turned it over in her mind, examining how she felt about it. There was grief, yes. The sense that she had lost something, but it didn't hurt quite so much anymore.

Something hurt, though. Deep within her chest, that much was clear. She could feel it, and if she tried to assess where that came from, she only heard the hum behind her ears again, and the burning of her mark, that deep sense that something was being communicated, something primal and without words. She rolled over onto her back, and realized that Cai was closer than she had thought. Now the arm that had been merely touching her hip, went all the way around her waist. She was lodged against the warrior's front, nestled almost into the crook of her elbow. The warrior murmured in her sleep and snuggled closer. It was amazing how much heat the woman gave off, but though Alaysha was grateful to be warm, she was uncomfortable lying so close to Cai. She eased the woman's arm off of her ribs and snuck out from the bedroll, gaining her bare feet and scanning the darkness, hoping her eyes would adjust to the night vision.

Mounds of sleeping forms assembled around the fire; directly across from her Gael hunched against a tree, his arms crossed, and the glint of his knife catching the firelight. She caught his eye and made her decision.

She crept about the sleeping forms, stepping over them when she couldn't get around them, and settled down next to Gael.

"She snores," he said.

Alaysha looked across the fire to where Cai was now sleeping flat on her back. "Really? I didn't hear anything."

"You must be already getting used her," he said, and his voice was harsh and almost hateful.

She tried to look at him but he was stubbornly facing the fire. "What's that supposed to mean?"

He said nothing for a short time, and she had to poke him, not playfully but angrily. "Tell me."

"You seemed awfully comfortable." Is what he said.

"Not really," Alaysha said. "I couldn't sleep." She sought out Isolde's form in the shadows, too shy to say what she really wanted: to be next to him.

"So you're to be a father," she said. "She's a good match for you, Gael; I think you'll be good together." Even as she spoke the words, she hoped he would deny it, tell her he didn't want the Enyalian at all, admit again that he loved her no matter who carried his child.

What he did was sigh and she felt her heart ache at the sound. He moved against her in a way that made her assume he was shrugging. "I suppose I should be grateful that Cai left her alive."

Again, it wasn't what she wanted to hear and in some peculiar way she wanted to punish him for it. "I was surprised as you to hear she'd killed the rest of them. I wonder how many others were with child..."

She felt his reaction to that rather than heard it, and she cringed, ashamed at her cruelty.

"She's difficult, I won't argue," he said carefully.

"Difficult wouldn't be the word I'd use," she said.

"No." Gael shuffled his feet in the dark. "She wants you," Gael said and the strange note was back in his voice.

"She has made that perfectly clear," Alaysha said. She thought for a moment, remembering, and then chuckled softly.

"What's so funny?"

"Just that for all her wanting, she's a warrior first. A Komandiri to the last. She even taught me how I can better harness my power, something she calls ti chai. It's really a rather long list of complex and slow movements meant to gather your energy." Alaysha practiced some of the hand movements in the dark as she sat next to Gael. "They're quite beautiful, although I would never tell Cai that."

"When has she had time to teach you that?"

Alaysha sought his jaw in the dark, wishing he would look at her. "The night I marked you both with the full ribbon. Afterwards. She said it would be something I'd never forget."

She thought she heard Gael chuckle, a low and throaty sound that made her want to reach out to him. "What?" she asked him.

"Nothing," he said. "And here I thought –oh, it doesn't matter now. Alaysha--"

What he thought was interrupted by a piercing shriek that Alaysha recognized as Saxon's. They were both on their feet in a heartbeat, Gael grasping for a torch in one hand, keeping his knife ahead of him in the other. They floundered in the dark, searching for Saxon where he lay between Aedus and Liliah. Gael thrust the torch over them, shedding light on the small forms.

"Not again," he groaned.

"Yes," Alaysha said, seeing the blisters rise. "Again."

Chapter 28

By the time they reached the outskirts of Sarum, a bedraggled, sore, and exhausted lot, Alaysha was so drained from feeding Saxon fluid to squelch the fire of his mark that she could barely keep her eyes open. Cai had noticed the toll it was taking on her a short time after as they left the mud village and gathered her in front as they sat the one large beast, giving up Barruch to Aedus and Liliah. Alaysha's bones had ached as they passed by the river where she had nearly lost Yenic, her heart hurt when they reached the gorge where she'd met Edulph and learned her half-sister Bronwyn had been abducted and her whole body trembled with a terrible energy as she caught sight of her father's homeland, the white stone walls towering above the pines and cypress trees.

She leaned against the Enyalian, anxious suddenly, knowing in her tissues that everything was coming to a head.

"We can't let this entire horde inside the city," Alaysha said.

Cai chuckled from behind her. "I was wondering when you would realize it," she said.

The Enyalian halted her beast and turned it ungainly back toward the assembly. "Which of us should go in?" She asked Alaysha.

"Me, Gael, and Saxon."

She felt the woman tense behind her. "You will be left unprotected,"

"I'll have Gael," Alaysha said wearily.

"As I said –"

"We won't be going in through the city gates," Alaysha told her. "I know a different way in."

In her mind, she thought about her little cave on the side of the mountain and for the first time was grateful her father had made her live there. In her flight from Sarum, she'd realized there were deep tunnels connected to her little cave. Tunnels that brought her to the deepest parts of the mountain, and some of them into the Crystal Cave where they'd found Edulph. She could get just about anywhere within the city just by going into her own little cave and searching out different branches. If they were still there, that was. She hadn't remembered them even being there when she was young, and Theron had said they moved: Liliah's magic protecting her secrets.

"And what am I to do with all of these?" The Enyalian spread her arm across the air to encompass the by now hundreds of hangers on, Highlanders and Enyalian boys alike.

"You should be safe here," Alaysha looked around her at the thickness of the trees and underbrush. It was far enough away from the city gates that she wasn't worried about being found, and if they were, Cai could make short work of any who stumbled upon them.

The Enyalian sighed audibly. It was obvious she wasn't happy about the arrangement. "And what will you do if they young one lets out a screech as he's been doing for the last few days?"

"What of it?" Alaysha asked. "He's just one more child crying in the city. No one will take any notice. Besides, I told you, I know a different way in."

"Must be some way," the Enyalian mumbled. Nonetheless, she flicked her wrist at Gael then wrapped her broad hands around Alaysha's waist and eased her onto the ground. "If anything happens to her, man, I will string all of your teeth, but I won't wear them. I'll wrap them about a crow's neck and let it fly so far from your homeland your spirit will never find peace."

Gael didn't seem the least put out. Rather, he grinned at the Enyalian as though he believed the threat was empty. Alaysha knew better. "Come," she said to Gael. "Let's get this thing done."

They set out on foot under cover of darkness, Gael carrying the child in the makeshift papoose they'd repaired at the oasis. Alaysha couldn't shake the feeling that they were being followed, but Gael seemed not to notice, so she pushed that thought aside. The growth around her nohma's cottage had grown since the last time Alaysha had been there. She tried to push aside thoughts that the last time she was here it was with Yenic. Instead, quietly she made her way into the old homestead and unburied the pouch of seeds she knew rested in the floor. Patting them against her ribs, she looked up at Gael and motioned that it was time to go.

They found themselves at the mouth of the cave by sunrise, and mere hours later, beneath the floor of Saxa's house. The tension in the tunnel was thick enough that it closed up Alaysha's throat. She felt for Gael anxiously in the darkness, her fingers clumsily meeting the leather beneath his arm. In no time, she was gathered close, his breath on her neck. "We're here," he whispered.

Saxon was between them, in his repaired papoose, and Alaysha could feel the fuzz of his head against her arm as Gael pressed close, the baby hanging in front of him squirming as though to wake. She shushed the boy, laying her palm on his head. Stroking and smoothing the hair down. "He's hot," she said to Gael.

"I know," he said. "But there's nothing better for an ailing child than his mother."

Alaysha drew in a breath, bracing herself. "Shall we?"

She expected an answer, but what she received was the feel of his lips on her forehead. They were hot as well, but in a different way. Automatically, Alaysha lifted her face in the darkness, hoping he'd be close enough that when she reached out to him and found his jaw with hers fingers, that he would not back away. In the second before his mouth claimed hers, she felt the middle of her chin burn and send a tingle to her toes. Her entire body sparked to his and when his tongue parted her lips and his hand went around her waist, pulling her close against him, she felt as though they were both being washed downstream by the fierce rushing of a swollen river. She was plunging beneath the water, feeling both buoyant and prickled by the loss of oxygen. It was exhilarating and fearsome at the same time. She broke from him, intending to apologize, thinking of the shame she felt for betraying Isolde. She was thinking of the unborn child, knowing that if the yoke of Enyalia was ever to be broken, Gael could break it.

"I'm sorry, Gael," she started to say and felt his finger against her lips.

"Don't be sorry, witch," he rasped. The emotion in his throat thickened his voice in a way that made her want to fling her arms around his neck and pull him closer.

"Before we go through with this any further," he said. "I have to tell you what I wanted to tell you days ago."

She shook her head, "don't," she said. "I don't think I could take it," she felt herself backing away imperceptibly, thinking he would tell her it was Isolde who needed him, that he had come to love. And while every instinct told her to go forward, the same fear was making her dizzy.

"Don't?" He asked. "I have to. I have to, witch. If it's not Cai you want, if you can stand to have me, I –"

He had time to throw his hand up to cover his eyes as light flooded the tunnel. Alaysha shielded her own eyes, peering through her fingers up into the face she thought she'd never see again.

"Saxa," she heard herself say.

There was no startled exclamation from the silver-haired woman, no bleat of excitement, only lean arms reaching in, tugging the boy from his papoose, lifting him, struggling upwards. Only then did Alaysha hear Saxa sob, but it was a soft, whimpering thing that made Alaysha reach for Gael's hand in the tunnel. Her fingers laced with his as they looked at each other, knowing that no matter what happened next, this one moment was worth it all.

The others were there: Yusmine, Bodicca. The latter sat sullenly on the stool in the corner, staring out into the room as though it was a distasteful place. For the moment, Alaysha ignored her, merely turned to the willowy woman who had loved her father and found herself gathered in the lean arms, the woman sobbing into her neck as the fingers of her free hand clutched the middle of her back. Alaysha could feel herself pressed tighter, feel the child squirming next her, his tiny feet pressing into his mother's chest, trying to pull himself free of such a tight grip. Before Alaysha could pull herself free, she was enveloped from behind, as Gael reached around the mall. They were all laughing and sobbing at the same time, the relief making Alaysha's legs tremble.

"I thought –"

"I had hoped to –"

"I wanted –"

Alaysha knew what they all meant as they spoke at once: that they'd all feared they'd never see each other again. And what could one say after that, after discovering that your loved ones were safe and unharmed.

Saxa had the boy lying on a bench in moments, peeking beneath his clothes, inspecting every inch of him.

"He's hale enough," she said in a worried tone. "But he has a fever." She was murmuring to herself, plucking at the course spun nap they'd put on him before they'd left the mucklands. She had changed him, wiping him clean, and was plucking the tunic off of him when she noticed the mark. Alaysha could see the way the woman clenched her bottom lip with her teeth, hear the sharp intake of breath. She caught Gael's eye. He looked as worried as she felt.

"We need to explain," Alaysha said.

Saxa waved away the words. "No need," she said. A strange look crossed her face, but without another word, the woman had the boy cleaned and re-changed and redressed so efficiently the boy didn't have time to protest before his mouth was being filled with spoonfuls of honey and something pungent smelling that Alaysha assumed was garlic.

It was trenchers of savory stew that lent a sort of thoughtful contemplation to the reunion. Saxa buzzed about the cottage, never settling, almost frenetic. Yusmine watched the woman closely, Alaysha noted, and she spooned a mouthful of stew into her own belly, chewed on the meat reflectively as she studied Yusmine who sat across from her.

"What does she know?" Alaysha asked the woman in Yenic's body.

The crystalline eyes turned on her. "By 'she' do you mean this woman Yuri loved or the fire witch who marked her?"

"I mean Saxa," Alaysha said. "What did you tell her?"

Bodicca staggered from her stool over to the table and laid her fingers on the surface. "She knows the Emir has returned."

Alaysha turned her eyes on the Enyalian. "This woman is not the Emir, Bodicca," Alaysha said patiently. "You put Saxa in danger bringing Yusmine here."

Bodicca shook her head obstinately. "You think I'm foolish," she said. "As even my people thought." She tapped her temple. "But who better to find her own stores than the Oracle who hid them?" She pointed to Yusmine. "Should this woman be some prophetess who can find the means to bring down the witch who stole the city, then who better to return it? If this woman is the Emir, then who better to wage battle against the witch who stole his city? If this woman is both, then tell me a better person to…"

"Enough," Alaysha said. "I understand what you're telling me. But I don't understand why you would put Yenic at risk. Saxa at risk."

The woman shrugged. "What risk has this woman with Yuri's best general at her beck and call?"

The superiority of Enyalia again: that implacable, unmoving sense that nothing or no one existed that could best him. Alaysha swiveled her gaze to Yusmine. "Has Aislin seen you?"

The woman shook her head. "I'm more cunning than that, you should know that, witch."

The words, the tone, were undoubtedly Yuri's. Alaysha shivered under the crystalline gaze. She reached for Gael's hand under the table and laced her fingers into his. He squeezed, giving her courage.

"I have the seeds," she told Yusmine.

The woman nodded. "That's fortunate."

"Fortunate?"

"Indeed. We have had a few… setbacks."

"Like what?"

"Like the tunnels being frozen, like Aislin finding the texts, like…" The woman's gaze darted to Saxa and the silver-haired woman rushed forward, refilling Alaysha's trencher with stew.

"My special recipe," she said. "Strengthens the blood."

Alaysha pulled the inside of her cheeks between her teeth, chewing reflectively. She studied Saxa and noted the woman was avoiding her gaze. Her eyes went to Yusmine, who was leaning back now, Yenic's arms crossed in front of her.

"What do you mean the tunnels are frozen?"

"I mean a witch has spilled blood in vengeance."

"There are only two witches in Sarum," Alaysha said.

Yusmine inclined her head. "Then it was one of those witches." The crystalline gaze narrowed and Alaysha felt as though something inside of her chest had whimpered.

"I could have killed Corrin for all the harm he did me," she murmured and watched Yusmine's face as she did so. The woman gave no indication that she was right or wrong, but Alaysha knew that even so, it wasn't quite accurate. She went on. "But I didn't kill him. Aislin did. She slit his throat in the bathhouse in revenge for Yenic's suffering there."

"Blood of vengeance spilled by a witch. Part of Liliah's puzzle. The tunnels shift to protect the magics within, of any objects--like amphorae to remain hidden. Blood stills them. And because the magic has made the tunnels remain still, he was able to find my texts. Those parchments stored away generations ago."

Alaysha couldn't stifle a groan of impatience and frustration. Yusmine looked at her in good humor. "Never fear for that, witch," she said. "I'm the one who wrote them, remember?

"The good thing is," the woman went on. "That while Aislin knew she was looking for texts, she had no idea she was looking for oils too." She looked at Bodicca. "My faithful general carried that back from the tunnel for me before Aislin could realize their significance." The hand that was Yenic's reached out and laid itself on Bodicca's shoulder. The Enyalian relaxed visibly and the face softened.

"It was nothing, my Emir."

"So we have what we need, then," Alaysha said.

"If you plan to lend your aid, witch, then we have all we need but for the witches," Yusmine said, giving Alaysha a knowing glance. "And all but their Arms and their blood witches." At this she looked away at the wall, uncomfortable, it seemed.

Suspicion snaked its way up Alaysha's spine. "What's wrong?"

Saxa fell onto a stool and laid her wringing hands upon the table. Her chest was shuddering, Alaysha could tell, and the delicate chin trembled slightly.

"What's wrong, Saxa?"

She sent a wary gaze to Gael, and though his expression was carefully crafted into a mask of calm, she could see the worry in his eyes.

"Saxa," he said. "What is it?"

Saxa said nothing, but she lifted blouse of her tunic on the left side and twisted towards them. There, black and sooty and red rimmed on that gracile, milky flesh were a series of marks that looked horribly familiar.

"She marked you," Alaysha heard herself say. "She remembered the look of consternation on Néve's face as she stared at the cairn where the fire witch's mother had lain. She was willing to bet Néve saw a difference in the arrangement, that she suspected what Alaysha now knew: someone had exhumed the fire witch before they got there. If not Aislin, then who else would have need of it?

Her voice was flat, but the feeling in her chest was one of dread. "Aislin took the body of her mother from that cairn and she incinerated her and she marked you with her tattaus."

Saxa's silver eyes brimmed with tears. "Yes, and I feel her," she whispered.

CHAPTER 29

Seeing that Saxa had been marked by Aislin was nothing to the shock they received when they snuck back through the tunnels to the outskirts of the camp, a pouch in her hand heavy with the seeds Alaysha had collected throughout her years.

It was Aedus who met them. She had gone back to wearing mud in her hair, and her idea of camouflage this time was to stick moss and bunches of lichen to her skin. She looked again like the wild thing that Alaysha had first met. And when she looked past her over her shoulder, Alaysha noticed that a good deal of the Highlanders had dressed themselves similarly.

She also noticed a peculiar swelling of the ranks.

"Who are they?" She asked Aedus, pointing to the half hundred new bodies milling about the makeshift bedrolls of branches and boughs.

The girl shrugged lightly. "Liliah's baubles, I guess." The girl hung her head, for what reason Alaysha wasn't sure, but there was something different in Aedus's posture.

"What is it?"

"She's gone,"

"Gone?" Alaysha caught Gael's eye, wondering if he understood what Aedus was telling them.

"The little goddess," Aedus said. "Liliah is gone."

For a heartbeat, Alaysha's heart swelled. She felt free, almost. As though there had been chains around her wrists and ankles and they had suddenly been struck off.

Then she remembered the plan they'd already put in motion just after they'd recovered from the shock of Saxa's marking and she knew better than to feel freed.

She remembered Yusmine's very clear, very succinct explanation. That the oil was spiced and made from linseed, an oil that could heat of its own accord enough that it could generate energy without ever sparking a flame. At her direction, they'd soaked linen strips in the oil, created packings of cattail cotton to insert into Aislin's ears and mouth and nose in order to block off the exit of Aislin's power as the linseed worked to contain her magic to mere smoldering ember and not outright spark and flame. If they could find a way to get Aislin wrapped in the linseed oil-soaked linen strips, her magic could be bound long enough for Liliah to ungod her.

Except Liliah was gone. Except the plan required Bodicca to face Aislin and tell her that she had Yenic in the caves. The old Enyalian would make some excuse about wanting Sarum back in Yuri's memory and that she would give her back her son if she'd leave the city. Except all of this meant that the plan set in motion without Liliah's presence would mean that Yenic would die as soon as Aislin realized it was Yusmine in his body.

It was Gael who asked the question that she should have asked in the first place.

"How long has she been gone?"

"Since you left," Aedus said.

Alaysha chewed her bottom lip thoughtfully. "Do you think she's off searching for more seeds?" She couldn't bear the thought of calling those people baubles; it reminded her too frighteningly of their episode in the Glades of the Highlands.

Aedus sighed. "I don't know. Really I don't. We just sort of noticed she was gone."

"But she was sleeping, Aedus." Alaysha's mind was moving fast, her eyes skirting the area just as quickly as she considered the problem. "She was sleeping. She couldn't just have gotten up and wandered off. You and Theron have managed her sedative quite well."

Aedus had a knowing look on her face, it was obviously something she'd considered already. "She must've been taken."

Alaysha nodded. "Taken, yes, but by whom?"

Gael stepped closer, touching Alaysha on the small of her back, awakening her tattau in ways that had nothing to do with the problem at hand.

"Worse even than that," he said. "Is what will happen when she wakes up?"

"Where is Cai?" Alaysha asked, scanning the group and coming up empty of the huge red Enyalian. "And Isolde," she added for Gael's sake.

"The last is doing well, "Aedus said. "Well enough to teach the younger girls to hold a sword." She laughed, then cut it off shortly, realizing the severity of the situation. "And Cai is out searching." Aedus said. "Ever since Liliah disappeared."

They found Néve and Ellison in deep conversation on the edge of the camp. Theron paced nearby in tune with Thera's steps, back and forth in front of a sitting clay witch and her Arm.

"Do you think it was Aislin who took her?" Alaysha asked of Néve.

Néve shook her head. ""And not remain to burn the rest of us to cinders?" She looked to Ellison for confirmation. "We've been discussing just the same thing, and we highly doubt she would leave us alive."

"Someone has been on our tail," Ellison said. "I've felt it since we left the Highlands."

"Me too," She said. There had been times when she felt the hairs prickle the back of her neck as though she was being watched. But the person or persons following were careful not to be seen, and as they gained numbers, Alaysha had come to believe that those following had simply been either Enyalian boys or more of Liliah's seeds.

"Could an Enyalian have taken her?"

Thera cut in, halting in front of Alaysha. "To what end? We would have no need of a simple child who was too powerful for us to control." She touched her chin where the sword mark had been burned into her flesh. "We're not afraid, but were not foolish either."

Alaysha sighed, having exhausted all of the other possibilities, she knew what the most likely answer was. "It's Edulph." She looked across at Gael. He nodded slightly. "We lost him in the muck lands and he's been following us ever since."

"We should have killed him long ago."

Alaysha tended to agree but there was nothing to do about it now. "He could be anywhere with her."

"Yes, but he has no idea what he'll have on his hands when she wakes."

"And when she does, he's in for a world of trouble."

"Well," Alaysha said. "I suppose in the meantime we could make use of all of these people." She turned to Gael. "What do you say? A good distraction at the gates of Sarum?"

Gael grinned. "Spoken like a true emir," he said.

She turned to the rest of them. "Then we'll make it so. All of these children who've accompanied us, all of these women, all of these Highlanders. We'll set them at the city gates begging for entrance. And while Sarum is dealing with a horde of hungry and afraid strangers beating at their doors, we'll slip back into the tunnels."

Theron stepped up. "And what of the little goddess? Such a group of foolish warriors still needs her."

"I don't think that will be a problem," he said. "I think we can find her with no problem."

Alaysha looked up, following his gaze to where man, woman, and child alike were lifting off from the ground, sailing glaze-eyed through the air, each one in the same direction.

"Oh dear deities," she heard herself say. "She's awake."

"And, judging by the direction her followers are taking," Gael said "she's heading toward Sarum."

CHAPTER 30

Néve and Ellison made quick work of herding the crew with some haste toward Sarum. Barruch led the horde of beasts with Isolde on his back. Alaysha had kissed him on the nose when he'd rolled his eyes at her in complaint, then she hung back, the tattau on her chin itching, her eyes searching the underbrush for signs of Cai.

She felt Gael's hands on her shoulders, felt herself being spun to face him. "We need to get going," he said.

"But Cai," she said.

"Cai is probably already following Edulph and Liliah. She's good at that."

Alaysha sighed, wanting to believe him. "It just wouldn't be right to leave her behind." She turned from him to follow the others and felt him hook her elbow.

"What?" She said.

"It's just that –"

She waited, watching the uncertainty flicker across his face. "Alaysha, I love you. I'd lost hope of you ever feeling the same way, what with Cai and…" He started to trail off, but she urged him on. He gathered a brave face. "When you admitted that you didn't return the Enyalian's feelings, I thought maybe I had a chance."

Alaysha's chest fluttered. "Isolde?"

"Isolde carries my child, but you carry my heart."

He reached out to her, tentatively, and his hands found her waist, inching towards the small of her back. Her fingers found his chin, rustling the stubble of his jaw line.

"I love you too, Gael." She smiled for him. "With everything I am."

He pulled her almost desperately toward him, both arms going so far around her she swore his hands must have met behind his back. She barely had time to turn her chin up to meet his lips before he was devouring her mouth and she was returning the kiss with equal fervor. She lost herself to him in that moment.

A sound from behind startled her. Rather than release her, Gael pressed her behind him. Standing there with her red brow arched, the sword trembling in her hand, stood Cai.

"It seems I have lost the battle after all, haven't I, little maga?"

Alaysha didn't have the heart to admit it. She hung her head. Almost with effort, the Enyalian brightened. "But at least there is another battle to wage." She took a step towards them. "And there's nothing better than the thrill of spilling blood to replace the sour taste of defeat."

CHAPTER 31

"She will come." Bodicca's voice, a bland, matter-of-fact thing in the torch lit cavern. Where torches were unavailable, oil lamps flickered, sending ghosts about the crystal walls, darkening again when the air moved.

They stood in a circle, all of them: Thera was closest to the door and on either side of her, Ellison and Néve; Bodicca was next, standing, feet splayed, beside Yenic, both of them facing the main entry--the one that looked like a nose in a hollow skull. Then came Yusmine, Aedus, Theron. Saxa clutched Saxon whom she'd decreed should be present: his birthright, she'd called it and Alaysha couldn't bear to argue. Gael breathed quietly next to her, funnelling his air in purposeful breaths.

Alaysha looked about the room, the crystal skull room that looked exactly the same as the last time she was here. The only difference being that Edulph was not in the deep pit screeching in pain from Aislin's torture. No. Edulph was off somewhere with Liliah. And Cai somewhere out there following Liliah's followers, believing they'd take her directly to the little goddess.

They were entirely unready.

"How do you know she'll come?" She asked Yusmine.

"Bodicca can be very convincing," Yusmine said, and Alaysha heard the undeniable note of Yuri in her voice. "I'm sure you've noticed."

Alaysha wasn't sure how long it would take before Aislin took the bait, and she was less sure that this would work anyway. She wished she'd not sent Cai after Edulph; he deserved death, but she should be here, next to her as was her rightful place. She'd been wrong and now she felt strangely empty without the Enyalian.

She shivered as she thought of how the Enyalian had refused to leave Alaysha's side.

"I'm Enyalia," the woman had said. "I choose my own purpose. No mere mark of soot and ash beneath my skin mark can make me do else wise." The woman had looked at her then, giving her a hard, careful study. Alaysha remembered squirming beneath it.

"You'll have need of my protection if the little one doesn't make it inside." She argued.

"But I need you to ensure that she does make it." Alaysha had countered.

"Send the man," Cai had jerked her chin at Gael. "He needs practice with children."

"I don't ask just because of Liliah," Alaysha said. "I need someone to make sure that Edulph doesn't make it."

She caught Gael's eye after the statement, and found that she could meet it easily. "He shouldn't make it," Alaysha said to him. "He needs to die."

Gael nodded, silently, and in a huff, the Enyalian had glared at him, almost saying with her eyes that he'd better look after his witch. She turned and pushed through the undergrowth, back bent, and disappeared without a word.

And so here they were, all of them waiting within the crystal skull cave, hoping against hope that Cai would find Liliah long before Aislin found her way into the cave to retrieve what she thought was her son.

Alaysha watched Yusmine scratch beneath her armpit absently. She knew the mark was dead now, but she had the feeling that the Oracle inside of Yenic's body could feel Yenic's spirit move within it. No doubt it made her uncomfortable.

"Do we have the oils and linen?" She asked Yusmine. In the absence of the goddess, the best they could hope for would be to overpower Aislin and wrap her in the linens in the hopes that the oil and spices alone would bind her magic. Just in case, Theron had stopped at his old apothecary and pocketed several pieces of yellow brimstone. It had taken a lot out of him, Alaysha could tell. He looked feeble on his feet as he stood next to Thera; in fact, it almost appeared as though his Enyalian daughter was holding him up.

Yusmine nodded toward the corner where almost out of sight stood several wide mouthed clay pots from Saxa's kitchens. It had been decided that Néve and Ellison would be responsible for lifting those clay pots, a simple enough feat that didn't require blood for the magic. When Aislin entered, Gael and Bodicca would strike her from behind and incapacitate her as the pots sailed to different hands only to be grabbed and wound around the witch as Aedus blew quills of purple beetle into the woman's neck.

Surely those two things would be enough that the remaining of them could wrap the linens about the woman's form and circle her with brimstone. It was a niggardly plan, after all, but in the absence of the goddess, Alaysha could think of none better.

Saxa was the one who revealed the ineffectiveness of the plan. They stood together, discussing the best means to immobilize Aislin on first sight when Saxa went rigid in the torchlight as she held onto Saxon. Seconds later the boy let out a howl that was both familiar and painful for Alaysha to hear. She fleeted a look to Gael. "She's coming," she mouthed.

Too late they realized that Aislin was already in the cavern. The milkiness of her eyes swivelled from Yenic to Saxon in confusion and in a split heartbeat, Alaysha realized the woman knew exactly what was wrong with her connection. Without a single word or change of expression, the fire witch reached out for Saxa, wordlessly demanding the boy. To Alaysha's shock, Saxa took several steps towards Aislin, obviously planning to pass the babe over. Both Néve and Ellison sprang to action; the clay pots in the corner rose unsteadily to the air, warbling their ways to eager hands throughout the cave. Alaysha thought she heard Aislin chuckle even as Thera, who was the closest to her sprang forward her sword raised, already swinging.

Alaysha didn't have time to cry out, to yell at Aedus to set the quill, to order Gael to leap for the woman, to even beg Thera to remain still. She had only the time to open her mouth before she heard the shaman's daughter inhale sharply. Thera began to let off curls of smoke from her hair. There was a whimper and another sharp intake of breath and then the woman's entire body leapt in flames. Alaysha heard a choking sound come from Theron's direction. She watched him stagger, clutching at his chest until he fell back against the dais, the feet in his sandals stone white, kicking at the air.

"Theron," she shouted finally, her hands in front of her as though she could stop what she saw happening with a mere wave of her hand. She heard a choked sob come from somewhere in her chest, as though she had hiccupped and it had caught in her throat. "No," she said, and wasn't sure if she was denying his death or the fact that her legs had turned to water.

The rest blurred, but Alaysha knew she had linen in her hands. She knew she could draw Aislin's fluid, and she pushed her energy out at Aislin as she advanced, trying her best to make her own fluid circulate: flush from moist lungs to tissue, from tissue to muscle, from muscle back again to heart. Inhale, Alaysha, she told herself, as she felt the certain, unflinching unfurling of heat deep in her chest. As she'd done for Saxon, Alaysha did for herself. Steady, focussed channelling.

Her vision greyed as she knew it would. Even still, she knew something was wrong. Where were the Arms, where Néve, and Aedus, and why was she spinning in the air, her legs dangling as though she was dancing.

She thought she heard a low guttural chuckle and tried desperately to seek out the source. By now she understood she was floating and struggled to regain enough of her vision to focus. There were hands on her arms, grappling for her shoulders, trying to keep her from spinning, trying to ground her. She had a peculiar sense that she was being peppered with bits of hail but she was trying so hard to keep the fire in her chest from setting to light that she couldn't be sure.

From somewhere in the distance, she heard Saxon howling, growing ever more screeching, heard Saxa's sobs begging Aislin to stop; please stop. She understood in that moment that the fire witch was hurting the poor child, punishing him for having her mark, a mark that couldn't function. And then suddenly the noise choked off. Someone was tugging at her feet, pulling her down to the floor of the cavern.

She heard the unmistakable sound of hail hitting the ground and mercifully, she felt the floor on her bare toes, then her soles, and then she was standing on her own power but gasping for air, clutching at her chest. She wheeled about, groping blindly, her fingers touching on skin, probing about to find a thick line of hair above a swollen lip.

"Edulph," she whispered.

"She's here," he answered. Instinct told her to send out her power in all directions, but she didn't dare pull it off of Aislin, and as she fought for air, she also fought that instinct within that told her to survive at all costs. She collapsed onto the cavern floor, blearily thinking that if she sat down, she could conserve some oxygen. She forced herself to stop sucking at air, to hold what she had deep in her chest. It was no good. It seemed to be pulling from her of its own accord, and just when she thought she would black out, she felt the heat within her chest dissipate. Robbed of its fuel.

Only when her vision returned, did Alaysha notice that what she'd thought was hail were hundreds of desiccated seeds pulled from her pouch. Saxa was crouched over Saxon's inert form, sobbing nearly incoherently.

"He's only sleeping," Edulph whispered, shoving a blower into Alaysha's hand, now empty of quills. Then he stood without looking back down at Alaysha to drive toward the fire witch, who Alaysha now saw was struggling in Cai's solid grasp even as the Enyalian began to smoke from the red roots of her hair. Edulph raised his hand, catching Aislin's attention, saluting her, revealing a thick line of crooked symbols on his ribcage. The witch grinned.

In the moment Alaysha realized he'd been the one to exhume the fire crone, and had somehow marked himself with the symbols he remembered. And Aislin believed he was hers.

Edulph wrenched Cai free of Aislin as though he planned to kill her with his own hands. Aislin let go her grip on the Enyalian and swung her gaze about the cavern, searching for her next victim.

It was Cai's voice that told Alaysha the witch's eye had settled on her. She heard in it panic and fear. "Gael," the Enyalian shouted, but beneath the commanding tenor of her voice was a peculiar huskiness, as though her lungs were singed. "The maga."

Alaysha only had time to register that the proud woman had used his name finally, when Gael collided into her, knocking her sideways. From the corner of her eye, she saw Edulph wrap a strip of linen about the fire witch's throat. He twisted.

Aislin's hands flew her to her neck even as her magic seemed to shiver away from Cai.

Edulph laughed as he pulled tight at the linen. "Try again, witch," he said against her ear. "I've got your crone in my mark, so try. Try again to burn me." His face became a twisted grimace even as the fire witch's dissolved to the realization that he was immune to her powers.

Aislin's chest heaved as she scrabbled for oxygen, and with one desperate twist, the fire witch rent the linen at her throat even as was Ellison creeping forward to wind linen strips around her ankles. She swung her wide-eyed gaze to him. Alaysha wanted to call out to warn him when several patches of purple bloomed on Aislin's throat. She sagged against Edulph so suddenly, he didn't have time to step away and ended up catching her instead. He was panting; Ellison working the linen up her ankles and shins.

And there, standing just behind them, stood Liliah, her blonde curls still twisting in the air, tears streaming down her face, her mouth open in a wailing O. Streaming in behind her through all three entrances, where her followers and Alaysha understood finally what was happening.

Like Liliah had smothered the fire in Alaysha's chest, she was doing the same to Aislin. Pulling the oxygen from her body, even as Aedus worked her own special kind of magic with the beetles she was so fond of.

Before Alaysha could process anything else, there was a pull somewhere inside of her that drew her to her feet. She noticed the same of Néve. The Arms came as well. All but Cai whose form lay unmoving on the stone floor. Not of their own accord, Alaysha, Néve, Ellison, Aedus, all of the marked moved to their places as though they had known exactly what they were all along. As though they had practiced on it for eons. They stood in a semi circle, toes facing in, blood witches behind them, Arms at their sides.

Still weeping, Liliah crept forward to close the gap. The torches guttered. The oil lamps went out.

The child looked heavenward, murmuring words that made no sense to Alaysha, and yet that sounded familiar and oddly soothing. She thought she caught one word: Etlantium and as she realized it, a strange and different kind of burning lodged at the bottom of her throat. She opened her mouth, thinking to free it, and at the same time heard her voice mingling with Liliah's and with Néve's. She saw Ellison draw a blade uncertainly, realizing there was no Thera any more to pass it to.

Instead, he ran the edge of it down his forearm as though skinning the flesh from his bones. Néve noticed and, smiling indulgently, took the blade from him, doing the same to herself. Saxa made the smallest of cuts on Aislin's palm, one of the only things that by now were free of the linen wrappings. Alaysha knew her turn was next and as she watched the beads of red blood drip onto the floor, she felt a surge of energy so strong she believed she could do it too, even without a blood witch to help her.

"Don't do it, witch," Gael croaked behind her. Liliah smiled a peculiar grin at him and shrugging, took the blade from Aedus. After kissing her lightly on the forehead, the toddler turned to run the edge along her own forearm. Where the letting of Néve and Ellison's blood made Alaysha burn with power, the spilling of the little goddess's fluid did something completely different.

This time, there was a shudder that moved throughout the entire cavern. The seeds along the floors jumped like beans on a hot skillet, and then streams of light streaked upwards. The cavern, made of crystal that was white and hard before, now turned translucent, as though light was shining from behind it.

The seeds beneath the streams of light begin to take shape. They wavered with colors that moved into and through each other like the colors of a rainbow shifted from one bar to the next, neither being one straight stripe nor being separate. She trembled as the shapes became more recognizable. They were people, Alaysha realized. Not solid forms, but flickering colors that wavered across themselves so constantly it seemed as though they were not of one plane but of many. One woman stepped forward, a slow, compassionate smile spreading across her face. Although she didn't look like her nohma, Alaysha realized that was exactly who it was. A slimmer, more mature woman stood next to her: her mother. A younger came next. Alaysha heard herself gasp. The sister. She felt water sting her eyes.

The seeds were all taking shape, all coming to form. And Alaysha realized that this was what she'd been collecting them for. So they could reclaim their spirits and return home. Home with Liliah.

But of the followers, no one shifted. They stood, all of them, shuffling back and forth in the darkness of the corners. She could see some of them stretching out in the tunnels beyond and they looked sad, grief stricken. They looked as though they were longing for something.

She caught Liliah's eye and realized in the moment exactly what the girl was planning to do. Alaysha called out to Edulph. "Stop her," Alaysha yelled. "Edulph, she's going to –"

The oxygen that fuelled her vocal cords quickly clamped off as the goddess's power stole it. She shuddered and fell backwards into Gael's arms. Unable to do any more than beseech the girl with her eyes, Alaysha lay against Gael, feeling his heart tremor against her back. She thought Edulph had crept behind Liliah and was about to grab the knife when he stopped short, his eyes fixed straight ahead. He murmured something that Alaysha didn't catch, but she noticed one of the wavering forms had stepped in front of him. And he fell to his knees, hands over his face. Sobbing.

When next Liliah drew the blade across her skin, Alaysha felt a strangled cry trying to escape. She wanted to lunge for the child, thinking to grab for her, stop up her wounds, to stitch them, heal them somehow. And as she looked at the fluid that leaked from one edge, she saw that it wasn't blood at all. Light was leaving her body in small drops of translucent liquid.

There was no extraction from skin, no stepping out of the flesh as though it was a tunic old and worn out. The girl simply transformed. And in her place stood a tall willowy silver form that was so beautiful Alaysha could barely stand to look at her. It was then, like lightning, that the followers shifted as well. Like Liliah, they wavered from something solid and made of flesh into translucent ribbons of color. There was a collective sigh as each of them shifted, and Alaysha heard in the sound a release of anguish, like the final push of a woman giving birth. There was ecstasy, there was relief. But also there was something else, something more indefinable that told Alaysha they had peace.

Liliah's gaze swung around the circle, lighting on Néve and Ellison and Yusmine. Each one of them nodded subtly. Caught up in the ecstasy, knowing they wanted to return home.

Liliah moved to where Aislin lay. With a wave of her hand, the wrapped form lifted into the air and floated over to the dais to ease onto the stone.

"Brother," said Liliah and her voice a musical sound that tinkled the crystal suspended over the stone, that reverberated through the forms hovering about the ceiling.

"Oh brother," Liliah swept across the cavern and laid her hand on the middle of Aislin's chest. A pulse of light came from her palm and shuddered through the linen wrappings into the body beneath.

"Is he ungodded?" Alaysha asked, her voice a hushed breath in the cavern.

With sadness, Liliah shook her head. "Quite the opposite," she said. "I have given him back his divine breath."

Alaysha didn't understand and it was obvious that Liliah realized it.

"He's my twin, little temptress," she said. "I love him. If I were to leave him here in this flesh of yours, he would eventually wither and die. Be reborn again. Over and over, forgetting who he is, never finding peace. Since there will no longer be temptresses with their long memories for him to reflesh into and realize what he is, he will be forever lost here."

"Beneath these wrappings, whatever magic remains will be bound here with him. But now at least he will not wither. He will lie here season after season until he remembers what he's lost. Until his remorse drives him to find forgiveness. And only then can he return to me. I hope it is soon. I miss him and I'm not whole without him."

The dais lifted from the floor then, and as though it were on ropes, lowered itself into the pit where Alaysha had found Edulph. She heard the grinding of stone meeting stone and even as it touched, the crystal light within the cave seemed to dim. Returning to stone, Alaysha realized. The torches grew brighter to compensate.

"And what of us," Alaysha asked, almost afraid of the answer.

"Those who wish to come with me, will come with me. Those who wish to stay, will stay."

Alaysha looked over at where Cai was lying and found she couldn't make herself take in the unmoving form. She had to look away and faced the goddess so she wouldn't have to look at the Enyalian. "She's dead, Liliah. Can you fix it?" She heard in her voice the high pitch of a child as she asked it.

Liliah shook her head. "She is Enyalia, child. They keep their own choices. All but the one who was the only Enyalian of Etlantium."

"My mother," Ellison said. And Liliah nodded. "She waits for you, child." She waved her hand towards the back of the cavern. "Go to her."

Even as he was striding away, Ellison's form began to shift and then Néve's with it. Everyone who had nodded began to change before Alaysha's eyes. And it was with a start that she realized the woman who had taken Yenic's body was standing in front of her.

"Sarum couldn't ask for a better Emir, Alaysha." The woman said but her voice was that of Yuri's. "You will be a far better Emir than I ever could be, tempering your rule with compassion." She turned and reached behind her, edging out of the way to reveal another .

"Yenic," Alaysha said, seeing the body that had been her bondsman waver to color in front of her.

The youth nodded. "I'm going home, Alaysha." he said.

She nodded stupidly. "Home," she repeated. "You deserve it."

Beyond him, Alaysha could see that the shaman had shifted as well. That he was holding the hand of a curvy shape, that they were melting into each other as though they had always been one body. It occurred to her that that's exactly what it had been like for him all along. They'd been sharing his mind since he lost her, so that she was never far from him. That's what she wanted with Gael. A love that could surpass even death.

Alaysha found Liliah's gaze. "Cai," she said to the goddess. "There's still Cai. She died for you. Please can you fix it?"

There was a fleeting movement of Liliah's mouth as though she were going to protest who the warrior had died for, but instead the goddess smiled. "Give me your hand," Liliah said.

Alaysha reached out, palm up. She winced as Liliah drew the blade across her skin.

"You can buy her with your blood," Liliah said. "Sacrificial blood is the most powerful. With it you can give her a choice. I can offer her life in this mortal flesh or I can make her of Etlantium."

Alaysha nodded dumbly. It wouldn't be so bad, going home. And if it meant she could save Cai…

"Please, Alaysha," Gael said from behind her. "Please don't."

She spun on him. "I have to."

"I'll do it," Gael said.

Alaysha clutched at his wrist feeling the pulse there. "No. Don't do that for me."

He tried a smile that didn't reach his eyes.

She was still clutching at him when Edulph eased the knife from Liliah's hand. At first, Alaysha thought he would use it on Gael, but instead he sliced at his wrist then moved to the other, drawing it lengthwise down the skin. The sharp coppery tang of blood rose to Alaysha's nostrils, making them twitch.

"What is this body to me," he said, looking down at the fluid as it leaked from his skin. "When my other half is gone to Etlantium."

She'd wanted him dead, believing him a cruel man, uncaring, and here her face was wet with tears for him. "Go home, Edulph," she whispered and he smiled thinly.

It was long moments after he collapsed before his wavering forms took shape in the cavern. It had such a different deportment than the physical Edulph that at first Alaysha wasn't sure it was him, but when it found its way to another shivering, wavering form of liquid crystal, she knew he'd found peace with his temptress.

Liliah moved to Cai's inert form.

Alaysha held her breath, looking down on the broad chest. She'd not understood how hard the woman had fought Aislin or what it had cost her. Now she did. The beautiful russet locks were nothing but a mat of singed hair. A smell came off her that reminded Alaysha of roasted apples and spitted boar. Alaysha told herself she wouldn't cry, not now. Now Liliah would do the same for her as she'd done for Yenic and the woman would rise. Alaysha told herself the Enyalian would rise. She would.

"She may already be in another body," Liliah murmured, taking in Alaysha's face as it turned to her. "It may already be too late."

Alaysha's fingers went to her throat, trying physically to press down a clump that she couldn't swallow. "She won't be," Alaysha said. "She wouldn't leave me. She… Loved me." She knelt next to Cai and placed her palm between the woman's breasts, snuggling the hand in, feeling for her heartbeat. "Do it."

Liliah reached down, the crystalline liquid of her hand swirling with color. There was a burst of light similar to that of the one she'd delivered to her brother.

Nothing.

Alaysha refused to look into Liliah's face. She felt Gael next to her, felt his hand pressed down next to hers. She didn't have the words to thank him for that.

"Again," Alaysha commanded the goddess. "Try again."

"I'm afraid it's useless."

"She's not gone. I would know it. She's not gone."

Long moments dissipated before anyone spoke again. In that time, Alaysha put all of the energy she could pull from within herself into willing Cai to wake. Futile though it may be, she felt more bereft than when Yenic had died because now she knew there was the possibility that she could rise. Somehow knowing that, and seeing the woman refused to move, was worse. The Enyalia could be so foolishly stubborn.

"Take it, Cai" she heard herself say. "Take the gift." Part of her worried that the spirit of the Enyalian refused it because in the end, Alaysha had refused her and chosen Gael. She dug deep to find some rationalization that might help.

"Will you truly let the man win?" Alaysha goaded the inert form.

This time there was an answer, but Alaysha didn't feel it through the revival of Cai's heartbeat. She felt it as a shiver up her spine, a coldness that wavered across her face as though a frigid wind was kissing her.

"She's here," Alaysha whispered. Her thumb found the woman's full lips and traveled from one end to the other. "She's here."

"And it seems she's made her choice," Liliah said.

Alaysha's gaze flew to the goddess. "What do you mean?"

Liliah drew Alaysha's attention to a shadow just behind her. Even as Alaysha watched, the inky blackness of the space began to waver like a breeze was moving through it. From one end to the other, colors began to shudder through. Finally, the sardonic grin, the superior expression, shivered into being. The eyes were different. Like the rest of Etlantium, the eyes swirled with color, but they were still Cai's eyes.

"It's the wrong choice," Alaysha told her, working to get the words through the thickness of her throat.

There was a movement in the form, the hush of the voice sending her images of a beautiful place, of herself and Gael and Alaysha finding peace.

"What is the wrong choice," the images told her. "When the one I've taken means I can be with you always and again."

"It's a short wait," Liliah murmured as though she'd heard. "I can see what your warrior has shown you. You know what waits for you, for all of Etlantium." There was a brief pause before Liliah spoke again. "Would you like to come home, Alaysha?"

"I would." Alaysha pulled her gaze from Cai's new form, the one that would be waiting for her eventually. She looked over at Saxa as she crooned to a now wakening Saxon, beyond to Aedus who crouched nearby, smoothing down the boy's fuzz. And then finally to Gael and she knew then what she wanted more than to simply go home.

"But I want them too. Here, in this flesh where I can have a normal life."

Liliah inclined her head gracefully. "It can be done. There is enough magic left here with Hel that you can all return to Etlantium when your savage flesh withers." She looked at Alaysha sadly. "But there can be no children, I'm afraid. You are not truly of the flesh you wear." Liliah was already fading, the vacillating form less wavering, more ghostly.

Alaysha thought of all those boys outside the city who'd never been mothered, of Aedus and Saxon and the child Isolde carried, of all she could learn from Saxa, and she smiled.

"That's all right," she said, reaching for Gael's hand and squeezing when he laced his fingers through hers. "We have plenty enough already."

-The End-

More by Thea:
Prequel Series of stories

- Seeds of the Soul
- Theron's Tale
- Sons of Alkaia

Stand Alone novels

- One Insular Tahiti
- Anomaly
- Throwing Clay Shadows
- Secret Language of Crows

Made in the USA
Lexington, KY
16 April 2018